ANGELS
ZERO

ANGELS ZERO

TEAM COLT
BOOK 2

ARLEIGH JACOBS

For those who stood beside me,
cheering through this past year. This book is for you,
for without your support, it never would have happened.

For Captain Jacobs,
My pilot.

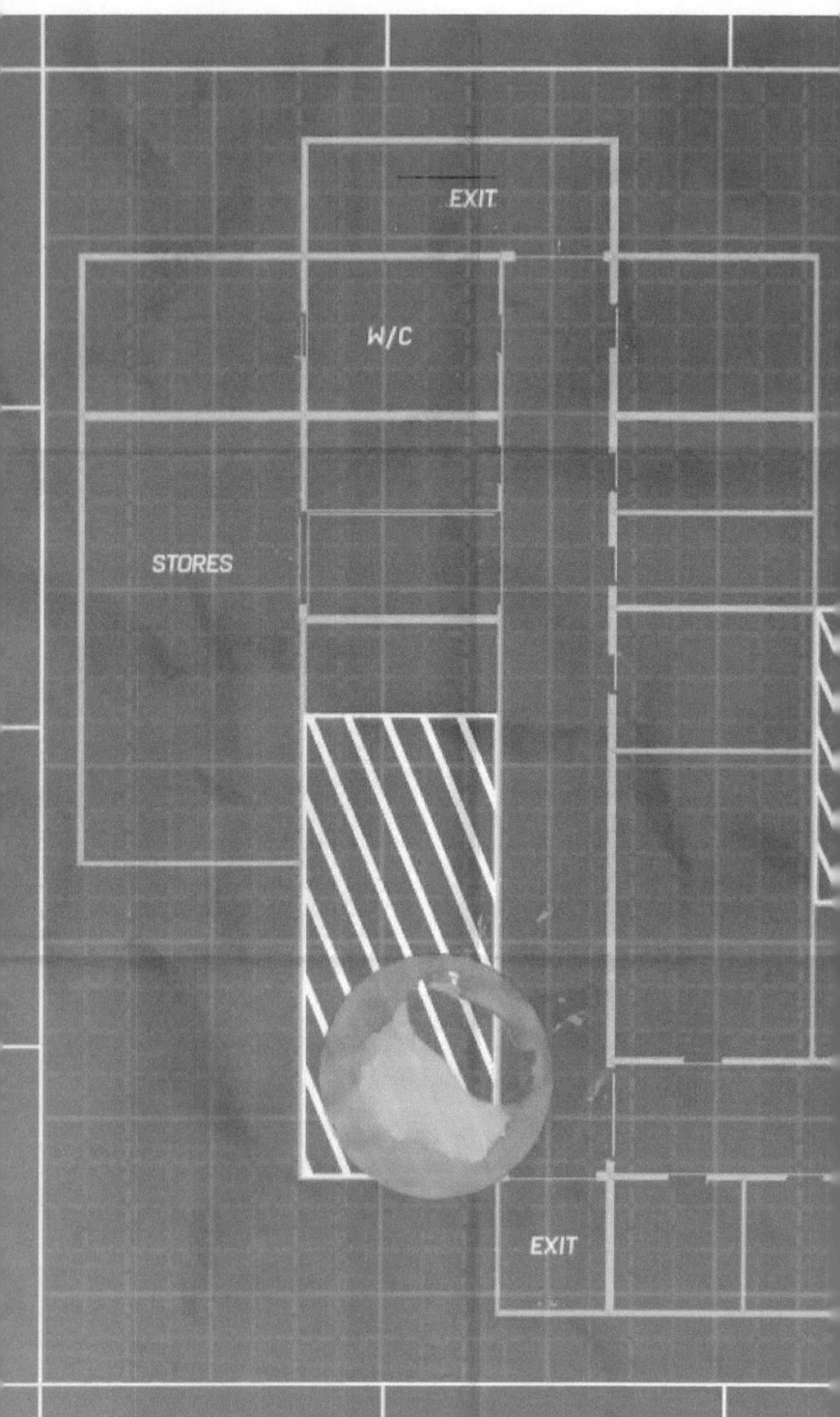

BUNKER 3-M5		
DESIGNED BY USEC 4B		13 APRIL 19??
JOB NUMBER	703-08	
CLIENT	USAF FORWARD SECTOR	

EXIT

1983

Only a small desk lamp illuminated the narrow office, as if turning on the overhead light would shine a beacon on the night sky. But there was no way for light to escape the underground bunker, and the only two people within a hundred miles to see it were in the office.

"You should have let her keep it, Katya," the man said. He was lean and tanned, silver flecks in his black hair. He stood, arms crossed, some feet from the desk.

"Too dangerous. The risk that it would identify her was too great." The woman spoke in a soft, accented voice. Like the man, she was in her fifties, but her hair was a smooth nut brown. Her hands were in her pockets as she, too, stood away from the desk. They didn't look at each other.

The desk held only a few items besides the lamp — a yellowing rotary telephone, a picture frame, a knife for opening letters, and the object of the current discussion.

The egg was only a few inches high, but enough diamonds encrusted its surface that it added a noticeable brightness to the room as the gems reflected the glow of the lamp.

"Are you going to sell it, then?"

There was the faintest note of desire in his voice, but she could hardly fault him for it. "No. Even now, it would be too dangerous."

"So why are you telling me about it? You've kept it a secret for so long — why now?"

Their whole relationship was built upon a solid foundation of secrets. He wasn't blaming her; it was a valid question, one she would answer, for as much as they kept secrets from and for one another, they never lied.

"My daughter is getting married," she said simply. "I wish to give her my desk." The handcrafted secretary was full of nooks and crannies and hidden panels, the perfect place to hide secrets. But it was also the only thing of value she owned, and she wanted her daughter to have it.

He nodded, understanding as she knew he would. "But why bring it here?"

She made a delicate motion with her hands. "I cannot risk it being found. And it is time you knew."

"If you don't trust that boy —"

"I trust him with my daughter. This is not about him." She cut him off. Now was not the time for that. "You've been a part of this, sharing the burden of the secret without knowing what it was. I cannot continue keeping it from you."

The truth was she was tired. Tired of the secrets, tired of being on edge, always one eye looking back. The fear was too deep now, too ingrained to just disappear by getting rid of one item. But she had to try.

"This could have made us a million dollars."

"The risk was too great. Our entire operation would have been exposed." She stepped forward, pressed a large diamond on the front of the egg. It opened, revealing an intricately designed golden chicken. In its beak hung a sapphire pendant. She lifted the necklace with care and folded it in a piece of velvet.

With a deep breath, she faced him. The whole truth. "There are people looking for it. Having them find it here will ruin everything."

His eyes hardened, understanding the danger that would mean.

"You need to go to Russia. Find out what you can. If we can return it, we will." Raising her chin, she waited for the questions.

He held the cloth bundle, eyes flicking to the egg on the desk. "The USSR isn't exactly welcoming Americans right now."

"I cannot go."

"If you're certain this is what needs to happen, then I'll go."

"It is. If we can return it to the family, then we must."

"What are you going to do?"

"Find a new hiding place. The necklace will be enough for you to verify. The real owners will recognize it."

"The girl?"

She shook her head. "She can't know. Too dangerous."

He slipped out the door, footsteps echoing in the concrete tunnel. Alone, her shoulders dropped, and she suddenly looked all of her fifty-plus years. "Too dangerous for all of us, I'm afraid."

1

Three Months Ago

Brody tossed the book into the box and reached for the next one. Why the old man had kept so many books and outdated flight manuals, he'd never know. At first, Brody had just swept the shelves clean, dividing the contents between what to take to the dump and what could be donated. Now he checked every book. The first hundred-dollar bill that had fallen out had surprised him. And he'd assumed it was a mistake. Nonetheless, he'd started flipping through the books. So far, he'd uncovered a stack of bills of all denominations equaling nearly eight hundred dollars, four old airline tickets, an expired check, and a receipt for a pawnshop item that hadn't been redeemed. The old man's pack rat tendencies didn't just extend to books. The entire house was full of the detritus of a long life. Brody had only glanced in the outbuildings. He'd already decided that the shed of lawn mowers, snowblowers, and other equipment wouldn't be touched. He didn't know enough to tell which was any good, and the next owners might need it. Maybe the price could be bumped up if he left it all there.

Either way, he didn't have time to clean it out and try to sell it all individually. He hadn't asked to be the executor of his uncle's will. The old man hadn't even called to say he was sick until the end. Hadn't wanted to bother, he'd told Brody. Yeah, right. He'd died a week later, saddling Brody with the responsibility of selling the property. The proceeds were to be divided among three cousins, so at least he'd get compensated for all his work.

Brody pulled another book from the shelf, causing the next one to tumble to the floor. It fell open, revealing the cutaway center. A black velvet bag sat in the hollowed-out pages. He picked up the book, a hefty tome of poetry whose presence he had wondered about. The bag was heavy, and he set the book back on the shelf to explore the contents. Gold coiled strings kept the bag closed, and it took a minute for him to unpick the knot. He tipped it up, spilling the contents into his palm. A simple gold chain filtered through his fingers. The light caught the gem in his hand, casting reflections in all directions. The oval stone was blue with a hint of green — sapphire, he guessed, about half an inch long. It hung on a simple yet delicate chain.

Grateful for the excuse to leave the books behind, Brody settled into the creaky recliner and pulled out his phone. A quick online search told him that the value of sapphires could be anywhere from fifty to five thousand dollars. Glancing around at the disaster of the living room, Brody made a snap decision. The afternoon was only half over. Plenty of time remaining to do a little investigation. Maybe a jeweler would be able to tell him its value. Perhaps even be willing to buy it off him. He slammed the door behind him. He might make some money off this dump sooner than expected.

Present Day

No time to think. The projectile was inches from her head when Talia "Colt" Levin snatched it out of the air. A size 13 Nike Lebron in pristine condition.

She stepped through the doorway to see what her roommate was up to.

"I need my own place." Mitch threw a second shoe out of the way so he could navigate his wheelchair through the doorway.

"Correction," Colt said, catching the shoe. "*We* need more space."

"I'm the one getting in your way, not the other way around," he argued.

She shrugged. "You're not in our way. This apartment is tiny."

Hawk joined them, his blond hair brushing against the top of the doorframe. "She's right. This was never meant to be permanent. Colt rented it so we'd have a place near the rehab facility while I was still doing daily therapy. Now that you and I are only going once a week, we could easily find a bigger place further out of town."

"Our lease is up at the end of the month, so it's a good time to consider new housing options." She lobbed Mitch's shoes in the direction of the front closet. Both Mitch and Hawk winced, for different reasons, she was sure.

"That still doesn't mean you guys need me underfoot," Mitch protested.

Colt cocked her head. "Wait, do you not want to be roommates with us anymore?" She'd taken it for granted that he was a permanent fixture, but maybe he didn't feel the same.

"What? No. I just...I'm kinda high maintenance." He gestured to his wheelchair and the equipment taking up a corner of the living room.

"Alright, good. That's settled then. We'll buy a bigger place together, yeah?" She started to leave the room.

"With what money? It's not like I can look for work right now."

The snark in Mitch's voice pulled her up short. She looked to Hawk for an explanation, but he was giving her one of those looks like she should know the answer to this already. She sighed. Reading people was not one of her strong suits.

"He's got a point. None of us have jobs at the moment," Hawk commented.

She flinched inwardly. There was no recrimination in Hawk's voice, but she knew what they were both thinking. She had turned down three different jobs in the past few months because she couldn't bear the thought of not flying. Biting her lip, she ran a hand through her brown hair. She flopped into a nearby seat.

"We are going to need money. I've got my eye on a place that would suit us, but it's a bit pricey." The men were eyeing her, so she dived forward. "Mitch, I hate to ask, but have you talked to your sister lately?"

"Kendra? Yeah, last week. Why?"

"Well, uh...did she mention the reward money at all?"

"Reward money?"

"Yeah, from helping with the kidnapping syndicate last year. The FBI promised there'd be a nice reward, but they've not contacted me about it, and I just wondered..." She trailed off, confused by the looks she was getting from both of them.

Hawk perched on the edge of the sofa. "You're telling us you've not been given the reward yet? Any of it?"

"No. Wait — you thought I had it and didn't share with you two? I wouldn't do that!"

"Colt, calm down." He leaned forward. "You're the one who did the hard part, risked your life. It would be fitting for you to keep the whole thing. You don't need to share with us. But we figured, as you kept turning down jobs, that you had a little extra cash on hand."

"Oh. No, that's not why. I'm sorry, guys." She looked between the two of them.

"Don't be. We'll figure something out together." Hawk offered a smile of reassurance.

Nodding in agreement, Mitch pulled out his cell phone. "Let me text Kendra. That money belongs to you. The FBI shouldn't be hanging on to it like that."

Colt slouched in her chair. She didn't want to be a nuisance, but the reward money held the key to her plans. She only hoped that Hawk and Mitch would agree to go along with it. Despite their protestations, they were integral to her helping bring down the kidnappers — in fact, without them, she wasn't sure that she and the other women would have survived. They were entitled to equal portions of the reward. Not that she knew how much they'd be getting. She figured maybe a few hundred thousand. She was counting on her share being enough for a down payment on the place she was considering, but if not, maybe she could wheedle Hawk into giving her a loan. Her secret wish was for the three of them to chip in together. She knew she could achieve her goal on her own if she had to, but in her mind, it was the three of them working together. And, not that she'd admit it out loud, she kinda liked having them around.

Mitch set his phone down. "Kendra says to meet her tomorrow morning at Riverside Park. She doesn't know what's up, but she'll try to find some answers for you before then."

Colt nodded, then pushed herself to her feet. She'd almost made it to her bedroom door before Hawk called her back. His voice held the weight of a father who knew exactly when an errant child was hiding something. She turned around, hands buried in her pockets.

"What aren't you telling us?"

She dug her toe into the carpet, looking back and forth between them. There was no anger, only curiosity, though there was a whole lot more skepticism on Mitch's face than Hawk's. She might as well tell them.

"I want to buy an airfield."

Malik Yasir Al Kandari laughed at the stale joke offered by his guest and reached for the wine bottle. The crisp white paired well with the salmon salad on his plate, but he found himself enjoying it more for its numbing properties than its flavor. As his guest paused for a bite of his own food, Malik took the opportunity to listen for noises within the house behind him. They were lunching on the expansive balcony over the lush gardens that belied the fact he lived in a desert climate. He knew he'd be unable to hear vehicles on the main road from here, obscured by the bird calls from the menagerie, and his butler could put a ninja to shame. Still, he hoped he could detect something that would indicate he would not have to entertain this absolute bore for much longer. He let his mind drift to the reason he had invited this man for lunch today. If he was right, it would be well worth the cost, and he might even forgive the dull conversation. He had flown the man from Italy to Kuwait for a single purpose, and that was not to listen to his attempts at humor.

"So, Mr. Alkanary, how many exotic birds do you have here?" his guest queried as a cockatoo flew overhead.

Malik gave a tight-lipped smile at the mispronunciation. "Please. Call me Mike."

Pietro Carpaggio blinked. "Mike? Yes, of course."

A play on his initials, it was a name that many people recognized. Malik leaned across the table to top up Carpaggio's glass, using the motion to hide his distaste. The nickname was one he had created for himself after discovering how many people wouldn't take the time to learn how to pronounce his name.

"Sir."

His butler's voice at his elbow made him jump. His eagerness for the expected message made him ignore his usual embarrassment over such a thing. "Yes?"

"The package has arrived. You requested that I inform you as soon as it was here."

"Yes, thank you. You've placed it in my office?"

"As instructed. And Mr. Driscoll is waiting for you."

"Excellent." Malik stood, dropping his napkin onto his plate. His appetite was forgotten in his excitement. "Mr. Carpaggio, won't you join me?"

Malik led the way to his office. Their footsteps echoed on the marble flooring. The office was a contrast to the bright white of the foyer and staircase. Paneled in dark oak, it was furnished with heavy, dark furniture and curtains in deep jewel tones. A young man with a shaved head sat on the black leather sofa. He stood as Malik and his guest entered.

Once introductions were finished, Malik got right to business. "You've brought it?"

"As requested." Driscoll motioned to a metal briefcase on the credenza.

Malik approached it, doing his best to hide his eagerness. Driscoll had no idea how much his delivery was worth. Oh, he'd been quite content with the agreed-upon delivery fee of three percent of the five million US dollars Malik had paid for the item, but if he suspected what Malik knew, Driscoll would have asked for ten times that amount. Carpaggio, unaware of his role in this, stood back, for which Malik was grateful. He didn't want the man to give away the truth before the transaction was complete.

Malik checked the case over, confirming the seal was still intact. The silver tape, emblazoned with the logo of the renowned New

York auction house, Rothschild's, showed no sign of tampering. He turned to the courier.

"Mr. Driscoll, my butler will take you to enjoy some refreshments and the rest of your payment." His butler appeared on cue, and Driscoll took his leave.

Once the door closed firmly behind the two, Malik pulled a tablet and a box of a similar size from a drawer in the credenza. Using the tablet, he made a call that was quickly answered by a small, silver-haired man.

"Mr. Rothschild," Malik said, "the parcel has arrived. I'm about to open it in the presence of my authenticator, Pietro Carpaggio."

Mr. Rothschild nodded. "Proceed."

Malik set the tablet down so the camera could pick up his movements. He opened the small box to reveal a penknife, several pairs of white cotton gloves, and a jeweler's loupe. Using the penknife, he carefully slit the tape. He peeled it back to reveal a fingerprint scanner. Laying his thumb against the small screen, he waited impatiently for the lock to release. It did so with a dull thunk. Malik carefully opened the case and lifted out a square velvet box that he set on the credenza.

Slipping on a pair of white cotton gloves, Malik raised the lid. The sunlight immediately caught the facets of the contents, flashing blue around the room. Malik swallowed hard. How had Rothschild missed the egg shape of the sapphire? It was described only as an oval stone, a description that failed to touch on the true opulence of the necklace before him. A simple gold chain held a single pendant, a large sapphire the size of the end of his pinky. It had been polished, revealing the depth of the stone, the variance in color between blue and green.

Rothschild began offering a litany of the necklace's specifications. Malik took the jeweler's loupe and studied the gem. To his amateur's eye, it was flawless. But he wasn't about to make the mistake of so many, claiming to recognize perfect stones when they were actually cut glass. He beckoned Carpaggio to join them. The man, understanding his purpose there at last, was all business. Wordlessly, he pulled on his own cotton gloves before reaching for the necklace. Malik watched him carefully. Saw the moment Carpaggio clued in. He drew back, and his Adam's apple bobbed. He looked at Malik, who gave him a slight shake of his head. Carpaggio lowered his head again to study the sapphire further. After a moment, he straightened and handed it back to Malik.

"It is as described," Carpaggio said, his voice clear.

"Thank you, gentlemen," Malik said as he returned the necklace to its box. "Mr. Rothschild, thank you. It has been a delight working with you as always."

"Your satisfaction makes it all worthwhile," Rothschild replied before ending the call. Once the screen went blank, Malik circled his desk and pulled a wooden cigar box from a drawer. He offered one to Carpaggio, feeling generous toward the man once again. He lit the cigars and settled into his favorite chair. Carpaggio took Driscoll's place on the sofa.

"Is it truly...?"

"That is what you are here for," Malik said, smiling around the cigar.

Carpaggio stowed his cigar on the ashtray and approached the credenza. "May I?"

"Go ahead," Malik replied, waving the cigar magnanimously.

Carpaggio lifted the box and, after a nod from Malik, settled behind the desk. He drew the lamp closer and adjusted his position to ensure the sunlight cast no shadows on the workspace. Pulling a suede roll out of his inner pocket, he draped it over the desk and selected a tool. Malik leaned back in his chair, enjoying the rich aroma of the cigar while Carpaggio worked. He was certain of his prize, but certainty was meaningless without confirmation. Carpaggio was the world's leading expert in the work of Peter Carl Fabergé. If Malik had truly uncovered a missing piece of the Imperial collection, he would know. Malik puffed away in silence while Carpaggio worked. He didn't care how long it took; it would be worth it. He had a large collection of rare and unusual items and was always on the lookout to add to it. When a sometimes rival hinted that a certain lost artwork had made it into his collection in recent years, Malik had searched exhaustively for his own.

At last, Carpaggio looked up, his gray face lit up with excitement. "Mr. Alkanary — Mike, I think you've done it. Based on my expertise and a thorough examination of this piece, I truly believe you have uncovered a missing Fabergé."

Malik smiled around his cigar and got to his feet. There was no reason to put off the celebration any longer.

"So tell me," Carpaggio said as he replaced the piece in its velvet nest. "Where did you find this delightful treasure?"

Malik opened the bottle of forty-year-old Balvenie whisky and poured them each a glass. "In the United States. The seller claims there is nothing more, but I'm not convinced. I've got people looking for more."

"You think the Egg still exists?" He removed his gloves and returned to the sofa.

Malik did not appreciate the note of eagerness in Carpaggio's voice, but he knew better than to let his face reveal his feelings. He handed the other man one of the glasses. "The pendant was found; I have to believe the Egg will be too. And when it is, it will become part of my collection."

"Surely the two would have been sold together? A complete set would draw more money than piecemeal." Carpaggio swirled the beverage around his glass before taking a cautious sip.

"Unless it was a strategic move to garner interest before revealing the Egg, thus pushing the demand and price much higher. He couldn't have known that I would buy it before it went to auction."

"You convinced Rothschild to sell it to you without an auction?"

That was better. Let Carpaggio be impressed at Malik's negotiation skills and business connections. Malik took an appreciative sniff of his whisky. "I've been paying him a healthy finder's fee for the past five years to keep an eye out for such rarities for me. But enough about me. Tell me more about the Fabergé pieces you've worked with in the past."

It was a topic carefully designed to get Carpaggio talking. Malik wasn't foolish enough to expect to identify work by the master on his own, but if he could eliminate obvious replicas before needing to pay the expert, he would. Before long though, Malik wished he hadn't asked. The hand on the grandfather clock took too long to march around its face. At last, the butler appeared, the signal that it was time for Carpaggio to leave for his flight back to Italy.

"Mike, I do thank you for allowing me the privilege of seeing the lost pendant. I trust you will call me should your fortune ever increase to attaining the Fabergé Egg."

Malik stood to walk him out. "I will do just that, *when* I add the Egg to my collection."

Carpaggio gave a short bow, hesitating before he spoke. "Greed has led to the downfall of many."

Malik returned the bow, smugly certain of his ability to get what he wanted. It wasn't greed; it was purpose.

"Well, this is the first time I've had clients arrive for a viewing in an airplane," the man said, looking at the Cessna. "I'm Walter Plouffe, of Greenstone Real Estate Company. I'm so glad you called."

Colt glanced at him. He was slightly taller than her but was dwarfed by both Mitch and Hawk. Dressed in khakis with a black polo sporting the logo of his company, he had the eager-to-please smile of a salesman. She completed her walk-around of the plane before directing her focus to the business of the day.

"Runway's in rough shape," Hawk observed.

"Yeah, not surprising though. I doubt it's been used much in the past few years." She stepped back, taking a broader look at their surroundings.

They were in the middle of a large forest, some distance from Scranton, Pennsylvania. The runway took up the larger leg of a backward L shape. Behind her on the outside edge was a lonely tower, painted gray, now faded and peeling. Opposite were two metal hangars with flaking paint. At the far end of the short leg was a cluster of smaller buildings. The whole place had an air of disrepair. Grass and weeds were sprouting through the cracks of the runway, and pine trees were encroaching on the cleared land beyond the tarmac.

Colt smiled. It was missing the bustle of her memories, the line of small planes parked along the apron, the friendly calls of the people working among the machines. The life of the airfield might have left for a time, but it was exactly how she remembered it.

"The price — that includes everything, right? The land, the house, the contents?" she asked, interrupting Walter's listing of the property value and how much they could get per square acre if they chose to subdivide.

"There's a house?" Hawk asked.

Colt pointed at the grouping of small buildings in the distance while waiting for Walter to flip through his paperwork for her answers.

"Yes." Walter consulted his notes. "Everything. As long as it's sold as is, no limitations. Pending inspection, of course."

"Of course," Colt agreed.

They moved to the tower, the agent opening the door with a ring of keys. Mitch opted to not climb the four flights of stairs with his prosthetics, but the others went up. Colt pointed out some of the landmarks while Hawk studied the equipment.

"You seem very familiar with this property," Walter said.

"I grew up here. My grandmother was part owner." Colt felt Hawk stiffen behind her. Of course. She should have told him. But she had hoped he'd take an unbiased look at the place. And it was nothing compared with the lovely house he'd grown up in. She knew he'd find out at some point, but she hadn't meant to let it slip like that. After a brief meeting with her estranged brother last year, she couldn't get his comments about their grandmother out of her head. She did a cursory search for anything related to her grandmother and stumbled across the obituary of the man who had co-owned the airfield. When the property came up for sale, the idea of buying it wouldn't leave her alone.

"Well!" Walter exclaimed, not picking up on the undercurrents in the room. "Buying this airfield will give you a chance to get to know your grandmother better!"

Colt shrugged. "I knew her pretty well. Buying this place won't change that."

"Still!" He beamed. "It's a bit of kismet, eh? You being back here, reconnecting."

Colt rolled her shoulders, choosing to ignore the comment.

They continued walking around the property, discussing the details. They only took the time to look inside the closer of the two hangars. It was mostly empty, with one sorry-looking Piper Cub in the center, its propeller propped up on the ground beside it. The periphery of the building was full of debris of sundry types.

"The other hangar is more or less the same, I'm afraid," Walter said. "Only with less clear space."

"Could we negotiate to have that removed?" Hawk asked.

"No, that won't be necessary," Colt interrupted before steering them toward the house.

For Mitch's sake, they piled into Walter's car and drove down the slight hill. The two-hundred-year-old farmhouse was surrounded by a large barn and two smaller ones.

"There's an old tractor, used for mowing and snow blowing, in the barn," Walter explained. "The seller is assuming you'll be wanting them, but if not, something can be arranged." He didn't sound eager to do the arranging.

"Why is he so interested in getting shot of everything? Seems a bit sketch to me," Mitch said. He'd been mostly silent.

"The current owner inherited the property from his uncle who passed away a few months ago. After sorting through the personal effects in the house, he decided it wasn't worth his time to sell everything piecemeal unless he had to. I believe the right buyer would be interested in the property as is." He looked at Colt as he spoke, a knowing grin on his face.

She turned to look out the window, not wanting to think about her grandmother. She focused on the barn. If the old man had felt a tractor was needed for clearing snow, who was she to argue?

As they pulled around the barn, a large man came into view. Walter stopped the car and went over to speak to him. Colt watched the exchange, frowning at how easily Walter seemed to accept the man's reason for being there. He flipped through his set of keys and unlocked the small side door.

"What was that about?" Hawk asked when Walter rejoined them.

"Oh, nothing. The owner apparently hired him to mow the grass but forgot to give him the key to the barn. Let's head inside."

Colt followed him, wondering how often grass needed to be mowed. It looked short to her, but she was far from an expert.

The house was full of character, touches of old and new as things had been renovated over the years. Two stories, it had a cellar-like basement under the original part of the house. The kitchen was the center of the house, with the other rooms leading off it. Hawk was impressed by the large pantry, even though he had to duck through the doorway to enter. Two sets of stairs led to the upstairs, one a straight set from the front hall, the other a disjointed jumble off the kitchen. Upstairs, three bedrooms of varying sizes were scattered around, connected by narrow halls, low doors, and intermittent steps. The main bathroom was large with an elegant clawfoot bathtub.

"All new wiring and downstairs windows," Walter told them proudly.

"Downstairs only has a half bath," Mitch said, his head stuck in a closet door.

"There's a bedroom down here, isn't there?" Colt asked. "The floor plan indicated one."

"Yes," Walter agreed, hurrying across the tiny kitchen in the center of the house. "It was probably a den at one point, but the old gentleman used it as a bedroom."

The three walked in. It was mostly empty now, just an old dresser and wooden rocker in the corner. Colt remembered the battered sofas and worn-out chairs where she and the other air cadets had spent their evenings. Things had changed but not that much. There was a familiarity to it.

"Well," Walter said as they headed back to the Cessna. "Are you interested in making an offer?"

Colt looked from Hawk to Mitch. They'd discussed it on the way down, whether it was a good idea and what they could do with the property. With any luck, the airplanes would be in good condition, and they could reopen the flight school Frank and Katya had run. Hawk gave her a ready nod.

"I think you should go for it," Mitch said. Colt noted his careful wording. Now wasn't the time, but something was bothering him.

"Yes," Colt said, scanning the tree line. "There's just one problem. I'm going to need a day to sort out the money."

Walter looked at his phone. "I've got other people who are interested in this place, but for you, I'll hold them off for twenty-four hours. Because of your grandmother."

"I'll call you before four o'clock tomorrow," Colt said, hoping that she'd be able to meet her deadline. She was counting on Kendra to make it happen.

"I'll get a contract drawn up and start working on the details. You call me tomorrow once you've arranged financing." Walter beamed at them. The property was for sale for one and a half million dollars, so he'd be earning a nice chunk from that commission. Colt couldn't blame him for being happy. "Are there any other conditions you'd like added?"

"No, we'll take it as is, the planes, tractor included. Any furniture he'd like to leave as well is fine. We've not got a huge variety."

Hawk joined the discussion. "What about the junk in the other hangar? Should we see about that being removed before we take possession?"

Colt shook her head. "No, that's fine."

"Are you sure? It'd be a lot to deal with."

"I'm sure. Everything as is." She shot him a look. She didn't dare look in the hangar now, not when everyone was watching. She wanted to find it on her own, when she could savor the discovery. And that was supposing it even still existed. She refused to consider that it might be gone. Frank's hoarding tendencies gave her hope that it was still there, but she wasn't ready to face the chance it was the one thing he'd gotten rid of.

"Alright, property in as-is condition, pending results of environmental and structural inspections." Walter spoke as he typed himself a note in his phone.

"Great. Talk to you tomorrow." Colt waited while Hawk climbed into the back of the Cessna. With his prosthetic legs, Mitch found it too difficult to maneuver into the rear seats, so Hawk had to fold his long legs into the cramped space. Colt was not looking forward to the day Hawk completed his license. At that point, logic and weight distribution would dictate that she sit back there, and she didn't like taking a back seat. Besides, she could barely see over the window ledge.

Normally, she'd prefer Hawk in the front with her. They were, after all, well trained to work together. But in this instance, she was grateful he wasn't beside her. And grateful for the noise of the engines. Although they could all talk via the radio headsets, it wasn't an environment conducive to deep conversations. And she wasn't ready to face her best friend's questions about her grandmother and the airfield just yet.

By now it was late enough in the day that the mountains had started to grow shadows, splashes of deep blue across the sea of green, all against a clear, boundless sky. Normally even a short flight like this would be enough to settle Colt's nerves, as tensions and concerns were drowned out by the noise of the engine, but this time there was a very pointed silence dampening the mood.

The tension grew as they landed and as she logged the flight with Simon in the office, and then finally broke once they made it to Hawk's pickup. He put the key into the ignition, sat for a second, then turned to Colt.

"Why didn't you tell us your grandmother owned that airfield before we went to see it?"

"Your grandmother what now?" Mitch said, leaning forward so he could catch Colt's eyes.

"I didn't want you to be biased." Colt let out a breath. "It wasn't going to be a big secret; I was going to tell you both once you'd seen the place. My grandmother Katya co-owned it with a man named Frank Farrell. They ran a flight school there, the one I proposed we re-open. If I'd told you that I grew up there, you wouldn't have been making a decision just about the house and airfield."

"Dude, obviously you should buy this place. It's your home," Mitch argued.

She shook her head. "I pitched this to you guys as our future because it would be. It's my past, yes, but this is the next few years of our lives. We can set up a flight school anywhere. I wanted to be sure we all felt this was the right place."

"This changes nothing for me," Hawk said. "It's a great property, with loads of potential." He twisted around so he could see Mitch. "What about you?"

"It's a great spot, and the fact your grandmother used to own it makes it even better."

Colt nodded, glad they understood. But still something bothered her. "Mitch, you keep leaving yourself out. What's that about?"

"It's just a lot of work, and you guys don't need me —"

"It *is* a lot of work," Hawk interrupted. "Which is why we do need you. Fixing up this place to get it back in working order."

"We won't force you, Mitch. It's your decision," Colt said, wondering what had changed since their first conversation about buying a bigger place.

Mitch sighed. "Look, guys, I'll think about it, okay? Either way, I think you guys should buy the place."

After a moment, Hawk cleared his throat. "There's one more question, Colt. Why do *you* want it?"

She cocked her head, thinking. It was a valid question, and the boys deserved a proper explanation. "Partly timing. We were ready for something new, and this came on the market at the right time. I'm familiar with the property and the business side of it as well."

Hawk nodded, accepting her response. He started the truck, and they headed back to the apartment. Watching the landscape roll by her window, Colt wondered why she wasn't satisfied with her own answer.

Malik stroked the velvet muzzle of the black stallion. The Arabian huffed into his hand, searching for more carrots. Malik obliged, unable to refuse Pozan's demands. Despite the heat and the low-key sandstorm that had been looming for the past three days, Pozan's coat was gleaming. Malik made a note to commend the groom on his excellent care of the stallion on the way out. For now, he was trying to concentrate on the numbers and statistics his head trainer was throwing at him. Several stables had applied for breeding opportunities now that the champion had retired from racing. Three straight wins at the end of his career meant the potential for stud fees had skyrocketed, something that pleased Malik greatly. He loved the thrill of owning racehorses, the status the magnificent animals brought him, but he was ever on the lookout to make sure the investment paid off. Pozan came from a small racing stable in Azerbaijan, and Malik was thrilled that the horse had lived up to his potential.

The quote the trainer had just outlined was excellent, but he was failing at hiding a smirk. Malik inclined his head.

"Out with it."

"We've received an offer from Bayda Natheel Stables."

Malik raised an eyebrow, waiting for the details. The Saudi stables were renowned in the region, but he wasn't about to let on that he was impressed just yet.

The trainer named a price nearly double the other offers. "They want to cover their mare, Karianna, who won several races a year ago. This will be her second foal. But they are also offering Kalina as well, full sister to Karianna, who didn't race after injuring herself during her first season. If we so choose, the foal of Kalina and Pozan is ours to purchase."

An interesting offer. Pozan was more than capable of providing covers for all the mares, but the fewer foals he sired, the more desirable he would be. However, the chance to own a foal of that lineage would be an excellent opportunity.

His phone vibrated in his pocket. Normally, he wouldn't take the call during a meeting, but this wasn't one he could delay. The trainer bowed and stepped back, giving Malik privacy.

"I'm in a good mood," Malik proclaimed as he answered the phone. "Tell me you're not going to ruin it."

"I think this is going to make you even happier," the caller replied. "I've been discreet like you said, but there's a property for sale. Old place, full of junk. Old guy died. Whoever is in charge of things doesn't seem interested in it. I'd say there's a good chance we can find what you're looking for there."

"How much?" He kept his voice calm. His hand clenched by his side, the thrill of the hunt flooding through him. Was this the right place?

"One point five mil. I'd say we could offer less, but there's already one offer in, and they seem ready to accept it."

Malik ran his hand along Pozan's neck, pondering his options. The horse tossed his head and snorted. Malik smiled. Pozan was right.

"Offer double. I want that property."

2

Colt stared at the vaulted ceiling of the Metropolitan Museum of Art as Hawk paid for four tickets. A few feet away, Mitch studied a floor map, trying to determine the best route to take for wheel-chair accessibility. Beside him, Mackenzie and Amanda chattered away about the exhibits. Colt relaxed as she listened to the two girls. In the year since the three of them had been kidnapped, the younger women had shown great resilience in their recovery.

Hawk finished with the customer service associate and joined the group, passing out the tickets to everyone except Colt. She checked her watch.

"Time for me to go. I'll catch up with you guys later." She waved goodbye and headed down the stone steps to the museum. With any luck, the others would be through the museum by the time she got back. Not that she minded experiencing art and history normally. But she was too on edge to relax enough to enjoy hours exploring the vast collection. Meeting Kendra and getting the reward money meant they could get things rolling for moving out of the cramped apartment.

The subway delivered her a block away from Kendra's latest stakeout spot. Posters for a pop-up art gallery opening that weekend were plastered all over the glass windows of the ground floor, and the lobby was full of people setting up displays. Colt dodged around an electrician on a ladder and ran up the stairs to the third floor. Signs indicated four different offices, and she chose the one without a nameplate. She rapped on the glass door. An FBI goon let her in and directed her to where Kendra stood by a window.

"Nice place," Colt said, noting the large desk and sleek furniture of the corner office.

"Thank you. We should be up and running by tomorrow."

Colt knew better than to ask for details on the investigation. After they exchanged pleasantries, Kendra got right to the point. Colt appreciated that about Mitch's sister.

"Mitch tells me you have not received your reward." She walked over to the desk and closed a file.

"That's right." Colt followed, noting the stack of art books on the corner of the desk.

Kendra made a sound that from anyone less refined would have been a snort. "What took you so long to inquire about it?"

Colt shrugged, the leather of her jacket creaking. "Had no idea how long it would take and didn't want to bother you."

"So why did you decide now to bother me?"

The tone was curious, not argumentative, so Colt went along with it. "The need for money has suddenly become a pressing concern on our end. I'm hoping that the usual time for processing rewards has passed."

"No other reason?" Kendra pressed.

"No? Should there be?"

"No." There was a pause as a technician carrying a large piece of equipment entered the room. He paused, then backpedaled out.

"Well, on behalf of the Federal Bureau of Investigation, I apologize for the delay in the forwarding of your funds. Details concerning the redemption of your reward can be found in this envelope. Such apology does not indicate in any way an assumption of guilt on the side of the Bureau." Kendra paused and handed a blank white envelope to Colt.

Colt accepted it and tucked it into her inside jacket pocket for safekeeping. She cocked an eyebrow at Kendra, waiting for the rest of the story. Kendra sighed, taking a seat in the executive chair.

"You were right." Her voice lost its official tone, dropping into conversation. She motioned for Colt to also sit. "You should have been given this months ago. Unfortunately, the Bureau decided to try something new with its larger rewards, and the ball was dropped along the way."

"Larger rewards?" Colt said hopefully. Maybe she could afford the airfield on her own after all.

"Yes. Obviously, based on the syndicate you helped take down, the reward would be equal in proportion." Before Colt could ask for clarification, Kendra's phone rang.

"Special Agent Mitchell," she answered crisply. There was a pause as she listened to the person on the other end of the call. "Yes, sir, I am aware... No, not until tomorrow." She looked sideways at Colt as she listened again.

Colt cocked an eyebrow, but Kendra pointedly turned away.

"Are you sure? ...Yes, of course. Thank you for letting me know, sir." Kendra ended the call and placed the phone on the desktop, adjusting the position until it sat squarely in the middle of the white marbled blotter. She took a deep breath before looking up at Colt.

Colt returned the look, waiting for Kendra to share the bad news.

"All of the charges against Mark Fisher have been dropped, including the kidnapping, unlawful imprisonment, and trafficking of the twenty women last year."

As the words hit, cold swept over Colt, wrapping around her chest. She sprang to her feet, moving to the window, but there was no air there either. "That's impossible."

"Unfortunately not. He has struck a plea deal to turn state's evidence in exchange for all charges being dropped against him."

Colt clenched her fists, fingernails driving painlessly into her palms. "So that's it? He gets off scot-free for everything he did to those women?" She didn't include herself as she didn't consider herself a victim, having chosen to put herself in that situation to uncover what was happening to the women who were taken.

Kendra nodded.

Colt spun on her heel, her fist lashing out. The drywall cracked from the force, sending dust flying.

Hawk pushed against the flow of people, wondering why everyone was avoiding the entrance to one of the many skyscrapers. At first, he assumed a celebrity had caused a cordon around the area, but his hopes sank as he noted the building number was the one he was looking for.

Colt paced a tight loop outside the formidable glass doors. A sidewalk in New York was not the most accessible place for pacing, but she was giving off such anger, the crowd was moving to the side to give her space. Hawk waited until she had turned around to face him before approaching. He knew better than to startle her at such a moment. She stopped in front of him, arms rigid at her sides, jaw locked, breathing fast.

"Mark is free!" she spewed. "They let him go because he says he'll testify against the others."

He frowned. "I know."

"He deserves to be punished."

"Our justice system at work." He didn't like it any more than she did.

"It's ridiculous. There was more than enough evidence against them. The lawyers shouldn't need his testimony." She crossed her arms. He could feel the rage coming off her.

"He would have information about the inner workings of the operation though." At least, he hoped the deal would be worth it.

He shrugged in response to the dirty look she shot him.

"Where are Mackenzie and Amanda?"

"I left them with Kendra. Amanda didn't take the news well, so I opted to give them space."

Colt nodded, danger lurking in her gray eyes. He needed to distract her before she decided to kill Mark herself.

"Now, tell me, why did you want to meet here of all places?" He gestured to the sign on the glass door, indicating they were outside a high-end investment and banking firm, Danforth & Briggs.

"Oh, right. Let's go inside." She led the way, explaining how the FBI had invested their reward money. Hawk followed along, making a note to pay attention to Colt's mental state over the next little while. After she had escaped from the kidnappers last year, she had been withdrawn and moody for weeks. He hoped this bad news wouldn't cause her to fall back into that.

They waited in line to speak with a teller, the opulence of the public banking area making them feel out of place. Or at least, Hawk felt out of place. He wasn't sure if Colt even noticed she wasn't wearing thousand-dollar ensembles like everyone around her. Certainly the woman behind them with coiffed hair and a Hermes purse noticed. She stood back, a slight curl to her lip whenever she glanced their way. Hawk planted himself behind Colt until it was their turn. Colt handed the teller a letter, explaining she wanted to withdraw all the funds in the account listed there. Apparently that was not a request the teller particularly wanted to grant, and the two soon found themselves seated in a fancy corner office on the twenty-fifth floor. Floor-to-ceiling windows on two sides offered them bright views of yet more glass-sided buildings. Hawk turned to Colt.

"What does the letter say, exactly? Are you not allowed to move the funds for some reason?"

She shrugged and handed him the paper. "Nothing like that. It's just the account number and my name, identifying me as the account holder. Shouldn't be that big of a deal."

Hawk accepted the letter, frowning at the flecks of blood caked on her knuckles. It didn't seem to bother her. But then, injuries never did. He wondered where her gloves were. "No, it shouldn't be a big deal. But evidently, it is." He pointed to the nameplate on the white and glass desk.

"Chauncey Danforth IV, vice president of accounts," she read. "Danforth, as in Danforth & Briggs?"

"I would assume so."

"Are we in trouble?" She shoved her hands in her back pockets and paced the room.

He skimmed the letter again. "No, trouble would mean security tosses us to the curb. Coffee means something else entirely." He nodded at the door that was opening to reveal the secretary returning with the promised refreshments on a tray. She moved with pinched steps, limited by the high heels and straight, knee-length skirt she wore. Bending awkwardly, she placed the tray on the table between two white leather sofas.

"Mr. Danforth will be right with you. Is there anything else I can bring?" She smiled up at Hawk, ignoring Colt.

He smiled right back. "Not at the moment, but that's awfully kind of you to ask." Ignoring Colt's sudden coughing attack, he held the door for the young woman as she returned to her desk.

Colt turned to the metal and glass shelving unit, studying a framed picture. "The guy's son is in the Navy," she observed. Hawk joined her. The picture was of a good-looking young man in Navy dress whites, standing at attention between a US flag and a tiny white-haired woman in a red velvet chair.

"Hmm, looks like he's in logistics. Wonder what ship he's on."

"Who knows, but guaranteed he's the payroll officer," Colt joked.

"I assure you, being a banker is about more than just handling stacks of cash," a voice said behind them. The pair spun around. Hawk couldn't help but notice Colt's hand went to her back, but she was smart enough to not bring her concealed piece into a bank.

"You," she said, somewhat stupidly.

"Yes, me." The man from the picture gave a suave smile and extended his hand in greeting. "I'm Chauncey Danforth. I understand you're here about an account you'd like to close?"

The two introduced themselves, then joined him at the sofas. He poured them coffee, and Colt handed over the letter.

"As you can see, we helped the FBI with solving a crime and as such were entitled to a reward. We only learned today that the reward is being held here, and we'd like to withdraw it to make a down payment on a property."

Danforth nodded, then flipped open a thin folder. "Do you have any idea how much money is in this account?"

"No, but I'm hoping it's at least two hundred thousand dollars for the down payment. But even if it's less, we can make it work. I just need it before 4 p.m. today." Colt finished by looking pointedly at the clock, which was inching nearer to three.

Danforth pulled a sheet of paper from the file and leaned across the table. "Your current balance is just over 5.1 million dollars. The initial deposit was five million, and as you can see, we've been rather successful in our investments, enabling us to add significant interest to the principal in just under a year. I'm sure we can —"

"Five million?" Colt's voice sounded a bit strained as she interrupted his spiel.

Hawk leaned over to read over her shoulder. There had to be some mistake, surely. They hadn't done anything worthy of five million dollars.

Colt showed him the page. "With that much, we wouldn't need a mortgage. We could buy the place outright. If you and Mitch are still okay with that?"

He looked at her, surprised she was still asking that question. "Of course we are. And even if Mitch didn't want to, there'd still be plenty. It's your money, after all."

"Our money," she said firmly before turning back to the banker. "How quickly can we have access to this?"

Danforth's mouth worked up and down for a minute. "You can't just take five million dollars from a bank. It's tied up in shares and mutual funds..."

"You're telling me you don't have five million dollars in your vault? What kind of bank are you?"

Hawk settled himself into the corner of the sofa. This would be fun.

"A very reputable one. What I'm saying is that *your* money isn't readily available, as we've put it into investments for you."

"On whose authority? I certainly didn't agree to that."

Danforth retreated to his folder. "We were instructed by the depositor..."

"Look, Mr. Danforth. I need 1.5 million dollars within the hour to buy an airfield." Screw the down payment and mortgage. If the FBI had given them five million, they could buy the place outright.

"An hour?"

Hawk hid a snicker. The man looked positively horrified.

"But it...it's tied up in mutual funds..."

Colt leaned forward, locking on Danforth with a glare. "I don't really care about your mutual funds, but I think it will be mutually beneficial if you got my money out of them."

Colt tucked the envelope of paperwork into her pocket, a triumphant smirk on her face. Hawk held the door, and they exited into a blast of wind.

She pulled out her cell phone, preferring the anonymity of the crowded sidewalks to the quiet eavesdroppers of the hushed marble lobby. "Hi, Walter? Yes, Talia Levin here. I've got the cash for the airfield."

"Cash?" Walter said at the other end of the line.

"Well, a wire transfer at any rate. Will that be okay?"

"For the total amount? Yes, of course. Good thing you called when you did," he added. "The other buyer has been hounding me all day, and I was about to give in."

"Yeah, well, you can blame the blokes at Danforth & Briggs. They were reluctant to give up my money." And she still wasn't entirely sure they had. Danforth had made a lot of excuses before offering an unconventional solution. She'd signed a lot of forms.

Danforth had promised to sort it all out in the coming weeks, but he swore it was the only way to get her access to immediate funds.

"Danforth & Briggs?" Walter sputtered.

"Uh, yeah. Is that okay? You'll take a transfer from them, or should I move it to another bank?" Colt raised an eyebrow at Hawk, who just shrugged in response. Would that delay mean they would miss out on the deal? Could she even do that with all the hoops Danforth had listed?

"No! No, that's fine. I'll get the paperwork drawn up, and you can come sign it as soon as it's ready."

She ended the call and slid her phone back into her pocket.

"How does it feel to be a millionaire?" Hawk asked.

Colt rolled her shoulders. "Don't really feel like one. You?"

"Colt, you know you don't have to share that. You're the one who —"

She moved in front of him, glaring. "Would you stop that? You helped. Mitch helped. I wouldn't have been able to do any of it without you. So no. I am not going to keep it all. You're taking your share, and that's that."

"Fine." He settled back on his heels, a slow smile forming. "We need to do something big to surprise Mitch with this."

"Agreed."

They tossed ideas back and forth as they headed toward the subway station. Colt's phone rang as they started down the steps. She checked the caller ID before answering. Mackenzie.

Colt made sure her voice was light as she answered. "Hey, Mackenzie, what's up?"

"They won't let me in to see her. Kendra came and told us. Amanda had a panic attack. They won't let me in." The words were rushed together, obscured by sobs.

"Where are you?"

A sniffle, then the teary voice. "At the hospital in Melbourne. I need to know if she's okay."

"Hang on, Mackenzie, we're on our way."

Colt glanced at the subway schedule board. The next train to where they had left their vehicles departed in two minutes. Hawk nodded, already on page with her. They increased their pace, making it through the turnstiles and jumping on board just as the doors closed.

Colt had had more than enough bureaucracy for one day.

Gray streaked the sky as they pulled into the hospital parking lot. Colt spotted Mackenzie as she and Hawk approached the main entrance. The girl wore an oversized hoodie over ripped jeans. Her long hair fell from the raised hood, a deliberate attempt not to be noticed.

Colt tried to catch her eye as they drew near, but Mackenzie looked away, scrubbing at her face with the too-long sleeve. Hawk stepped forward, his arms an open invitation.

Mackenzie collapsed against Hawk's broad chest, shoulders heaving. Colt stepped back. Chin up, arms folded, she took up a defensive position.

"Shhh, it's okay," Hawk said, rubbing Mackenzie's back.

Muffled, incoherent words came from behind the curtain of blond hair. Colt looked at Hawk, hoping he had understood. He ignored her, murmuring comforting words as the sobs continued. Colt shoved her hands in her back pockets and scanned the parking lot. A small group of people carrying giant balloons glanced their way before averting their gaze. Colt narrowed her eyes at them. It's not like tearful scenes were unheard of outside hospitals.

At last, Mackenzie pulled away from Hawk, mopping her face with her sleeves. Hawk pulled a clean, folded handkerchief from his pocket and gave it to her. She nodded in thanks. Once she was cleaned up, she turned to Colt and fell on her with a tight hug.

"Oh, Colt!"

Colt stiffened, fighting the urge to jerk away. Thankfully, Mackenzie let go before the feeling got too strong.

"They won't let me in to see her or tell me anything about her condition. Her parents are on their way but won't be here for a while."

Colt straightened her jacket, giving herself a minute to recover from the hug attack. Hawk had told her what had happened at the museum during their drive. "I'm sure she's fine. The doctors will take good care of her."

"Do you really think so?" The hopeful look on Mackenzie's face made Colt flinch. What if she were wrong?

"Let's go find out."

"They won't let us in," Mackenzie reminded them as they moved toward the main doors of the hospital.

"We'll figure something out," Colt promised.

A security desk sat directly in front of them, with a bank of elevators to their left. To the right, the area opened up to provide seating space for a small cafe. Hawk stepped toward the security desk to ask for Amanda's room, but Colt grabbed his sleeve.

A man wearing a three-letter jacket and carrying two coffees wove between the tables of the cafe. Colt turned and got to the elevator before him. The doors opened, and they all filed in.

"What floor?" Hawk asked as the agent juggled the hot beverages.

"Four, thanks," he replied.

Hawk pressed the button for the fourth floor as well as the sixth. They rode in silence. When the doors slid open, Colt stayed still, letting the agent get off first. Better to let him think they weren't following him and circle back after.

He turned, raising an eyebrow. "You coming?"

Colt gave him a questioning look.

"Kendra said a giant, a pixie, and their friend would be arriving soon. Come on, I'll take you to her."

Colt glared at his back as they followed him down the wide hallway to a family room. He could have let on that he knew who they were. She rolled her shoulders to shift the sense of unease.

Kendra and Mitch were both waiting for them as they entered. The agent nodded and continued on down the hall.

"Mackenzie, there you are. I am so sorry you got separated from Amanda. They ran some tests then brought her up here for further observation."

"So she's okay?" Mackenzie peered up through her curtain of hair.

"Yes, the doctor is with her now, but you should be able to join her as soon as he is finished."

Mackenzie slumped in relief. Hawk rubbed her shoulder.

Colt motioned to the door. "What's with the G-men?"

Kendra wrinkled her nose at the term but didn't comment. "Just for the night. We thought it best that the young women had protection after this morning's news."

Colt snorted. "You think one night is going to deter Mark if he has something planned?"

"No, but I spoke with Amanda's parents a few minutes ago. They want to send Amanda, and Mackenzie too, if she would like, back to the secure facility they stayed at last year."

Mackenzie drew near, her hands still hidden in the sleeves of her sweater. "Why?"

"With Amanda's reaction to hearing the news, they are worried that she will have a setback with her PTSD symptoms and want her to have support on hand to ensure she has the best care. They also believe the extra security at Willow Grove Retreat will help, not least for peace of mind."

It made sense. "Mackenzie, what do you think?" Colt asked.

She scrubbed her hair out of her face with her sleeve. "Yes, please. I mean, if Amanda wants to, I will."

A nurse stuck his head around the corner and smiled at the room. "Dr. Jones is finished now. You can go in, but only two at a time."

Colt went with Mackenzie, identifying the correct room by the familiar FBI agent sitting in a chair opposite the door.

"Excuse me, I'm going to need to see some ID before I can let you in," he said as he stood up, his voice deepening to the official agent voice so many of them practiced.

Colt rolled her eyes at him. He grinned as she bypassed him and headed for the door. She knocked loudly, then pulled it open for Mackenzie to go in first.

Amanda was propped up on a mountain of pillows. Blankets were pulled up to her chest. Her face was pale, her eyes wide with purple shadows. Mackenzie ran to her, and the friends hugged. Colt waited until they broke apart to approach.

"You okay?"

Amanda nodded shyly. "Yes. I'm sorry for making such a fuss. They've got me on fluids in case I'm dehydrated." She lifted her arm to show the IV tubing running out of it to a bag hanging beside the bed. "They're keeping me overnight."

"I can stay, can't I?" Mackenzie begged.

"I don't see why not. It makes the most sense." She wasn't sure if Amanda knew she was being guarded and didn't want to be the one to tell her.

After a few minutes, Colt left and rejoined the others in the family room. The four of them exited the hospital together. She rolled her shoulders, trying to dislodge the overwhelming desire to introduce Mark's face to a baseball bat. She drew a deep breath as the warm afternoon air hit her. After the closeness of the hospital, it was refreshing. As she followed Hawk and Mitch to the truck, she couldn't help but wonder how many more surprises were in store.

Malik leaned down to kiss his mother goodbye and stepped outside to answer his ringing phone. He'd been waiting impatiently for the call, hoping to use it as an excuse to cut short his weekly visit. He'd brought her an antique cuckoo clock from the Black Forest, knowing how much she'd enjoy it. As expected, her eyes had lit up, filling her face with life for a few short minutes before it slipped away again. Those moments were becoming few and far between, causing Malik to stretch his imagination for ways to make her smile. He wasn't ready to admit his mother was getting old, her grasp on the present slipping away.

He decided then and there that when he acquired the Fabergé Egg, he would tell no one. His mother's birthday was in just over a month, and he would present it to her on that day. Surely the disease that was ravaging her body would give him that long to bring back her smile. Fate couldn't be so cruel to steal such a beautiful and gracious lady before her seventieth birthday. Yes, he would give her the Egg, at a lavish party. All her friends would be there, all his. It would be the party of the year.

It would be a huge loss to his collection, but for his mother, he would make the sacrifice. She deserved a fitting gift.

He was in a good mood as he answered his phone, taking the time to smile at his driver. He nodded as the man opened the door to allow him to slide into the back.

"Tell me I now own a new runway."

There was a pause. Pauses weren't good. Pauses interrupted him, his ideas. Held him back. Not this time. Not when his mother needed this to get better.

"It sold. Even offered triple the price, offered the bonus to the agent directly. Too late. They closed on the property before I could speak to him in person."

Malik pressed his lips together, a trick he'd learned long ago from his father. *Never take your anger out on those below you; you're above that. Take a moment, then guide them along the correct path.* He counted to five. "What about the new buyers?"

"I got the impression they had some connection to the place. They're former military and probably not easily convinced to sell already."

"Hmm. Do you have any good news today?"

Shuffling papers signaled the caller's discomfort. "Not yet."

"But you have the name of the seller?"

"Yes. But wouldn't he have taken anything of value with him?"

Malik rubbed his head. He purposely chose not to tell this man everything, but he hadn't expected to do *all* the thinking.

"It was an estate sale. He might not have realized what was of value and what was not. Find out what he knows."

"Oh. Right."

"And remember — be discreet."

3

Colt climbed out of the box truck and stretched. The ringing in her ears faded, brought on by more than two hours behind the wheel of the moving van. Hawk and Mitch were a few minutes behind her, so she leaned against the truck and sipped her coffee. Her phone vibrated in her pocket, so she pulled it out to check her messages.

Glitch, the hacker she'd met on the dark web last year during her search for her brother, had texted her a link with the comment, "Found you."

With a smile tugging at her lips, Colt tapped the link. It took her to a video filmed at an airshow several years prior. She squinted at the three aircraft that zoomed across the screen, then groaned. He hadn't, had he? She glanced at the title that indicated the date and location of the show. He had.

Not long after she had earned her wings in the Navy, she and Hawk had attended an airshow with the rest of their squadron. Due to a shortage of pilots, she had ended up piloting a vintage Grumman F6F Hellcat during a demonstration of World War II aircraft.

She turned her attention back to the video. After the first couple of maneuvers, she had ended up out of position. The only way to get the display back on track had been to try something risky. The three planes disappeared in the distance, then reappeared, the Hellcat leading the way at a much higher altitude. Colt held her breath as the Hellcat on the screen began quickly losing altitude, the first part of the Night Witch maneuver.

"When the enemy thinks they've got you, cut the engine and scream to your death," she muttered.

The Japanese Zeros roared by above the Hellcat, unable to attack. The powerful engine of the Hellcat restarted, bringing it up behind the Zeros to complete the maneuver.

The video ended, and Colt grinned. As much as she hadn't wanted to fly that day, it had been a rush to pilot the vintage aircraft. She flipped back to Glitch's message and tapped out a reply.

"You know too much. Now I'm going to have to vanish."

His response was instantaneous. "Aww, we were just getting to be friends."

Colt sent him an emoji, then slid her phone back into her pocket. Hawk's pickup was pulling into the parking lot, so she put her empty coffee cup away and grabbed her keys.

She walked over as Hawk and Mitch climbed out. Hawk handed her a steaming cup of coffee when she joined them. She had just finished one, but she wasn't about to tell him that. The past two weeks of packing up their apartment and getting everything ready to move had only increased her caffeine addiction.

"We good?"

"Yes'm."

"Final check. You guys are good with this? Joint owners?"

"Colt, seriously. Starting a flight school is a great idea for us. We're with you," Hawk assured her.

Mitch sighed dramatically. "If you don't stop asking, I'm taking my million dollars and moving to San Cabo. I'll live out my days on the beach, drinking Coronas, waited on by pretty girls in bikinis. Now shut up and get in there."

Colt grinned at him. It was the response she'd been waiting for. Mitch had agreed before, but until he got exasperated, she couldn't be certain he was fully into it. The trio entered the real estate office and found Walter just arriving as well.

"You guys keep bankers' hours?" Hawk joked.

Walter shrugged sheepishly. "We often work late, doing evening showings. Mornings tend to be quite productive times though, so there is a bit of give and take. But it's barely eight — you guys must have been up quite early."

"No point in wasting the day," Colt said. "We might as well get things moving along and have the rest of the day sorting out stuff at the property."

"Oh, taking ownership today?" Walter looked up from the papers he was sorting through.

"If we can. There's no reason not to — you said the owner has already moved out."

"Yes, he has. I just had the date marked down for Monday, but that's easily changed, as long as he agrees. He should be here shortly."

Walter spent the next half hour explaining all the paperwork to them and indicating the sundry places the three of them needed to sign or initial. The seller still hadn't arrived by the time they were done. Another twenty minutes passed before he wandered in.

Colt sized him up. Over thirty, in jeans and a button-down shirt under a casual jacket. His light brown hair was stuck up in scattered spikes, and he kept his sunglasses on. He seemed unconcerned that he had kept them waiting as he flashed a smile around the room.

"Ah, Mr. Farrell. Good to see you again," Walter greeted him.

Farrell? Colt looked at the new arrival again. It had been a long time since she had last seen him, but now that she knew, she could see the familiar face. The boyish features were lost beneath the stubble and overpriced clothing, but she kicked herself for not clueing in sooner. She had played with him when they were kids.

"Hi there. Sorry for being late. Traffic, you know." The comment was meant to break the ice, but only Hawk chuckled in response.

Walter showed him the various places to sign. "The new owners would like to take possession of the property immediately, if that's okay with you?"

Brody looked around as if seeing them for the first time. "Sure, it's okay with me. You'll need all the time you can get to make that place livable. If I get my money today, you can have the property today. No money, no deal, hey baby?" He laughed again. A good old boy with the misfortune of having sudden money. "Wait. I know you. Tara, right? How the heck are ya?" He moved toward her, arms open for a hug.

Colt stepped back, arms crossing. He faltered, then changed his tactic to a handshake. After a moment, she accepted it. "It's Talia. Been a while, Brody."

"Talia, right. Wow. And you're back home now. Cool, cool."

Small talk seemed required, so she made an effort. "Something like that. What about you?"

"Oh, I'm over in Allentown. Is this your boyfriend?" He turned to include Hawk in the conversation.

"No, these are my business partners."

Hawk offered his hand. "Justin Halversen, and this is Franklin Mitchell."

Brody had the decency to look embarrassed at not noticing Mitch. He shook hands with both of them. "Great to meet you both. I knew Tara here back in the day."

They chatted for a few minutes, Colt letting Hawk take the lead. What do you say to someone you haven't seen in ten years and who you're buying property from? The whole thing felt awkward. Thankfully Walter stepped in.

"Alright, here are your copies of all the paperwork. The money has been released from escrow and should appear in your account in the next couple of hours, Mr. Farrell."

Colt took the folder and flipped through it, glad of something to do with her hands. Brody fished a mass of keys out of his pocket and handed them to Colt with a flourish. "I guess these are yours now. Good luck fixing up the place. It'll take you a year before you can move in." He laughed again. "Give me a call. We should catch up." He made a point of saying goodbye to each of them before sauntering off.

Walter gave them a big smile. "Congratulations. I hope you'll enjoy your new home."

Colt hefted the keys in her hand. "I think we will, starting with the puzzle of what key opens what."

They rumbled up the drive to the house, following the dirt road as it circled the old place. Colt backed the moving van up to the side door, and Hawk parked his pickup nearby. Their clothing was in the back seat while the bed held a few awkward pieces of furniture that hadn't fit in the moving van. The chain at the bottom of the hill had given them a few minutes of frustration as they tried several keys to undo the padlock. Colt had finally noticed that there were five on a separate ring, all with new, colored tags on them. The second one fit the padlock, and she returned to that same set to find the key to the house.

They explored the house again, this time with the right of ownership. Each room had a few pieces of furniture left in it. They could fix up and update as necessary, but at least the place wouldn't feel barren until then. Hawk stared in shock at the massive table and matching chairs in the dining room. Colt and Mitch left him exclaiming over the workmanship as they continued the tour.

"This one okay for you?" Colt asked, stepping into the room by the kitchen.

"You sure you don't want it?" he countered.

"I like my coffee, but I think I can handle walking down a flight of stairs to get it."

Still, Mitch hesitated.

"Look, take it for now," she said. "I know those stairs are going to be difficult for you. Don't take this as a defeat — take it as a strategic move. Once you're more comfortable with steps, you can decide to move up."

"But this room would make more sense as a den."

"What do we need with a den? The living room is large enough for anything we need. And there's three large rooms upstairs for Hawk and I to fight over."

Mitch raised a hand in surrender. "Okay, okay, I'll take this room."

"Good. We'll get this bathroom upgraded too. There's room for a shower in there." She moved through the room to the other side. A door led into a narrow hall, then out onto the porch. Two doors opened next to each other, one into a tiny closet and one into a half bath.

"Uh, no, there's not."

"Sure there is. What do we need this closet for? Paint cans and light bulbs can go somewhere else."

Hawk joined them. "Is there room for the wheelchair to get through here?"

Mitch shrugged. "I don't need it for the bathroom most of the time."

"Not that," Hawk said. "We could easily put a ramp up to the porch, giving you an easy way in and out. The ground to this door is smoother than the flagstones leading to the side door, so it makes sense."

"Guys, I don't want you making all this fuss for me," Mitch said, rubbing his hand on the back of his neck.

Colt looked at him in surprise. "You're part owner. Therefore, the house should fit your needs as much as ours. Besides, you don't want to hear what he's got planned for upstairs."

Mitch conceded, and they decided to start unloading the trucks. When Hawk asked Colt which room she wanted, she told him to just pick one; she didn't care.

When she went up later, she discovered he had neatly stacked her boxes in one corner of the master bedroom and put his own in the smaller room over the stairs. She dumped his suitcase on the bed in the master bedroom, then quietly moved her three boxes of belongings to the back bedroom — the one with the view of the airfield. Leaving Mitch to take a nap, despite his protests he didn't need one, Colt and Hawk returned the moving van to the local depot and arrived back at the house with pizza. After they finished eating, Colt declared that they had done enough for the day, and it was time to explore.

They had already opened the barn and the sheds earlier, looking for the best place to stow Colt's motorcycle, so they opted to skip those and head to the airstrip. Sorting through old lawn mowers, paint cans, broken chairs, and golf carts could wait for another day. Hawk drove, and Colt directed him to the second hangar.

"But we've not really looked around the first one," he protested.

"What you saw is what you get. It was the public one, where the other owners stowed their planes. There's Frank's old plane left, and tools, and empty oil cans. Not much else."

"And this hangar?" Mitch asked as they pulled to a stop in front of it.

Colt climbed out, jangling the keys. "Wait till you see." She'd done some thinking over the past couple of weeks and decided to share this moment. Trolling online forums gave her hope that she was right, and it'd be more fun to see their faces.

It was both more and less impressive than she'd expected. It certainly held far more than the first hangar, but in her mind it had seemed more like a trove of wonders, not the mass of junk that filled the entire space before her now.

"Is that a P-51 Mustang?" Hawk said, pointing to a tail fin that stood out above an old farm implement.

"Probably," she replied, hiding her grin. She started picking her way through the boxes, moving things out of her way as she went.

"And that's an F6F Hellcat!" Hawk's voice squeaked as he started identifying the aircraft crammed in the hangar.

She couldn't hide her smirk this time.

"You knew."

"Of course I did. Why do you think I didn't want you agreeing to sell all the junk?"

Hawk bumped her shoulder with his fist. "Sneaky."

"Couldn't have someone running off with these babies. The Mustang has one of the rare Rolls-Royce engines instead of the Merlin."

Mitch whistled, running his hand over the engine cowling of the Mustang. "You think this baby would go again?"

Colt nodded. "I used to fly it. So yes, it was working in the past fifteen years; I'm sure it will again. Just need to find someone to look at it." She bent over a heavy box in her way. There was another plane here, she was sure. Or at least parts of it should be.

"I could," Mitch said. He set his crutch against the plane and leaned into the open cockpit. Hawk joined him, and she tuned out their conversation as they discussed the various aspects of the plane, Hawk listing the famous battles the Mustang had featured in while Mitch prodded the engine.

Colt crossed her legs and sat down on the dirty floor, peeling the cracked tape off the top of the box. She brushed the dust off the top and opened the cardboard flaps. Immediately the smell of old leather, oil, and lilacs filled the air. She reached in and lifted out one of the books inside, holding it like it could fall apart at any moment.

It was an old leather-bound volume, worn smooth but now hard. A leather tie was wrapped around it and knotted to keep it closed. Delicately, she used her nails to pry the knot apart and let the book fall open in her lap. The smell of lilacs grew stronger, and she swallowed hard. The pages were full of a familiar cursive script, and an image filled her mind. One of a dainty white-haired lady bent over an old desk, fountain pen in hand, her precise handwriting filling the pages. Colt ran a shaking hand over the journal. The words were in Russian, written with beautiful calligraphy.

"Colt?"

She looked up to see the boys looking at her, realizing she had missed their question before.

"Mitch wants to know if he can work on the Mustang."

She looked at him in surprise. "You can do that?"

He gave her an odd look. "Do they throw beads at Mardi Gras?"

Colt blinked. "Yes?"

Mitch rolled his eyes. "Yes, it means yes. It's just an engine. I grew up working at my uncle's garage. I know mechanical things."

Colt looked from Mitch to the plane. That explained his obsession with *Top Gear*. "Sure, go for it then."

"Awesome. We'll have to see about pulling it out of here, maybe take it to the other hangar where there's more room. I saw some tools over there too. Get some fresh oil in it, new fuel. Take a look at the spark plugs…"

Hawk caught her eye and grinned. She nodded back. Mitch hadn't been this excited about anything since she met him. His career as a Marine helicopter pilot had been ripped away by the SAM that tore through his Blackhawk. She and Hawk hadn't met him until after the accident. It was nice to finally see a spark of life about something positive for a change.

She turned back to the box at her feet and hefted it into her arms. She wanted a chance to sort through the journals, savor them, and she couldn't do that here. As she made her way through the junk to a room at the back, she heard the boys discussing the best approach to fixing the Mustang.

"Maybe we can get you a chair with a scissor lift," Hawk proposed.

Mitch's answer was obscured by her phone ringing.

Malik stepped into his car, anger seething off him. The doctor was a fool. Surely there was something more he could do for Malik's mother beyond "making her comfortable." Pah. What did that even mean? The woman was not yet seventy — she had years left to live. Her grandchildren, his sister's children, needed their grandmother to see them grow and thrive. Why didn't that idiot doctor understand that? Malik texted a doctor friend of his, asking for recommendations for another cancer expert in the country. Never mind the man currently in charge of his mother's care was considered the leading expert. Clearly he knew nothing, and a second opinion was needed.

The car slowed to make a turn. Malik looked out the window to see the garish red and white sign of a fast-food restaurant. "What are you doing?" he demanded of his driver.

"Do you want your usual, sir?" the man asked.

"No, I do not want my usual! Didn't I say straight home?"

"Apologies, sir. I thought you meant after this stop." He flipped the turn signal off and pulled back into the flow of traffic.

Donkey, Malik thought. *Why am I surrounded by donkeys today?* He closed his eyes and leaned his head back against the leather headrest of his Mercedes-Maybach. His phone buzzed in his pocket, but he was too annoyed to answer it. It was probably his sister calling to rant at him for not coming back to visit his mother after walking the doctor out. He'd figured his mother would be asleep again by that point, and he hadn't wanted to wake her. Not that Amna would listen. He had a plan to make it all better. They just needed to be patient a little while longer.

He climbed the stairs from the inner courtyard to his office, not giving his butler a chance to greet him. Somehow the man managed to reach the office before him, a tray of hot tea in his hand. Malik sank into his favorite chair and let the warmth of the tea soothe him. It was only when he was on his second cup that he pulled out his phone to check his messages. Two calls from his American contact. Ire at the bumbling fool filled him, despite the fact he was the one who hadn't answered the calls. He hit redial, tapping his fingers on the arm of the chair.

"I found the man selling the property. A few drinks and a couple hundred bucks, and he spilled the beans. He found the necklace in a bunch of junk in the house. The guy went through everything in the house and found nothing else of value."

Malik bit back his anger. There was no way he was accepting defeat at this stage. "He must have been hiding something."

"I don't think so. But he said there were a bunch of outbuildings on the property. A big hangar apparently full of junk. Boxes, old furniture, that sort of thing. He didn't want to bother sorting through it; it's possible the new owners won't want to either."

"Buy it."

"We tried that, boss."

"Not the whole property. The hangar. Everything that's inside of it. Rent a warehouse, haul everything back there, and go through it with a fine-tooth comb."

"That's going to take manpower."

Malik sipped his tea. Of course the man wanted more money. But at this point, Malik didn't care. Whatever he spent paying some poor saps to sort junk would be pennies in comparison with the value of the Egg. "The funds will be in your account by morning."

Colt shoved the door open, the door handle catching on her hip. She dropped the case of books on the nearest surface, an old bunk bed. A cloud of dust plumed into the air, making her cough. Digging her phone out of her pocket, she fumbled to answer it while choking.

"Talia? Hi, this is Walter. I've got an offer for you."

Colt frowned, waving dust away from her face, peering through the gloom for a better look at her surroundings. "An offer?"

"Yes, you remember I told you that I had another buyer interested in your property? Well, they've called with a very generous offer. They'd like to purchase all the junk in the outbuildings and haul it all away for you. No charge to you. They want to buy it."

"No." A glass cabinet caught her attention, and she navigated toward it. The room wasn't as crowded as the main hangar, but there were a few chairs and boxes scattered around.

"No? But I told them you'd jump at the offer! It's perfect. You make a bit of cash and have all that stuff out of your way."

"Don't want it out of my way." What was in that cabinet? Years of grime clung to the glass, obscuring what lay within.

"But the other day, Justin mentioned…"

"Did he already arrange this with you?"

"No, but based on that conversation, I thought..."

"Okay, so the answer is still no. We bought and paid for everything on this property. All structures intact, all sundries included, did we not?"

"Yes, of course. But what am I going to tell the other party?"

Colt tugged on the cabinet's handle. "The truth?" She was being rude but not sure what else she was supposed to say.

"I mean...but...well, what are you going to do with all that stuff?" He was flailing, but she wasn't really paying attention.

"We're going to turn the place into a scrap metal yard. All this junk will be a good place to start." She ended the call and slid the phone back into her pocket. The door was swollen shut. She'd need something to pry it open. She turned to find a tool, only to see Hawk in her way.

"A scrap metal yard?"

She snorted. "Don't be ridiculous. Walter apparently promised some dude he could have all this stuff."

Hawk looked around at the stack of broken chairs. "Might not be a bad idea."

"Sounded like an all-or-nothing sort of deal. So all the planes, Mitch's new project..."

"This box of books?" Hawk held up one of the journals.

"Yeah."

"It's in Russian."

She bit back a sarcastic reply. He wasn't being dense. He was giving her the chance to be open about it. But she couldn't. She couldn't open her mouth to tell him.

He cocked his head, waiting. She clenched her hands, willing her mouth to open to tell her best friend the amazing gift she had found, but she couldn't. Her mouth was as sealed as her juvie file. His eyes softened, and the expectant look on his face faded to one of concern. She hated the pity as much as she hated herself in that moment.

"They were your grandmother's?" He held the book gently in one large hand. The other hovered over the pages as if sensing the personal connection the book held.

She nodded her head.

"She had beautiful handwriting," he said with a final look. He closed the journal with care and replaced it in the box.

"She did," Colt finally broke her silence.

He gave her a smile. "Can you read it?"

"I can. It's been a while, but it shouldn't be too hard." She shook off the moment and turned to the cabinet. "Here, see if you can open this."

Between them, they managed to pry open the damp-swollen doors, revealing a number of trophies, ribbons, and other awards. All had been awarded to pilots of the flight club over the years. Colt dug behind a row of marble statues with metal airplanes and pulled out a silver biplane. She handed it to Hawk with a slight grin.

"To Talia, the best little pilot on the field." Hawk read aloud the plaque mounted on the bottom.

"The other pilots gave it to me after I landed a plane on my own."

"This was given to you when you were what, eight? You flew solo at that age?"

She took it from him, wiping the dust off. "Nine, actually. And I wasn't technically solo, but Gram let me do everything on my own. She was there in case something went wrong, but that landing was all me." She forced a smile at him. "Come on, we better go make sure Mitch hasn't taken apart all the airplanes yet."

"Thanks for sharing this with me, Colt." He held up the trophy before placing it carefully back on the shelf.

She squirmed at the look of pride on his face. Why could she tell him about this but not talk about her grandmother's diaries? She didn't have an answer for herself. But what she did know was that she was glad Hawk was here.

A dinner of leftover pizza found them stretched out on the ragged furniture in the living room. Colt was the first to move, opening boxes and digging through them. After her fourth abandonment, Hawk pried himself out of his chair.

"What are you looking for?"

"The coffee maker. Going to need it in the morning, so figured better to find it now rather than when we're barely functioning."

Hawk led the way to the kitchen and pointed to a reusable shopping bag on the floor. He lifted out their coffee maker and set it on a small stand by the window. Next, he unearthed the can of coffee and the two bottles of flavoring Mitch insisted on using.

"Milk?" she asked, just to annoy him. He had an air of smugness about him that she felt was uncalled for.

"In the fridge. But I'm planning to go grocery shopping tomorrow. Add what you want to the list."

She shrugged. "The usual is good."

"Colt, you need to eat more than just chicken, salad, and peanut butter."

"Why? Actually, that sounds good. Do we have a toaster?"

Hawk sighed and dug back into his bag. "One toaster. Bread is in the pantry."

"Regular Mary Poppins, you are," she said, accepting the toaster and plunking it on the counter.

"Aren't you full from all the pizza?" He started unpacking other things.

"This is dessert. I think I'll go back to the hangar, dig around a bit more. You want to come?" She found the bread and peanut butter in the pantry and loaded the toaster.

"No, I'll stay here. Give the kitchen a bit of a wipedown, sort out things." He stacked a row of cleaners next to the sink.

Her face fell. "Oh. I should help you with that."

"Don't be silly. It won't take me long, and I'm behind on my podcasts anyway. It'll be a good chance to catch up."

She rolled her eyes, catching the toast in the air as the toaster expelled it. "More true crime stories?"

"What? They're fun. If I ever write a novel, I've got lots of ideas."

"Fair enough." She smeared thick peanut butter on the toast. "Right, I'm off. Don't wait up."

She munched the snack as she walked up the hill toward the airfield. The evening air was warm, interrupted by a light breeze. The sun was dipping below the tree line, leaving behind a wash of pale oranges and pinks.

She wiped the last of the crumbs off her face and tucked the napkin into her pocket. She thought about opening the big doors to capture the last of the sunlight, but they were noisy, and she decided not to disturb the peace. A flicker of brown by the tower made her glad of her choice. Three deer grazed, taking turns to watch for predators. There must be a hole in the fence somewhere if they had gotten through. Deer on the runway would not be a good landing in a Piper Cub. She made a note to repair the fence soon. Colt slipped into the hangar, careful to close the door softly. The overhead lights flooded the space, revealing once again the piles of things to sort through. Why she was so intent on cleaning it out now, she wasn't sure. But she decided to give herself the weekend and focus on the more important tasks next week. Hawk wouldn't be happy until he had the house in perfect order, and it was often best to stay out of his way. If he needed her, he'd let her know.

A long workbench occupied a stretch of wall to her left. She made her way over to it and started digging through the boxes that covered it. They were filled with paperwork, old maintenance records, flight logs, bills from thirty years ago. Of little interest to her, but the squirrels and mice had already put a lot of it to good use. She dragged a bin of spare parts out of the way and stacked the boxes of paper on the floor. As she worked, her mind kept drifting to the journals she had found earlier in the day. After yet another box of uninteresting bits of rusted metal, she gave up.

Working toward the back of the hangar, she did little more than rearrange boxes to make a wider path. Mitch's expertise as a mechanic would come in handy. He'd have a better idea of what was useful and what could be tossed from all these spare parts. She was glad he was there. He added a balance to the dynamic that was her and Hawk. Take this, for instance. She'd be inclined to toss anything that didn't have an immediate use, and Hawk would want to keep it all in case it was needed later. Mitch would have a better approach.

A curved board caught her eye, and she straightened to get a better look. She traced the outline of the P-51 Mustang and then the F6F Hellcat. A grin tugged at the corner of her mouth. There were definitely three rudders. The two American fighters had square ones, not rounded. And that stack of boards leaned against the upper wings of a biplane. She grinned for real. It *was* here.

She thought about texting Hawk to share the news but decided it would be more fun to show him in the morning. It was too late now to unbury it anyway.

Continuing on, she made it to the bunk room and flicked on the lights. Not an overly cozy sight. She shut off the lights to the main hangar and moved inside.

Four stacks of bunks lined the back wall of the hangar. To her right, a pair of doors led to separate bathrooms. To the left was a kitchenette, complete with fridge, stove, and microwave. Two narrow tables were pushed up against the wall, and sofas filled in more of the wall space. The result was a long, narrow room. Colt liked it though. It had a camp feel, reminding her of boot camp days but with the added air of relaxation that the pilot rooms on the carrier had. It was currently overfilled with random boxes and extra chairs, but she could see the potential. The box of journals was still sitting on one of the bunks, where she had left it. The mattresses were old, striped, and sagging. A bag of pillows was stuffed on one of the top bunks, and she spotted a couple of sleeping bags, rolled up and tucked away.

She moved to the bunk that offered the best view of the door, then changed her mind. If anyone came in, she wanted a few seconds to prepare. The bunk two down would let her see who entered before they spotted her, as the door opened inward. She flipped the mattress over, sending up more clouds of dust. There were a few marks from the wooden slats, but otherwise it seemed in decent condition. Pulling the bag of pillows down, she beat the dust off it and shoved it in the corner for a backrest. Finally, she set the box of journals in the middle of the bunk and settled in beside it.

It took her a few minutes to put them all in order. They covered a range of years, some missing. There was no set format to the entries. One journal covered only a three-month period while another held sparse records over four years. Colt picked up the earliest one she could find and settled in to read it. It took her a few minutes to get into her grandmother's writing style and grow accustomed to the penmanship. With a Russian translation app open on her phone, she lost herself in learning about her grandmother.

Masha called today. It's been too long, but as always, there is a risk. I understand why she wanted to talk today though. Her grandson has decided to join the Navy. He's so pleased to be able to continue the family tradition of serving, but Masha is heartbroken that she can't share the true extent of that tradition. The dear boy believes that he's the fifth generation to serve his country, but the truth is, the tradition extends not just through his father and grandfather. Masha's family also served, even if that country wasn't the United States. I'm so thankful I don't have to hide that from my own granddaughter. I fear she's already eager to sign up. But I pray she will never experience the war that I did.

The office was darkened against the midday sun. The first day all week without a sandstorm, and the sun was intent upon making up for the missed light. Malik closed the accounting report and opened a separate spreadsheet. On his taxes, he reported certain items under "discretionary" or "research." Here in this report, he broke them down into actual expenditures. The money sent to his contact in the US was starting to add up, and he couldn't help but wonder how much of that was being pocketed and not passed on to the sources who supposedly had pertinent information. He sighed, reminding himself it would be worth it when he had the Egg in his possession.

He checked the time again. His nephews were due to arrive shortly, but his American man was late calling. Malik knew better than to take the call when the boys were over. They'd report the conversation to their mother, and if he stepped away to talk, his sister would lambast him for doing business during family time, something they long ago had agreed never to do. If only Americans were as respectful of others' time...

A light knock sounded on the door, and he called for his butler to enter. "Your nephews just pulled in, sir."

Malik stood, brushing the wrinkles from his jacket. "Very well. I —" The phone on the desk rang. He sighed. "I'll be right there. Show the boys into the sitting room and offer tea."

The butler nodded, closing the door silently behind him. Malik let the phone ring a couple more times before answering, giving himself time to separate from his impatience. "What news have you?"

"Well, I've got both good news and bad. The new owners aren't interested in selling the junk. Claim they want it to start a scrap metal yard. They're going to sort through everything and find stuff worth selling, I guess."

Malik paced the length of his office. "Tell me that isn't the good news."

"Nope. But I'm not sure you're going to like the good news."

"What is it?"

"The place is sold but needs a ton of work. No one's going to be moving in anytime soon. So maybe we could take a little visit and do some sorting of our own."

Malik let the silence sit as he evaluated the options. Breaking and entering was a crime but not one he could be connected to. And if this was what needed to be done to put the missing Fabergé Egg in his possession... "Do it. Keep it small, only people you trust. Don't let on what we're looking for."

"Leave the details to me. It might take us a few days if there's as much junk as the seller implied."

"This had better work. I'm not interested in hearing any more excuses." Malik ended the call and headed down the stairs to the giggles of his nephews. They had their own tradition. If their uncle didn't greet them at the door, a full-scale game of hide and seek broke out. "Ready or not, here I come," he shouted.

4

Clang!

The noise pulled Colt from sleep in an instant. Her hand slid to her back, to the reassuring feel of hard metal. Scuffling sounds from the main hangar drew her attention. The journal lay open on her stomach, and she slid it to one side before getting to her feet. She moved to the door, careful not to step on anything that might make noise, and pressed her ear against the wood.

More scuffling sounds. Not the steady tread she'd expect if it was Hawk coming to check on her. No clump of Mitch's crutches or squeak of the rubber wheels on his chair. She flicked the lights off in her room, plunging herself into darkness. She let her eyes adjust, then dropped to the floor. Peering through the crack, she could see moving lights sweeping back and forth. Murmured conversation reached her.

That settled it.

That was not Hawk nor Mitch. Which meant whoever was out there should not be.

She got to her feet, checking the Beretta M9 on her back again. Hesitated. She could go out and start shooting. But what if it was a couple of kids out for a dare? No, she'd wait. She did loosen it in the holster, making sure she could pull it out smoothly should she need it.

The door handle clicked as she turned it, and she held her breath, waiting long seconds to see if it had been noticed. The scuffling continued without a pause, so she eased the door open. Crouching to one side, she let it fall open a few inches.

Still no response from whoever was in the hangar. She peered around the corner.

Three spots of light bobbed around the hangar. It took her a moment to discern they were headlamps attached to three figures. Two were digging through boxes, and one was climbing into the P-51 Mustang.

"There's nothing here but junk!" the nearest voice whined.

"Keep digging," growled another.

"You believe him?" asked the first voice.

"Is true," replied a third, accented voice. "Treasure was found here."

Treasure? What was he rambling about? Either way. They weren't supposed to be here. She watched for another moment, but when the sound of ripping material came from the Mustang, she'd had enough. She mapped out the path she'd made earlier in her mind. Creeping out the door, she made her way along the wall, trusting that any sounds she made would be lost amid their own digging.

They certainly weren't concerned with being caught. She was surprised they hadn't turned the overhead lights on, but perhaps they were worried it might be spotted from a distance.

"Do we know what we're looking for?" The whiny voice broke the silence again.

"Shut up and look."

"I am looking, but it's easier to look when you know what you're looking for."

"Is Russian treasure," stated the accented voice, the one working on the far side of the hangar.

Colt slid one foot at a time along the path, keeping an eye on Whiny, who was only a few feet from her. He hadn't ventured too far from the path.

"Russian?" snorted Grumpy from his perch in the Mustang. "I'd say more likely German. Probably smuggled over with a bunch of Nazis. All these planes are from World War II. Wouldn't be surprised if missing artwork was buried in here someplace."

She stifled a laugh. Yeah, right. If they were looking for stolen art from Nazi Germany, they were out of luck.

"So we're looking for paintings?" Whiny stretched, twisting back and forth. Colt froze, directly behind him in the shadows.

Grumpy shrugged. "He said small, heavy. I'm thinking more like gold bars."

"You idiot," said the Russian. "You think we find gold here? Durak."

"Yeah? What do you think we're looking for?"

"Small treasure from Russia? Is jewels. Russian oligarchs had many riches — diamonds, rubies, emeralds. Romanov wealth has never been found."

Whiny kicked a box at his feet. "If we're looking for diamonds in this mess, we could be here for years and never find them."

"We will be if you keep jabbering. Get back to work." Grumpy obviously considered himself the leader. Whiny complied even though he continued muttering under his breath. Colt took the opportunity while they were distracted to move through the darkness to the door. She wanted to be between them and their exit before alerting them to her presence. Treasure or no, this was her property, and they were in for a surprise if they thought they could get away with digging through it.

Closing her eyes to protect her vision, she reached for the switch. The massive space immediately flooded with lights and shouts. Whiny bolted, heading straight for the door beside her. She let him go. Grumpy was in the process of climbing out of the plane, and the surprise made him lose his footing. He fell with a thump, the knife and other items he was carrying in one hand clattering to the cement floor. He stood slowly, brushing himself off with muffled curses. The Russian was watching her, eyes hidden in the depths of the balaclava he wore. He circled through the piles. From the way he stepped, she guessed he had purposely left himself an escape route. She was proven right when he made it to the opposite personnel door. It was locked, but the deadbolt was on the inside. She thought about pulling her gun, but something about the way he had stared at her made her think she wouldn't get anything from him.

Grumpy, on the other hand — now there was a tough guy to carry her message. They'd mentioned someone else, someone who had sent them.

He was back on his feet by now, the short knife in his hand. He was grinning, confident he could beat her, a woman several inches shorter than him.

"Get out," she told him, knowing she was blocking his path. Unlike Whiny, he hadn't cared if he stepped on things or got dirty. And unlike the Russian, he hadn't planned an escape route.

"Give me the treasure, and I will." He swaggered toward her as best he could, following the path Mitch and Hawk had made earlier in the day.

This was the part Colt hated the most. Big tough guys assuming she was a pushover because she was a woman. She'd dealt with enough like him all through school and had quickly learned how to handle them. The gun at her back was an option, but she still didn't feel threatened enough to use it.

"No," she told him. "There's nothing here worth anything, and even if there was, it's mine, not yours."

He came closer, wiggling the knife in his hand. "You really want to argue with me about that? You show me the treasure, then maybe you and I could have a little fun."

The space by the door was the clearest, scuffed up by the many footsteps that had passed through there that day. She made sure there was nothing under her feet that might compromise her footing and waited for him to come nearer.

He obliged, striding forward with a broad, threatening stance in an attempt to intimidate her.

Colt rolled her eyes.

One more step, and the knife exploded from his hand as her foot shot up. The blade flew up into the air and landed in the boxes behind him, but Colt didn't bother waiting to see where it went. She followed up the kick with a double tap to his stomach and a right cross to the jaw.

He slumped to the ground.

"Get out," she said again.

"He won't give up so easily," Grumpy said, holding his face. "Not when he wants something this badly."

"Whatever he thinks is here, isn't. Now get out of my hangar, and don't come back."

He staggered to his feet and made his way outside. Colt watched him go, feeling her racing heart slowly return to normal. Was she a fool for letting them go?

She looked around the hangar. They had tossed things around, but there was no noticeable damage, and they hadn't made off with anything. What worried her the most was the implication they'd be back. And the mysterious person behind the break-in, who seemed convinced there was something worth a lot of money in all this mess.

Footsteps outside the hangar had her reaching for her weapon. She was too tired and annoyed to fight them again, and if they were foolish enough to come back, she wasn't in the mood for chitchat.

"Colt?" Hawk called as he pulled open the door.

She dropped her hand in relief. "What's up?"

He blinked at her standing in the hangar, not doing anything. "I should ask you that."

"Did you see anybody out there?"

"No, should I have?"

"There were three of them, poking around. I chased them off, but I don't know... They seemed pretty sure we were overrun with wealth here."

Hawk looked around. "Did they say what they were looking for?"

"Nothing that made any sense." She puffed out her breath, blowing her hair off her forehead. "Whatever it was, it's worth a lot of money."

"You okay?" he asked.

"Yeah, fine. Why?"

"Your hand."

She glanced down at her bloody fist. "Oh, that. I punched one of them. What are you doing here, anyway?"

Hawk pulled a clean handkerchief from his pocket and handed it to her. "Woke up for a drink, noticed you hadn't come back, saw all the lights on, and decided to come see what was up."

"Thanks," she said, bunching the cloth in her hand. Hawk reached over and took it from her, keeping hold of her hand. He dabbed gently at the blood.

"Did they say anything else, anything to identify them?"

"No, but one was carrying a knife...a Ka-Bar, I think." She pulled away, turning to the boxes. "He dropped it here somewhere." She bent over to search for it.

Hawk's sharp intake of breath had her straightening immediately. "What's wrong?"

He had a pained expression on his face. "You fell asleep with your holster on, didn't you?"

"How do you know I was asleep?"

"Messy ponytail, creases on your face, and bruises on your back."

Her hands moved as he pointed out the evidence. "Oh."

"Turn around, lean forward." She complied, holding still as he pulled the holster away from her skin. He removed the Beretta, checking it before passing it to her. With gentle hands, he unclipped the holster from her belt and lifted it free. He then took a picture of her back and showed it to her.

He was right. Sleeping with a holster on was a bad idea. The small of her back was one large bruise, and patches of skin were rubbed raw from the webbing of the holster.

"I've got some antibiotic cream back at the house you can put on it. But you need to let the skin heal. No pancake holster until it's a hundred percent better."

She made a face at him but nodded. Who knew how long that had been building? The last few days had been busy packing and arranging things for the move. She hadn't taken the time to do a full body inspection every night. She knew better.

Hawk dropped an arm on her shoulders. "Come on, let's grab some sleep. It's 4 a.m. We can get a couple of hours in before Mitch wakes up."

Colt groaned. "Does he have to sing *every* morning?"

"He says it's the only thing that gets him through the mandated exercises. We can't begrudge him that."

"At least your new room isn't right above his. I've got that to look forward to."

"Fair point, but that was your choice. I gave you the master."

Colt didn't reply, unable to argue that point. They continued on, Hawk's arm dropping after a few steps. It was too hard to walk like that, but she found she missed the contact.

Hawk was still looking out for her. He was better at it than she was. He remembered her condition more than she did. She kicked herself for letting him see the injury, but she couldn't deny needing the wake-up call. As someone with Hereditary Sensory and Autonomic Neuropathy Type V, she was predisposed to injuring herself without noticing. It was better described by its other name, congenital insensitivity to pain with partial anhidrosis, meaning she felt no pain or discomfort and rarely sweated. Congenital meant it was genetic, and she'd been dealing with it ever since she was a child. Her grandmother had helped her develop habits to look after herself, including the one to check herself all over each morning and night for injuries. The cursory approach she'd taken over the past few days meant she had missed her back. Thank goodness for Hawk. It would only take a couple of days for the raw skin to heal, but if she'd carried on, it could have gotten much worse. Thankfully, without feeling the pain, the bruises would do little to bother her. They'd heal, and she'd do better at not falling asleep with a hard metal object underneath her.

Still, not having the familiar weight of the Beretta on her belt was odd. It felt as though she were forgetting something important, something she would need later.

5

Malik did not appreciate being yelled at. Certainly not by an underling. However, in this instance, he felt the man had the right to vent, and so he counted in his head, distancing himself from the anger and focusing on his next steps. He flipped through the sheaf of fabric samples his sister had sent over. She was redecorating their mother's sitting room. As he was paying for it, she wanted his input. Not that she'd listen to him.

"... She was lying in wait! They knew we were coming! Who else did you tell?"

The words started to sink in. "What did you just say?"

"I said, who else did you tell about this? I thought I had your trust, and you go spilling —"

"No, before that. Someone was there?"

"That's what I've been trying to tell you! My men were am-bushed, thanks to you!"

Malik tapped down his anger. "If I recall correctly, you were the one who said the property would be empty. In fact, you assured me that no one would be able to move in for several weeks."

"It is! The place is a disaster, according to the seller."

Malik shoved the book of samples away from him, knocking over a pen stand. "Clearly the buyers didn't agree with him. Didn't your men notice their vehicles?"

The man's voice turned belligerent. "They came in the back way, away from the house. Any cars would have been parked there, not up by the hangar."

"Did your men learn anything from the people who ambushed them?"

"They're...not the brightest. My lead guy claims he fought off three attackers, while one swears they were surrounded, and the other says it was just one woman."

Malik rubbed his forehead. At this rate, he'd be bald before the Egg was in his possession. "Please tell me they didn't let on what they were searching for?"

Again the man hesitated. "Two said they got out of there as quickly as possible. But the other guy..."

"Why did you trust him for this if he can't keep his mouth shut?"

"Because he has a reputation for being good with locks and spotting things of value. He won't go blabbing though."

"He better not."

"Isn't it a good sign though? If they had a guard posted at the hangar, they must know there's something of value there, right?"

"If they didn't before, they do now."

"So what do you want me to do? Should we try again tonight?"

Picking up the toppled pen, Malik tapped it against the desk. "Send me the property details. I want blueprints, satellite photos, whatever you can find. Obviously I can't trust you to do this on your own."

Colt poured herself a second cup of coffee and another for Hawk. Mitch's voice echoed from his room as he sang along to the latest country hits, broken by occasional grunts and huffs as he did his exercise routine to keep his limbs mobile.

"Get any sleep?" Hawk said, accepting the mug with relief.

Colt nodded at the mess of eggs, bacon, and hash browns in a large frying pan on the stove. "Some. Too busy thinking about what those guys said. I should call Farrell, see if he knows anything about this treasure. I can't think of anything, but he's been here more than I have in recent years."

Hawk filled his plate with a pile of the breakfast mash and topped it off liberally with sweet chili sauce. "Was it like this when you were here? Was your grandmother or the old man a pack rat?"

Colt sipped her coffee, contemplating the question. "Not my grandmother. She was pretty minimal with her purchases. But she left all her belongings to the old man. I was at sea when she died, unable to come home. Most of her money, minus funeral expenses, was left to me, and he got her things. He sent me a box of stuff he thought I might like, but it looks like everything from her apartment was just shoved into the hangar."

"And you don't think there was anything in the apartment that could have caused this kind of uproar?"

She shook her head. "No. If there was, I'm certain she would have told me. Before I deployed, she showed me her will, explained her wishes. She wasn't doing well then, and I think she knew she wouldn't live much longer. Anything she wanted me to know, she would have told me then. She didn't have a lot."

"And the old man? Maybe he picked up stuff at a flea market?"

She wiggled her hand. "He wasn't one to throw things out, certain they would come in handy at some point in the future, but he didn't spend his Saturdays trolling the local garage sales. And the guys last night mentioned it might be Russian. That means it would have come from my grandmother, not him."

"None of this makes sense."

"No. Brody must know something. He's the only one who's been around since the old man died."

"Well, good luck with that call. Maybe he'll ask you out on that date."

"What date?"

"Come on, Colt, he was clearly hitting on you."

She gave him a dead look.

"Uh, you know what, I'm probably wrong." Hawk snatched up his coffee and retreated to the dining room with his breakfast.

The paperwork for the sale was on the desk in the living room, and it only took a minute with that and the internet to find Brody Farrell's phone number. It rang twice before he answered.

"Hey, this is Talia C — Levin." Belatedly she remembered that he would know her by her real last name. One of these days, she was going to have to make the new name official.

"Who?"

"The person who bought the airfield."

"Oh, hey, great to hear from you. Hope you're not looking for a refund." He gave a laugh. Magnanimous, gregarious.

"No. We had some…visitors last night, and I was wondering if you might know why."

"Folks interested in your scrap metal yard already? Well done!"

How did he know that? Maybe Walter had told him. Still, it sat oddly. "That's not what I mean. They seemed to be looking for something specific, mentioned a Russian treasure. Does that mean anything to you?"

"Treasure? Wow, that's cool." There was something in his voice. Was he mocking her? "I'm sorry you had to deal with that. If there's anything I can do to help, let me know."

"I am. I want to know if you've seen any sort of Russian artifacts around the place?"

"Yeah, no. Can't think of anything. Look, I've got to run. But give me a call. We should catch up." He hung up before she could reply.

"Good news?" Hawk asked, having returned to eavesdrop on her end of the conversation.

"Intriguing, at the very least." She slid the phone into her pocket and picked up her coffee again. It was cold, and she debated topping it up. "He claims not to know anything, but I'm pretty sure he was holding back."

"Strange."

"Yeah. I can't say I'm fond of the idea of people thinking something like that is here."

"Agreed. Although it'd make a great story for the true-crime podcast I listen to."

Colt rolled her eyes and threw a dish towel at him.

Colt pushed the sense of unease to the back of her mind as Mitch made an appearance and demolished what was left of the breakfast. She helped tidy the kitchen, letting the conversation keep her focused on their plans for the day.

"What was this place like when you lived here?" Mitch asked, wiping a plate.

Colt took the dried mugs to the cupboard. "I didn't live here, exactly. We lived in town but spent all our time here. When I was little, Gram let us spend the night here with Brody."

"Wait, you knew him?" Hawk turned, dripping dishwater on the floor.

Colt realized she hadn't explained that part to them before. "Yes, he's older, but we were all friends as kids that age do when there aren't a lot of others around."

"What was he like then?"

She shrugged. "A bit spoiled but otherwise a decent kid. I don't even know if he was really the old man's nephew; we all called him 'uncle.' He spent all his summers here when he was younger."

Mitch shook out the dishcloth. "He is still a spoiled brat, so that's not changed."

She laughed. "Maybe. But maybe not. Come on, let's see what else we can uncover in the hangars."

They piled in the truck and drove up the dirt path to the airstrip. They spent a minute discussing how the thieves had gotten in. Even though Colt hadn't locked the hangar behind her, they did have a chain across the main driveway. Hawk pitched the idea of a security system, but Colt pointed out there wasn't much point to securing a hangar full of rusted equipment.

"So what's the plan for today?" Hawk asked once they were inside.

Colt punched the button to open the massive roller doors. The clattering and rumbling blocked out any hope of conversation, so she used the time to evaluate the space before them.

"Well, first, I think we should get the three planes cleared out." She nonchalantly stood where she could see their reactions.

"Three? We've only got two in here," Hawk said.

"Do we?" she asked.

The boys looked at her, then scrutinized the mess in the hangar.

Mitch whistled. "Well, blow me down and pick me up. She's right."

Hawk stood on tiptoes, then bent down to see from a lower altitude. "I'm missing something."

"Count the rudders," she told him, rocking up on her toes.

He did so, then laughed. "How did we miss an entire plane before?"

"I don't know, but this is the one I've been trying to find."

"What is it?" Hawk walked around the pile, looking for a better angle.

"A Polikarpov Po-2. NATO reporting name 'Mule,' flown by the Russians in World War II," she recited, pleased that she'd stumped him.

Mitch rubbed his hands together. "Nice, a real vintage bird."

"Right," Colt said, pleased with how her surprise had gone down. "There's plenty of room in the other hangar, so maybe we can get the Mustang out of here and into the other one for

Mitch to work on. But if we're moving stuff around, we may as well organize things as we go."

The other two agreed, and she showed them where she had started to stack boxes of paperwork near the workbench. Hawk hefted the bin of spare parts onto the bench, and Mitch got settled on an old bar stool to sort through the contents. They fell into a rhythm of sorting and stacking boxes and plane parts. Soon piles started to appear outside the hangar — things to burn, things to take to the dump.

"Your grandmother certainly had good taste in airplanes," Hawk said, running his hand over the P-51 Mustang. "This thing was a queen of flight."

Colt nodded to the Mule. "She flew one of those in the war."

"Really? A shuttle pilot?"

Colt hefted a box of folded fabric into her arms and headed for the stack of similar items by the door. "No, in combat. The Soviet Union was the first modern country to allow women in combat. The 588th bomber unit was staffed solely by women. They flew hundreds of sorties and had an impressive success rate."

Mitch looked from her to the plane. "No way. That's from the 1920s. Even the Russians had moved on from biplanes by the '40s."

The next boxes were hidden under a pile of rusty metal bits. Colt picked them up one at a time and lobbed them into the pile outside the hangar, blinking against the brightness of the sun. "Not the all-female squadrons. They got old planes, old equipment, no parachutes. Didn't matter to them. They still flew the pants off the Nazis. The 588th was so effective at terrorizing the Germans they got the nickname 'Night Witches.'"

Hawk whistled. "They outflew Messerschmitts in that thing?"

"Max airspeed was lower than the Germans' stall speed."

"Which was what, about 100 mph?" Hawk asked.

Mitch shook his head. "Top speed was over 500. No way it'd have that much of a variation."

Colt tuned out their argument. It wasn't the sun that was blinding her. It was light reflecting off something on the far side of the runway, near the fuel tanks. She squinted. It was just an old bottle or something littering the forest. There was enough garbage around the place. She lobbed a rolled-up carpet onto the junk pile and turned back to the mess before her. Nothing to worry about. Nothing at all.

The day passed quickly. The boys headed back to the house for lunch, but Colt opted to keep working. She wasn't keen on leaving the hangar open and unattended. Hawk had argued to stay with her, but she assured him she'd be fine for the short while they were gone. The old black radio was set up on the workbench, its antenna at a sharp angle to catch the local station. The strains of the latest Imagine Dragons song blared through the hangar. Colt hummed along as she shuffled more things around. The stack of boxes containing the personal effects of Katya Levin was growing, but Colt did her best to ignore it. The journals were more than enough to deal with at the moment. These boxes held items Colt would recognize from the years she lived with her grandmother. She wasn't ready for that yet.

The song changed to an old one from The Score. She let the music distract her as she lugged boxes of old encyclopedias out to the apron. A discordant note rang through the hangar, making her pause.

Her phone. She jumped over the boxes, dashing to turn the volume down on the radio.

"Hello?" she puffed.

"Ms. Levin?" the voice on the other end of the line asked.

"Yes, this is Talia." She forced herself to steady her breathing. "How can I help you?"

"This is Chauncey Danforth, of Danforth and Briggs."

"Has something gone wrong?" Surely the money transfer had worked. They weren't about to be kicked off the property, were they?

"No, nothing like that," he assured her. His voice was confident, suave. Thank goodness he couldn't see her lip curling over the phone. "This is a long shot, but my father mentioned something this morning, and I thought it might be of interest to you."

"Why's that?" She immediately decided that no matter what he said, she wasn't going to be interested. Not when he was so supremely confident that she would be.

"Well, it involves the estate of a recently deceased landowner in Pennsylvania. I immediately thought of you."

Colt tossed a bag of coat hangers outside, pleased with the noise it made on landing. "Last I checked, I'm still alive."

"Yes, but not the previous owner of your property." He was trying way too hard to sound casual. "Anyway, apparently a rare piece of jewelry was uncovered. My father has been unable to find out more details, but it was sold for quite a sum of money." He added a few extra facts that she mostly tuned out.

"That's nice," Colt said, pulling a tarp that was covering a pile of stuff against the wall.

"Yes, it is. But it's certainly causing a stir in certain circles."

She stood back, taking in the old secretary desk. It had once sat in the corner of her mother's bedroom, then later in Katya's living room. "Like yours?"

Danforth gave a little laugh. "Well, in a way, yes. My grandmother is quite interested in the story."

"Look, Danforth, unless your grandmother is interested in eighty-year-old planes or scratched furniture, I don't think there's much here to interest her."

He laughed again, gaining control back. "I'm sure it's nothing. But will you grant me a favor? If you do stumble across something, will you call me first? I'll make sure you're well compensated."

She lowered the front panel of the desk, revealing the inner shelves and drawers. The heady scent of lilac poured out, mingled with musty wood and something more. "Sure, but I doubt there is anything here that would interest you."

Danforth thanked her and hung up. Colt set her phone down and started opening the little drawers. Hawk approached.

"What was that about?" He joined her in admiring the desk.

"Danforth's grandmother seems to think something expensive is hidden here at the airfield." She told him about the rest of the information Danforth had shared about the uncovered jewelry.

Hawk shook his head when she had finished. "There seems to be a lot of interest in this place lately. I wonder why."

"It's foolish though, isn't it?" She waved a hand at the stuff in front of them. "How could anyone expect to find expensive diamonds or emeralds in this stuff? People keep that sort of thing in the house, their jewelry boxes, or a safety deposit box."

"You did say that all your grandmother's belongings were brought here. Maybe people figured her jewelry was stashed here too."

"Maybe, but it's crazy to think she had anything of great value. I mean, this desk is the most expensive thing she had, besides the planes. The old man couldn't have been the only person with property to die in Pennsylvania recently."

"You're right. They must have confused him with someone else."

"If our nighttime visitors return, maybe we can suggest that to them." She raised the lid on the desk again and turned the key to lock it.

"Good plan. For now, we've got bigger issues. Mitch's bathroom's flooding, and we're going to need a plumber."

"I'm going to regret home owning, aren't I?" She sighed as they headed for Hawk's truck.

The sound of ripping boards and tile saws filled the house. Hawk left Mitch hovering in his room as the carpenters ripped apart his bathroom to install a flat-entry shower. The leak had revealed rot behind the toilet, so that was being replaced as well. Brody had come by, the second time now in the week since Colt had called, insisting on helping paint. Hawk made sure he had the right supplies to finish the dining room, then headed up the main stairs.

Colt sat atop a ladder, painting the trim around the windows in Hawk's room. He picked up a roller and applied a fresh coat to the ceiling, hoping for a chance to bring up something she wasn't going to want to talk about.

"You're sure this dries white?" he asked, applying a liberal layer of pink paint.

"That's what the lady said. Goes on pink, dries white. Helps you see if you've missed any patches."

Hawk made an unconvinced sound but kept rolling.

"Speaking of pink," he broke the silence several minutes later.

"We were?" Colt said, looking up.

"Yes."

"Okay." She glanced up and pointed. "You missed a spot."

"That's not what I meant." He redirected his roller to where she had indicated.

"Sorry."

He sighed. "You're not making this easy."

"Sorry?"

"Fine, I give up. Colt, why are you still sleeping in the hangar?"

Her paintbrush stilled. "Uh, no reason?"

"We've got three bedrooms upstairs here. You can have your pick of them."

"It's not that... I just am still working in the hangar and end up falling asleep out there."

He narrowed his eyes at her, but she kept her back turned. She dabbed paint with great care on a corner block. He let a few minutes pass before speaking again.

"How are your grandmother's journals? The Russian giving you any trouble?"

She still didn't turn around, and he waited for her answer.

After a long minute, she spun around and pointed the paint-brush at him. "How do you do that?"

"Do what?"

"Always know when something's up and how to wrestle it out?"

"I...don't know?"

She blew a piece of hair out of her eyes and rested her elbow on her knees.

"So is everything okay?"

"Yeah, it's fine. Really good, actually. Reading her diaries, it's like getting an insight into who she really was. There's gaps though, and I wish I could find the missing diaries."

"Maybe there's another box out there."

"Maybe, but I've not seen anything that looks similar. The journals aren't all identical, but she definitely had a preference — heavy paper, leather bound, with either a tie or a clasp. I bought her one for Christmas one year, and I haven't found that one yet either."

"And the Russian? You're doing okay reading it?"

"It's a challenge, but I shouldn't have let myself get so rusty. There's some stuff though that I don't really understand. It's almost like she's purposely using the wrong words. I can't figure it out."

Hawk watched Colt talk about the mystery and smiled to himself. A mystery or puzzle to solve, and Colt was happier than a kid with a new toy. She might be content to fall asleep in the hangar over the old journals, but he decided he'd fix up the back bedroom for her anyway. It had an outside entrance and a balcony with stairs to the back of the house. He understood her need to be uninterrupted while delving into her grandmother's life. Journals were private enough as it was without feeling like someone was hovering nearby. He would love to read them, fascinated by the history the woman would have seen unravel; but more than that, what had she been like, the woman who shaped his best friend? For some reason, he pictured them as very similar.

"Did you ever keep a journal?" he asked without thinking.

"Me? No," she scoffed, then thought about it. "She tried to get me to do so at one point, said it would be therapeutic."

"Why didn't you?"

"I was a very angry teenager, and pretty much anything adults suggested as good for me I ditched." Colt dropped her paintbrush into the container holding her paint and climbed down the ladder. "I did keep very thorough flight logs though that may have included my mood before and after the flight."

He grinned at her. "Of course you did."

"Don't get your hopes up. I definitely tried various forms of redaction later on."

His face fell, giving himself away.

She burst out laughing. "Don't look so sad. I'd say it was pretty predictable: sulky teen makes a big deal about being forced to fly, only to come back and be grumpy that the flight had ended."

"You really couldn't have done anything else other than become a fighter pilot, could you?"

She set the ladder by the next window. "Nope, in my blood."

"What about your parents? Were they pilots as well?" The words slipped out without thinking. He wanted to take them back as soon as they were out. She didn't move for far too long, and he felt the pain in his own chest for the past she couldn't talk about.

"I need a new brush," she announced, spinning on her heel. She left without looking at him. He finished the room alone, berating himself the whole time.

6

"Give her back!"

The shout echoed through the house. Colt and Hawk looked at each other over the top of the dresser they were moving and set it down in one move. They raced down the stairs to find Mitch blocking the door, a burly man trying to push his way in. He was shouting incoherently, demanding he either be let in or somebody be returned to him. The man was shorter than Mitch but as big around. Not that he was going to get anywhere — the former Marine made a formidable wall.

Hawk slipped out the other door to circle around behind the guy while Colt wandered over to see if Mitch could explain what was going on.

From the look on his face, he could not. He stood squarely in front of the screen door, arms folded. With a second look, Colt covered a smirk. He was purposely clenching his hands around his elbows, pumping his biceps to make them look bigger. It was working; the sleeves on his shirt were threatening to burst.

The intimidation did little to impede the man on the other side of the door. He was moving all over the place, shouting, shaking his fists. He was maybe sixty years old, but he carried it well. A big, solid man, Colt was sure his heft was as much muscle as it was fat. He had a hard face, bearing marks of old fights. He also seemed familiar.

"Give her back! You stole her! I know she's here!" He kept repeating the phrases, alternating between English and Russian.

After a minute of waiting to see if he'd calm down, Colt spotted Hawk in position at the corner of the house. She stepped into view.

"Sir, there's no one here. I'm the only woman on the property. There's no one else."

He ignored her, his shouts turning into screams. Colt looked at Mitch. "Time to take out the trash?"

"I think so," he said. He dropped his arms and took two steps forward, through the screen door. The wooden frame cracked, a board crashing into the man. He jumped back as the huge man bore down on him. Colt followed Mitch out, impressed with his range of motion as he stepped over the broken door without tripping.

She could tell that he used his hands to break down the flimsy door, but to the man outside, it looked like he had stepped through it. The man stumbled backward into the brick wall that was Hawk. Hawk wrapped him in a bear hug, squeezing slowly against the man's struggles.

Colt walked up to him, stopping just short of where he could kick her. "Look, I don't know what you want, but whatever it is, it's not here. This is our property now, and you need to leave." She waited as Hawk tightened his grip, and the man stopped screaming to focus on breathing. "Do you understand?"

A few seconds more of Hawk's bear hug, and the man began nodding. Hawk held on a moment longer, then let go. The man sank to his knees, catching his breath. Colt watched him.

"Leave."

"I will get her back," he gasped, pushing himself to his feet. He stumbled down the drive to a battered blue Neon parked in the weeds. "I will find her!" He shouted one last time.

"*Get out!*" Colt roared at him.

He fell into his car and drove off.

Hawk straightened his sleeves. "That was disconcerting."

Colt was watching the empty drive, arms crossed. "Did he look familiar to either of you?"

Mitch cocked his head, thinking. "Maybe?"

Hawk bent to pick up pieces of the screen door. "I've not seen him before. Why?"

She tapped her finger. "He was shouting in Russian. And I think he might have been one of the men who broke into the hangar the other night."

"That makes no sense. First he's after jewelry, and now he's looking for a woman?" Hawk held up two pieces of board, trying to fit them back together.

"You must have made quite the impression on him, Colt," Mitch said.

She made a face at him. "Very funny. But I don't like what's going on here. None of it makes sense."

Mitch snapped his fingers. "The lawn guy. The day we viewed the place. Walter talked to someone mowing the lawn."

"You think it's the same guy?"

"Could be. I didn't pay too much attention to him that day."

"I didn't get a good look at him either." He frowned, then sighed. "Mitch, did you have to completely destroy the door?"

Mitch shrugged. "You said it needed to be replaced."

With Hawk distracted by the door, Colt took the opportunity to slip away. If she stuck around, he would go full big brother, and she needed to text Kendra. Too much weirdness was going on, too many people showing up chasing stories and ghosts.

There's nothing quite like the smell of sawdust in the morning. Except Hawk had yet to make the first cut, and the morning was almost over. He measured the board one more time, then forced himself to put the tape measure aside and the pencil behind his ear. Setting the board on the bench, he lowered the saw, checking that the blade lined up with his marks. He raised the saw, then flipped the switch on the side to turn on the power. Hesitating, he ran over the safety protocols in his head for the sixth time, then kicked himself.

The saw was new. The tape measure was new. The pencil was new. Even the extension cord he'd run from the barn was new.

This wasn't the first time he'd used any of these tools. He'd grown up helping his dad fix stuff around the house, had even built his sisters a playhouse when he was in high school. He scolded himself for wanting to call his dad. He was a grown man, and the saw wasn't about to bite. He hoped.

Grasping the handle once more, he depressed the trigger. The motor roared, and the blade spun to life. It ripped through the wood cleanly, sending sawdust in a cloud around him. The air filled with the woodsy scent at last. Confidence restored, he rotated the board and made the second cut, then switched off the power.

"You look like a pro with that."

The words made him jump, and he looked up to see Brody leaning against the barn. The shorter man peeled his sunglasses off and approached.

"Sorry for startling you. Didn't want to interrupt while you had the wheel of death going."

Hawk beat the dust off his hands. "Appreciate that. No work today?"

"This economy is killing me. I did an install not far from here this morning. Got nothing else on the go, so figured I'd swing by and see if I could be of use."

"Well, there's no shortage of work here, that's for sure." Hawk picked up the freshly cut board and led the way into the house. He wondered, not for the first time, what it was Brody did for a living. When asked during a previous visit, he gave the vague response of "computers." The topic was broad, but Hawk was surprised he hadn't elaborated.

He carried the board up the main stairs to the top step where the first tread was missing. Brody took the back flight up and met him in the hallway. He pushed Hawk's carefully laid-out tools to make room for himself to crouch down.

Hawk ignored it for now. Before securing the step in place, he needed to check that he'd cut it the right length. It caught on one corner, so he hammered it in with his fist. Other than that one spot, it was a perfect fit. He pulled the board out and scraped the tight corner with his utility knife.

"Pass the glue, would you?" he asked.

It took Brody a minute to find the long tube and gun in the pile of tools he'd moved. Hawk applied a liberal layer to the underside of the tread and pushed it back into place. He picked up the nail gun and drove in finishing nails. The air compressor sprang to life, the chattering sound as it refilled blocking out all chance of conversation.

Not that either of them were talking. Hawk was too focused on getting the stairs right to chat, but he wondered why Brody was unusually quiet today.

Once he was satisfied with the step, Hawk moved down the stairs until he found the next damaged one. At some point, all the treads would need to be replaced, but for now, he was focusing on the few that posed a tripping hazard. After prying the broken tread off, he measured the space, then headed back outside to the saw. Brody followed, making small talk about the property.

This time the cuts were a lot easier to make, and the two returned inside, Brody again perching on the top of the stairs. As Hawk nudged the step into position, Brody stopped him.

"Aren't you going to check for hidden treasure?"

Hawk gave him an odd look. "Brody, there's no treasure hidden in the staircase."

"You sure? I mean, those other guys seemed to think so."

"Didn't you used to live here? There's another flight of stairs under this one, down to the basement." Hawk lifted the board out and slathered it in glue.

"Oh, yeah. Guess I was too busy chasing Talia through the air to pay much attention to the house." Brody gave a cheeky grin, waggling his eyebrows.

Hawk cringed. He wasn't sure what Brody was trying to imply, but he wasn't falling for it. "From my understanding, she didn't let you catch up to her."

Brody leaned back. "Oh, sure. She outflew us all, as much as I hated to admit it then. Her gran was too old to go up much, but she taught Talia all her tricks and would watch from the ground."

The note of resentment was interesting. Hawk wondered what caused it. That Colt was better than Brody even as a teenager or that Katya hadn't taught him as well?

"Bet that didn't last though, huh? You know, once she met real pilots, like you."

Hawk laughed, looking up from his task. "I'm not a pilot. And Colt was one of the best pilots in our squadron. She topped the boards six months running."

Brody gave a half laugh. "Something must have happened that she's not flying anymore though."

"She left because of me." Hawk glared at Brody. He was over-simplifying the truth, but at that moment, he wasn't willing to go into details. For someone who grew up with Colt, Brody clearly didn't know her at all.

Brody made his excuses shortly after that, leaving Hawk to finish the stairs on his own. A lot of time passed before he heard Brody's car start up and leave.

The engine of the Ferrari F8 Tributo growled as the car rumbled over the cattle grate. Malik barely slowed as he swept under the ornate stone archway of the stables onto the road. He shifted gears, the engine settling into a contented purr as he accelerated. If he ever caught his brother driving his car like this, he'd rip him a new one. But today was not a day for poking down the road. He shifted again, longing for the worries pressing down on him to vanish as swiftly as the tarmac disappeared under his tires.

The trainer had just informed him that Pozan had an infection, so the process for starting his life at stud was on hold, forcing a delay in payments. He had already allocated that money to his sister for her redecorating project, and his banker wasn't going to be pleased with the change in cash flow.

On top of that, his sister was pressuring him to take in their mother for the two weeks the workmen would be in the house. Malik wasn't sure why it was going to take them two weeks to repaint a room, but he was more concerned with how his mother would handle the move. The doctor visited every other day now, continuing to make grave faces as he left. Malik wavered between insisting on talking to the doctor after each visit and avoiding the man, unable to bear more bad news. Offers of more money had done nothing to encourage the doctor to speed up the treatment.

"It's a delicate balance," he'd told Malik that morning. "The chemotherapy kills the cancer cells, but it also kills good cells. Her body needs the chance to recover between each treatment, and at this point, we're not seeing that recovery like we'd hoped."

"Then do something to help her," Malik had growled.

"Your mother is nearly seventy years old. There's not a magic drug we can pump into her to solve everything. And frankly, you should ask your mother if that's even what she wants."

"What are you saying?"

The doctor had shaken his head. "That's not for me to say. You need to speak with her."

Instead of taking the doctor's advice, Malik had left without even seeing his mother, something that hadn't gone unnoticed, judging by the missed calls and unanswered texts on his phone. He didn't care.

He pulled onto the highway, shifting gears again, pushing the car till the engine roared with power. The thought of losing his mother loomed over him, a dark, red storm ready to engulf him, a never-ending sandstorm full of abrasive grit stealing his air. The fact the doctor thought she didn't want to live made it all the worse.

He had one chance to convince her otherwise. If he could only get the Egg for her, she would see that there was still beauty and wonder in this life. He smacked his hand on the steering wheel, giving way to the anger he kept hidden from anyone else.

The link to the Egg was becoming tenuous, the forays thus far coming up empty. He'd already sanctioned one illegal act, one that had been deemed harmless at first. Now there were injuries, injuries he was responsible for. Further action would risk lives, either sending people to jail or worse, solely based on his decision. Who knew how many people would be in danger if he gave the word?

As he left the city behind, the rocky mountains beckoning, he found he didn't care. A legion of lives would be worth it if it saved his mother.

After three days of hard work, they were finally ready to move the Mustang. The plumbers were still ripping apart the bathrooms in the house, so the trio opted to stay out of the way and focus on the hangars. Mitch had the main hangar swept out, tidied, the workbench all set up and ready to go. The detritus had been cleared out around the plane and a tow rope anchored to the tail wheel axle. Hawk backed his truck into the hangar, and they secured the rope to the tail hitch. Colt took the wheel, and Mitch levered himself into the plane to spot it as they moved it. Hawk brought up the rear in case the nose needed to be swung around.

It felt like a momentous affair, a parade. Sans viewers or streamers, but still. They were moving their first plane along their very own runway. Colt found her favorite upbeat song and plugged it into the truck's sound system.

She drove straight into the hangar, making a wide sweep. With only a tow rope, she didn't have the capacity to push it backward, but the hangar had enough space for her to park the plane and maneuver the truck out with little difficulty.

"Looks good there," Hawk said as she climbed out of the truck.

"Yeah, it does." She undid the knots from the towline. "Reminds me of the day my grandmother was finally able to fly her Polikarpov, the crop duster in the back corner."

"Now that sounds like a story," Mitch said, pushing his wheeled toolbox next to the fuselage. Hawk brought a set of rolling stairs alongside, an early investment to ensure Mitch could move about the planes without too much trouble.

Colt nodded. "There weren't many left by the end of the Cold War, but as soon as the Wall fell, she started writing letters, contacting everyone she could find. Finally found someone willing to sell one. Charged a ridiculous amount, and my grandmother said she was nervous it was a scam. She paid him only part up front, then flew to Russia to bring it home. It was in pieces, crashed in his field, covered in overgrowth. She had to dig it out herself, then spent another month in Russia, tracking down spare parts.

At last, she got everything together, put it on board a container ship, and Russian officials arrested her for trying to smuggle war secrets out of the country. She managed to pay all their fines and administrative fees, only to face similar issues when the container landed here. The US government wanted to investigate that she wasn't bringing in weapons to target locals. When they found out it was a war plane, they thought they could take it apart to learn Russian technology." She grabbed a wrench, working at removing the propeller while she talked.

"The expert they brought in to check it out ripped into them, mocking them for not knowing the difference between a fast jet and a crop duster. To cover their embarrassment, they fined her again.

"She moved everything into the hangar, spent months working on it by herself, fixing it, singing to it. At last, she hauled it out, just like we did. It was beautiful."

Hawk grinned at her. "After all that, she still let you fly it?"

She threw a screwdriver at him. "Yes, she did. Flew better than that old thing your uncle's got."

Hawk gave a mock shudder, ignoring the projectile as it hit his shoulder and fell to the floor. "I think the Wright Flyer flew better than that plane. I'm never convinced it will get off the ground with me in it."

Mitch and Hawk lowered the seat to the ground. Mitch went back to taking apart the inside of the plane. "There's something stuck here," he said. He pried it out. "This is new. It can't have been under there long. It's not covered in dust."

The other two crowded around as he turned the envelope over. It was blank on the outside, the flap already ripped open. He nudged the flap out of the way, and out spilled a stack of photographs. The three stared in amazement.

Mitch fanned them out, then passed them to Colt one by one, who handed them off to Hawk after staring at them a moment. "What is this stuff?"

"Items worth a lot of money, I would say," Mitch said, flipping through them a second time. "Gemstones, sculptures, necklaces, even gold boxes." He whistled. "Not to mention a Fabergé Egg."

Colt took the bundle and shuffled through them again. "These are all old — look at the styles. None of these are modern designs. The thieves...they mentioned Nazi treasure. The Germans confiscated anything of value from the Jews. All this stuff predates the '40s, wouldn't you say?"

They shared the photos around again.

"I'd agree with that analysis," Hawk said. "So what? They think stolen art made its way to a farmhouse in Pennsylvania after the war?"

"They must, but how?"

"Your grandmother was a pilot, but what about the old man? Did he serve in Germany?"

Colt shook her head, trying to remember. "No, I think he was stationed in London...logistics or something. But seriously, guys, the man was bordering on broke his entire life. Any penny he got, he sank back into this place. Does this look like the airfield of a man sitting on millions of dollars' worth of art and jewels?"

"No, but maybe he couldn't move any of it without drawing too much attention?"

"Maybe. But not all of this stuff would have been that identifiable. Especially as more time passed." Remembering the call from Danforth, she pulled a photo from the stack. It showed an opulent gold and emerald necklace, a style she wouldn't be caught dead wearing. "He nearly went bankrupt once. The bank threatened to foreclose the airfield, and he had to scramble to come up with the funds. Surely if he was sitting on something like this, he would have done something to make some money."

"I don't know, Colt. A lot of people are convinced that there's treasure of some sort hidden here. Is there any chance any of it is true?"

She shook her head stubbornly. "I just don't see it."

"Nothing like a little mystery on a sunny afternoon," Mitch said, stuffing the pictures back into the envelope. He handed it to Colt. "But it's not getting this plane fixed. So if you'll excuse me…"

Colt flipped through the photos one more time. They weren't high quality, some showing a ruler for accurate dimensions of a piece and others shown on display. They looked like images pulled from the internet. But why these ones? And why here?

7

Colt went back to Hangar 2, tapping the envelope against her palm as she walked. The grumpy thief must have kept these images to himself for some reason, based on Whiny's discouraged approach to searching and the conversation she'd overheard. She spread out the pictures on the workbench. The most recognizable one was the Fabergé Egg, so she did a search on her phone. The first article had a comprehensive list of the Romanov Eggs. The photo in her hand was a print of an image on the website. It was one of the Eggs in the Metropolitan Museum of Art. So the photos had been included as an example of what to look for, not the exact items.

She looked up a few more of the pictures, doing her best to use the correct keywords. The jewelry box could have been one of hundreds of gem-encrusted boxes. Either way, she got the impression that all these items were extremely rare and expensive. But who could she contact to find out more about them?

Danforth. He moved in the wealthy world and had even mentioned the other day that his family had interests in expensive and rare items. She also got the impression that he knew how to be discreet. Surely as a client of his bank, of sorts, there would be some sort of banker-client privilege, and anything she shared with him would be kept between them. She drummed her fingers on the desk, debating, eyes running over the photographs again. If only he weren't such a tool.

His secretary answered and seemed disinclined to patch her through to Danforth's line. Colt told her to relay the message that the call was regarding the information he had asked her about the other day.

He called back less than ten minutes later.

"I need to know more about the item you said had been found here."

"Why the sudden change of heart?" She could hear the superiority in his voice, how he enjoyed the fact she was coming to him for help.

She stared at the picture of a necklace so laden with gems she wondered how any woman could hold her head up with it around her neck. "Let's just say there's been some interesting developments here over the past few days, and I think that item might be connected." She explained about the break-in, the Russian man's odd claims of a missing woman. She didn't mention anything about her grandmother's journals. There was nothing in them that specifically mentioned treasure or wealth.

He took a moment to deliberate what she had told him. "I might be able to help you, but you need to come into my office."

"It'll take me two hours to get there, traffic permitting. Can't you just tell me now?"

"Come tomorrow morning. Whenever you can; I'll adjust my schedule. I promise, it will be much better if you come in."

"Fine. We'll be there at eight." Hawk would hate her dragging his butt out of bed so early, but she planned on avoiding as much of the city traffic as she could.

"Bring anything you've got that gives any insight into the previous owners of the property. It may give us an idea of what we're looking for," Danforth said before he hung up.

She gritted her teeth. He was going to have to get over that ordering-her-around thing and fast. For one, she wouldn't be bringing any information with her. It wouldn't be necessary. She could tell him anything he wanted to know about her grandmother or the old man, of that she was certain.

The night was closing in on the city, but you wouldn't know it from the light that drowned out the stars. Only the sound of the occasional overpowered car driven by someone needing to prove their worth reached Malik in his office. In the aviary, his pet cockatoo protested an unknown disturbance. At any moment, the parrots would wake up and join her. Not for the first time, Malik considered opening the cage and letting them all go free. Unfortunately, he doubted that would do much. They were so used to being fat and happy, they'd return no matter what he did. He pressed a hand to his eyes, trying and failing to ignore the incessant calling.

Slouching further in his seat, he tipped the last of his whisky into his mouth, savoring the hints of citrus, vanilla, and oak. The sherry and honey finish lingered in his mouth, not quite washing away the bitterness of the day. Once he'd opened the bottle of Balvenie to celebrate finding the necklace, it had been hard to rationalize not drinking it. But now it only served to mock him and his inability to find the Egg that went with the sapphire. It shouldn't be this hard. All indications, all the rumors, pointed to the necklace and the Egg being kept together. It's not like someone would sell the one without the other. Unlike most beautiful jewelry, whose cases only served to highlight the piece, the Fabergé Eggs were exquisitely designed artwork. The jewelry pieces were delightful treasures found within but of lesser value than their housing.

His eyes flicked to the mahogany paneled wall that hid a walk-in safe. The necklace was securely hidden there, resting in the understated black velvet box. He had shown it to no one yet, not even his sister or his girlfriend. They would both want to wear it, although the setting was much simpler than his girlfriend's usual tastes. Even she would be able to spot the quality of the gem. Maybe someday, if he couldn't find the Egg, he would allow her to wear it, but not yet.

He stood suddenly, setting the glass down on the table with a clatter. He crossed the office, fingers sliding into the groove that would release the mahogany panel. It opened, and he laid his palm on the biometric scanner. A thumbprint would have sufficed, but he had given in to the thrill of having a full hand scan like in the movies. The safe door released with a sigh, and he pulled it back, the lights turning on automatically. The cooler air within only added to the sense of stepping into a refrigerator.

Malik opened the box and stared at the necklace, imagining it on the neck of a beautiful woman. Without gloves on, he refrained from touching it, admiring the light reflecting off the many facets of the gem. After a moment, he returned it to its shelf and locked up. It was late in Kuwait, but the afternoon was still going strong in the United States. He rang his contact, pacing around the office as he waited for the man to pick up.

"Find out everything you can about the man who used to live at the airfield. Dig up old records; go back thirty, forty years if you have to. I want to know who was in his life, especially women. And find out more about the property. There's got to be more to it than a strip of land with a bunch of dilapidated buildings." He ended the call, not giving the man a chance to reply. Too on edge to consider sleep, he headed outside to have a chat with a certain cockatoo.

Hawk slumped against the passenger door, snores emanating softly from behind the ball cap pulled down low over his eyes. Colt was thankful he was asleep. They'd hashed out everything about this little adventure the previous evening, going in circles. Mitch had been against bringing in Danforth, especially if there was no treasure at all. And if there was, would the banker expect a cut?

Colt had insisted there was no treasure, but she wanted to know more about what people were looking for. If she knew what they wanted, she would have a better idea of why they were looking here. And it would be easier to guide them someplace else once they were able to solidly prove there was no treasure at the run-down airfield.

Hawk had been concerned for her, wondering if she was ready to face evidence that her grandmother kept secrets from her. Colt stubbornly refused to accept that possibility, convinced everyone had the wrong place.

Either way, Hawk had agreed to make this journey with her, despite the early hour. She'd had his coffee ready in a travel mug when he came down the stairs. He'd accepted it with a grunt of thanks and handed her his keys. As the sun climbed over the horizon, the light threatened to wake him, so he'd roused enough to dig out the old ball cap to cover his eyes. She let him sleep an hour before turning into a drive-through. She wanted breakfast, so he was going to wake up, whether or not he wanted to.

The second round of coffee did the trick.

"So you think Danforth has information that could help us?" Hawk asked, wiping the crumbs from a bacon and egg bagel off his coat.

"He's got a better chance than we do on our own."

They parked in the private client slots below the office tower. The elevator shot them straight up to the offices, forgoing the lobby. A receptionist guided them through the halls to another elevator, where Danforth was waiting for them when they got off, looking as though he'd just walked out of an Armani showroom. He led them into his office.

"Coffee?" he offered.

"Please," Hawk said, almost begging.

Danforth pressed the plunger on the French press and poured them each a glassful. Each movement was precise and fluid. A man in control of his surroundings. Colt studied the mug. It was double walled to insulate the hot liquid, but she felt it was a bit of a rip-off. She could see the inner cup was a lot smaller than the outside. After a few minutes of pleasantries and wafer-thin cookies filled with dulce de leche, Danforth got down to business. A press of a button turned the clear glass windows to darkly tinted, and another press lowered a screen from the ceiling. He proceeded to walk them through the history of the Fabergé Eggs, from the first one ordered by Tsar Alexander III in 1885 for his wife through the last one, delivered shortly before the death of the Imperial family. He finished with pictures of the few that were still in existence, then moved to sketches of ones believed lost. The final slide showed a blue lapis lazuli egg, yellow yolk open. A gem-encrusted chicken sat in the center, a large sapphire pendant beside it.

Colt sat forward, studying the Egg. How had he jumped from rumors of a necklace to Imperial Russia? "You really think there's a Fabergé Egg out there? Hidden for all this time?"

Danforth leaned back, crossing his legs. "It's entirely possible. One was discovered in a flea market not that long ago. One can always dream the impossible."

Hawk set his coffee down. "But why that? Why not any of these other things in the photos we found?"

Danforth got to his feet. "Ah, yes. That." He moved to his desk, returning with two copies of a full-size glossy brochure. He hand-ed one to each of them. "This is the most recent catalog of items at the premier auction house here in New York. Rothschild's Auction House only handles the most expensive and rare articles, items that attract collectors from around the world. If you'd turn to the page I've marked..."

Colt stopped flicking through the first pages and turned to the one flagged with a black sticky note. Several necklaces were displayed, their particulars and starting bids listed. But one took up two-thirds of the page, a large sapphire pendant on a simple chain. She scanned the description, seeing nothing that indicated its origin, aside from an estimate of its age. It was believed to be more than eighty years old.

"This one?" she asked, tapping the sapphire picture.

"Yes. It fits the age, the styling of the hidden prize that was often found in the works of Fabergé."

"Have you seen it?"

"No." He sounded disappointed. "It was purchased by a private collector before it could go to auction. He paid three times the lowest bid for the honor."

She pointed to the screen, still showing the hen and sapphire Fabergé Egg sketch. "You really think someone found that at the airfield?"

"No. I think someone found the necklace and sold it without realizing its value. Whether or not the Egg still exists is impossible to predict." He paused, steepling his hands as he chose his words. "If this were to be found, it would be worth a lot of money."

"How much are we talking?" Hawk asked.

"A minimum of fifty million dollars."

Colt's mug wobbled, splashing coffee over the edge. She set it on the table, accepting the napkin Hawk passed her, neither of them removing their gaze from Danforth's face. A long moment passed.

"You're not joking, are you?" Colt asked when he added nothing more after several seconds.

"I am not." He stood again, heading to the small stand by his desk. He lifted the box sitting there with great care, placing it in the center of the coffee table.

"Go ahead, open it."

Colt exchanged a look with Hawk. She wiped her hands again, then reached for it. Black velvet, a foot tall, eight inches square. She lifted the top off, hands steady as it slid up and off the contents.

She felt Hawk's reaction before seeing what was inside and forced herself to go even slower, ensuring the lid was well clear before moving it aside to set down.

A diamond-encrusted Egg sat before her, glittering in supreme glory. It lay nestled in its black velvet cocoon, safe and oh so haughty. It was identical to the images Danforth had just shown them, of an Egg believed to be lost forever. The word *replica* floated into her brain even as she struggled to accept the luxurious item before her wasn't real. Or, at least, wasn't the original. Danforth leaned over and pressed the diamond set in its center. The top half of the golden Egg sprang up, revealing a dazzling array of diamonds. After the initial shock, Colt saw the gems were set into the shape of a small round chicken. In its beak, it held a sapphire pendant.

Beside her, Hawk's jaw dropped with an audible pop as he struggled to find words. She knew what he meant, able to do little more than motion at the screen with her hand. Danforth understood the request and clicked the pointer. The six-foot picture changed, and a ginormous version of the pendant appeared. It looked identical to the one before her. She reached for the auction house brochure to double-check.

The artist's concept in the slideshow was close, very close. The color was different, sapphires having several different shades. The artist had chosen deep indigo to represent the gem, its rich tones leaping off the screen.

The one in the model, the recreation, was peacock in color, as was the one in the brochure. Colt tapped the picture.

"That's uncanny. Where did you get this model?"

Danforth sipped his coffee, unable to hide his smirk. "It belongs to my grandmother. She had it commissioned several years ago, having always had a fascination with them. When I asked her why she chose that particular color, she said it was an arbitrary choice but figured 'peacock' kept with the theme of birds."

"Fabergé must have had the same idea."

She studied them again. The settings between the model and the brochure were also very similar — simple and elegant. "It's almost as if your grandmother had seen the original."

Danforth laughed. "I can't imagine that happened, but she has long loved art in all forms. In fact, that's how my grandfather met her — she was working at an art gallery. She studied Fabergé's style for a long time, so she had an insight into his style and knew him well enough to make similar choices for settings and styles."

"Has she made other replicas?"

"Two. This is her favorite."

Colt used her fingernail to turn the Egg, careful of getting fingerprints on it. Every facet was impeccable, from the smooth gold outer shell to the diamond clasp to the jewel-studded chicken. It might not have been created by Fabergé himself, lacking the historical element of it, but she still guessed its value would be well into the millions. This wasn't a gold-plated piece with cubic zirconia adding the sparkle. This was as authentic as anything the artist would have made a hundred years ago. Original or not, it was an incredibly valuable piece.

"Thank your grandmother for letting us see this. That was very kind of her," Hawk said as Colt memorized the details.

"I should get this back to her." Danforth slid the lid back on the box, then gave a small laugh. "My grandmother shared this clue — maybe yours has the next one."

Colt stilled. "What did you say?"

"The property you bought belonged to your grandmother, didn't it? It would be a fitting continuation if both our grandmothers were connected to this piece."

The words scraped down her spine like fingernails on a chalkboard. Colt stood, shoving her hands in her pockets. "Thank you for your time. We'll be getting back now." She held back the shiver until she and Hawk were safely on the elevator. Why was everyone so insistent her grandmother was involved somehow?

"Colt, you —"

"No." She cut him off. "Katya has nothing to do with this. I'll prove it to you."

Malik's normally orderly office was in disarray. His jacket was off, slung over the sofa, his shirt unbuttoned. Stacks of books and open files lay scattered across the desk, and a half-empty French press sat beside dirty coffee cups on the credenza. The door to the walk-in safe was open, ledgers from its shelves tossed on the sofa. Malik flicked through a ledger, searching for the reference he needed.

"It was a minor donation. Perhaps we didn't record it on your accounts," said the other man in the room, helping himself to a mango skewer, one of the few remaining delicacies from the tray of refreshments that had been brought in an hour before.

"If so, then this error will be coming out of your fee. You were supposed to check the legitimacy of these so-called charities *before* we made donations to them. Not after." Malik sighed. Hours stuck in the office with the corpulent accountant had put him on edge. "Where did we even come across them?"

Another bite disappeared. "Your nephews' school, if I recall correctly."

A sound close to a growl left Malik's lips as he tossed the file onto the desk with the others. "So these fools preyed on children? I want proof of my donation, and you had better find it."

"Yes, of course, but if I may remind you, Mr. Al Kandari, we do have the record of the payment coming from your account..."

"Yes, but not where it went!" He bit back the rest of the words as a knock sounded at the door. "Come in," he called, welcoming the interruption.

His butler stepped in. "Ms. Baby is here, sir."

A woman, several years his junior, swooped in. "Oh, you know that there's no reason to announce me! Malik, I'm back! Did you miss me, honeybear?" She grabbed his arm and leaned up to give him a kiss on the cheek.

Malik cleared his throat pointedly. She looked around, a pout appearing on her shapely lips. "You have visitors. Did you forget I was coming home today?"

"No, of course not. Mr. Osman was just leaving." Malik welcomed the excuse to send the man away.

Osman was slow to take the hint, helping himself to another canapé as the butler bustled him out the door. Dalal dropped her purse and scarf in a chair and spun around.

"Do you like my new pantsuit, honeybear? I think it shows off my waist perfectly. Of course, the color meant I *had* to get these new shoes to match because I had nothing to go with it."

He dropped his hands on her shoulders and kissed her forehead. "You look lovely. Why don't you settle in the den with some tea, and I'll join you as soon as I clean up here?"

She stood still, taking in the disaster for the first time. "Don't send me away. I can help. Then we can watch a movie together."

"Very well. Help me put the books away." He pointed to the space on the shelves where the law books belonged and moved to his desk. The files were all out of order, so he took the time to return them to the cabinet where they belonged. Dalal finished with the books and wandered over to the desk, picking up the ledgers.

"Where do these go?" she asked.

"In the safe — you'll see the shelf of them." He didn't turn around, one hand holding open three different slots in the files while the other tried to balance the folders.

She returned quickly. "Did you get me a present? You sly man! This is why you didn't want my help. You were going to surprise me!"

"What? No?" Malik turned to see her coming out of the walk-in safe, holding a square black velvet box. He dropped the folders on top of the cabinet and moved to take the box from her.

He was too late. She opened it, spinning around to drop into the corner of the sofa. "Ooo, that's super precious! That blue is just my color!" She raised a finger to probe the sapphire.

Malik reached down and slid the box out of her grasp. "Ah. No. That's not for you."

"What do you mean it's not for me? Who's it for? Your cow of a sister then?" She narrowed her eyes.

Malik pressed his lips together, letting the insult go for now. "No. It's for no one."

Dalal stood, one elegantly manicured finger pointing at him. "You'd better explain that, mister. Because if this 'no one' has a name, we're going to have words."

He sighed. "No. It's not like that. This is an antique, a collectible. No one is going to be wearing it." The light caught the gem, and he tilted the box to admire it more. Dalal came around to lean over his shoulder to look at it with him.

"There's a story, isn't there?" Her voice was softer, reminding him more of the curious, intelligent woman he'd fallen for.

He smiled down at her, then nudged her to join him as he sat on the sofa. He kept the box open in his hands. She curled her legs under her, leaning on his arm. For a moment, he debated how much to tell her. He trusted her, but he also knew how much she enjoyed sharing exciting news with her friends. "A long time ago, a rich young ruler had a beautiful wife. He wanted to give her a present that was as beautiful as she. He sought high and low for an artist who could meet such a demand. At last, he found one, and the gift was delivered some months later. It was exquisite, a set of sapphire pieces of such quality, the ruler knew that it was perfect for his wife." Dalal shifted closer, and he paused to drop a kiss on her forehead. "On her next birthday, he gave his wife the jewelry. She vowed to wear it the next evening to a dinner with foreign visitors, showing off the greatness of her husband. Before the guests arrived, the palace was attacked, and everyone fled for their lives as it burned to the ground. Many lives were lost, along with the riches held within. This necklace alone survived."

They sat in silence a moment. Dalal brushed her finger along the velvet beside the gold chain. "That's heartbreaking. But it's such a lovely piece. It shouldn't be hidden in your vault."

Malik snapped the box shut. He had hoped she'd understand, but he'd been wrong.

"Something like that deserves to be shared," she said. "As a way to honor the queen who never got to wear it."

He stood, carrying the box to the vault. "No. It's too valuable. I can't risk it being damaged." His words were harsher than he'd meant.

"Fine. I need to get home anyway." She grabbed her coat and left.

As he put the box on the shelf and locked up the vault, Malik knew he was right. He couldn't risk anything happening to the necklace. Not yet. He needed to have both pieces in his hands first.

It was late by the time Colt and Hawk got back to the airfield. While they were out, they decided to stop at various stores and load up on supplies for the projects they had going on. Colt checked a number of things off her list while Hawk spent half an hour in the toilet aisle, trying to find the best option for Mitch's reconfigured bathroom. In the end, he walked away with a slew of brochures from the poor clerk who couldn't answer all his questions. After unloading the stack of two-by-fours and paint in the smaller of the two barns, Hawk presented Mitch with the brochures.

Mitch took them with a skeptical look.

"To help you find the best one," Hawk explained.

"Any toilet is fine," Mitch said. "My butt isn't the bit that's missing."

"Oh, right." Hawk stood there awkwardly. "Sorry."

Colt stared at them for a second. "Oh, come on, you morons. Mitch made gumbo. Let's eat before it gets cold. We can discuss porcelain decor later." They filled their bowls while Colt and Hawk recounted to Mitch what Danforth had told them.

"So there is a good chance that necklace was found here?"

"Absolutely not," Colt said, dunking her cheese bread in her bowl. "Katya and Frank weren't into buying art or trolling flea markets for eclectic vases. They bought and flew planes. In the summers, the place was so busy with the cadet camps, they didn't have time for anything else."

"How long ago did they buy it? The house is over a hundred and fifty years old; any chance the necklace was here before them?" Hawk asked as he filled his bowl for the second time.

"The paperwork said the property hadn't changed hands since the '60s, and before that, it was a government air base."

Hawk snagged a piece of cheese bread and started pacing out the dining room, tapping the walls as he went. "Maybe there's hidden compartments in the walls? Is this room shorter than it should be?"

Mitch's laptop was open at the end of the table, and he pulled it toward himself. "The airfield was built during the Cold War? Wonder if there's any records online."

Colt hunkered over her bowl of gumbo as the boys ran with their ideas. If they wanted to explore this, then fine. She had better things to do. She pulled out her phone, checking the list of supplies she needed against what she'd bought that day. Repairing the cement floor of the hangars would have to wait until they got more of the junk cleared out, and she needed to do more research on the best place to buy canvas...

"Hey, check this out." Mitch spun his laptop around for her to see the screen. "A number of these old bases had underground tunnels. Partly for ease of movement during the winter but also as nuclear fallout bunkers."

Colt ran her finger over the mousepad, scrolling back and forth over the layout he had found. Fine. If they wanted a treasure hunt, she'd give them one. It'd give her a chance to prove them wrong. "It could be unrelated, but I remember we used to play near something like this. We thought it was a cave or maybe an old mine shaft. It only went back a few feet before it was blocked by a pile of rocks."

"Sweet, let's go find it!" Hawk said, leaning over her shoulder.

Stabbing a shrimp with her fork, Colt waved it at the darkened windows. "No chance of finding it this late."

"First thing tomorrow then!"

Colt cocked an eyebrow at Hawk. He was far too excited about this. "What's got you all wound up?"

"Come on, Colt. Secret tunnels, buried treasure. It's like being in a Hardy Boys novel!"

She turned to Mitch for an explanation.

He shrugged. "Don't look at me for a translation. I grew up reading Luke Cage and Blade."

Colt blinked at him.

"Aw, come on, Colt. You did have a childhood, didn't you?"

"Sure. I spent it here. Flying planes." For some of it. The other years she preferred to pretend didn't happen. Memories threatened to resurface, and she shoved them away. She gathered up her dishes and carried them to the kitchen. Maybe coming back to the airfield wasn't such a great idea after all. It was certainly a lot more work than what she remembered.

8

Hawk followed Colt through the woods. The early morning mist lingered over the airfield, wrapping the world in a soothing blanket. Layers of pink and purple mingled with gray as the sun hid behind the tree line. Instead of heading up the hill toward the hangars, they entered the woods behind the barn. Two towering oaks marked the promise of a path, but it quickly petered out. He'd been meaning to explore it since they'd moved in but hadn't had the time. He was pleased with this chance to explore the property with Colt. They were dressed alike in hiking boots, jeans, and flannel overcoats. Colt led the way, hatchet in hand. Along with his own hatchet, Hawk carried a small backpack with water, rope, and a collapsible shovel. He held his phone in his hand, using a map app to track their path. There was evidence they were on an old trail, but pine trees had grown up between the stands of oak and maple, intent on wiping out the footprint of man.

"We should open this trail up again. It'd be nice to be able to walk through here without being attacked by trees." Hawk shoved a branch out of his face as he walked.

"That'd take a bulldozer, wouldn't it?" Colt hacked at a particularly stubborn branch in her way.

"Not necessarily. There's a BushHog mower in the barn with the tractor, along with some other implements that could come in handy."

"Need something bigger than a mower to take out these trees though." She pushed through a couple of trees and vanished from his view. He circled around, searching for a way through that didn't involve getting soaked by the dew-laden needles.

"Chainsaw will take care of it." Although a chainsaw would ruin the tranquility of the morning. Despite the noise they were making, squirrels and chipmunks hung around, more curious than frightened. Birdsong chorused around them. All the sounds of the woods and none of the world. It was hard to believe they were only a half mile from the highway.

She cocked her head as she walked. "I think if we did, and found the connecting trails, we could make a loop of three miles, easy."

"That would be a good running track then, if we could get the ground smoothed out enough."

She grinned at him. "Little trail running never hurt anyone."

He stumbled, his foot caught under a half-buried branch. "No, I'm pretty sure it's hurt lots of people. At least we should make sure there's no hidden tripping hazards like that one."

"Weakling." She paused, nearly causing him to bump into her.

Before them, the hill opened up. To the right, it climbed steeply, a vague pathway curving up along the slope. A few yards ahead lay a fallen oak, its massive trunk blocking their route. On the left, the ground swooped away, covered in rocks and heavy undergrowth. Looking at the height of the trees, Hawk could just distinguish a swath that was uniformly shorter than those around them.

"Which way?" he asked, digging in his bag for water and handing one of the bottles to Colt.

Colt considered the terrain as she took a drink. "I know for sure this path continues up, but it looks like there's one that goes downhill too. I don't remember it, but it would make sense to go lower if we're looking for a cave."

"You don't remember? I thought you grew up here?"

"I did. Off and on." She tossed the bottle back in his bag and headed for the lower path, slashing at a branch with her hatchet.

Hawk slung the bag back over his shoulder, hurrying to follow her. "But you lived here in high school. That wasn't that long ago."

She let out a puff of air. "I did, but we lived in town at that point. A lot had changed by then."

Hawk considered her words, confused. "The trophy you showed me...you were a lot younger then."

"Not everyone had a perfect, stable family life, Hawk." She hacked at a branch and shoved her way between two trees.

He stilled, her harsh words knocking him off-balance. He hadn't meant to pry, but he'd let his curiosity push too far. She moved ahead, and he let her have the space. From experience, he knew better than to apologize. Better to let the topic die. They pushed forward in silence for some time until she let him catch up to her.

"I was only three when my parents...died." Her quiet voice startled him, and he nearly missed the hesitation. "My grandmother took in my brother and I. It was wonderful. For three years, everything was perfect. Then social services got involved. Gram fought to keep us, but we were shuffled around a lot. She was unwell, but we didn't know at the time." The words seemed to tumble out of her. Colt concentrated on the trees as she talked, chopping branches left and right with clean, precise movements. Hawk let her go on without interruption, putting his own hatchet to use. He took each detail she offered and tucked it away in a safe place. She wouldn't share twice.

"We were allowed to come for visits, stay with her for holidays. She had a stroke while we were flying one day. I was nine, and I landed the plane on my own. She was unconscious, but I thought she was dead."

The trophy. It wasn't to celebrate a young pilot's greatest achievement. It was a distraction for a young girl's heartache. How long was it before she could face a cockpit again? Hawk's chest tightened, and he wanted to wrap her in a hug the way he would have done with any of his sisters. But the hatchet in her hand didn't stop, and he knew physical contact right now would be as unwelcome as the trees in their way.

"After that, we were put in a group home." Chop. "My brother was eventually adopted." Chop. "When I was fifteen, I ran away and came back here." Chop chop chop. She slowed, shoving hair out of her face. "Gram was doing a lot better and had an apartment in town. Social services agreed I could stay. Probably because I threatened to keep running away if they took me." She finally looked at him again, a cheeky smile threatening. "Gram adopted me, I changed my last name to hers, and all my records were sealed. She taught me to fly, for real this time." She wrapped up the story in a few quick words, methodically chopping at a particularly thick branch that didn't really need to come down. It fell, swinging in slow motion against the trunk.

"She died the year after I joined the Navy."

The finality of the words hit him like a felled tree. Hawk stopped cutting and turned to her. "No wonder this place holds such meaning for you." His heart ached for her, this friend who'd had to defend herself alone for so long. She stood there now, head thrown back, jaw tight, eyes daring him to say anything. As much as he wanted to declare his everlasting friendship, he offered her a lifeline instead.

"There's a spider on your shoulder."

She craned her head to see it, then flicked it off. "No shortage of those around the place."

They moved on, letting the conversation drift to more casual topics. "In Minnesota, we valued the land based on output per acre. Here, it's a different sort of value, isn't it? The trees, the peacefulness of being secluded from the world."

"Yes, but that's about all the value there is. I can guarantee there's no money here." They reached a section where the trees were stunted, allowing them to make progress without stopping to chop and hack.

"Somebody certainly thinks otherwise," Hawk pointed out. He didn't want to bring up a sore point again, but they were on a hunt to find a tunnel that might confirm the rumors.

More rocks littered the hillside, and they had to concentrate on their footing. At last, the path leveled out as the trees thinned. Beside them, the hill rose away from a pile of rubble.

"That looks like an entrance to something," Hawk observed.

Colt kicked a rotting beam. "An entrance that's definitely not an access point anymore."

Colt used the shovel to lever a piece of beam out of her way. The rotting wood had once been ten by ten and a good eight feet long. Now it crumbled away at the edges, broken into three. She leaned her weight against the fulcrum, focused on moving this obstacle from her path. She avoided looking at Hawk as much as possible.

After what she'd told him, he was going to be extra nice and kind, and she didn't want to deal with that.

Hawk lifted a stone and tossed it to the side, breaking her concentration. It landed with a heavy thunk. He stopped to wipe the sweat from his forehead. "This is fruitless. We need to get the tractor out here to clear this out."

A final shove and the beam shifted, causing a mini avalanche of stones to tumble down the hill. "Or some dynamite. Who knows how far in the entrance collapsed."

"Any chance you remember a huge steel door with nuclear warning signs?"

She gave him a look.

"Just asking." He stripped off the flannel jacket and hung it on a branch.

They worked for a while, trying to clear enough away to find the defined lines of the opening. Some of the stones showed tool marks, evidence of being shaped to fit against each other. After an hour, they found one of the upright beams, still in place, framing the left side of the entrance.

Hawk sank onto the pile of cleared stones, panting. He fished the last bottle of water out of the backpack and offered it to her. She shook her head.

"Go for it. I'll be fine until we get back."

"You need to drink." He tossed it to her.

She caught it and hiked it back in one movement. "Nope. One advantage to not sweating. I don't lose water the same way you do. Replace what you've lost before you stop sweating altogether."

She was relieved when he acquiesced, downing half the bottle in one gulp. They gathered up their gear to head back. Hawk checked his map, dropping a pin on their location to make the cave-in easier to find next time. Clutching her hatchet, Colt held it ready in case she needed an outlet on their walk back. She half-expected Hawk to bring up their earlier conversation again. Memories of that time lurked at the edge of her thoughts, but she shoved them away, concentrating on what needed to be done to the property.

"Does the tractor have an attachment to level the road up to the hangar? I thought it was paved, but it's not. We should get it flattened for Mitch's wheelchair. Although that's a long hill."

"We'd need a box blade for that, which I've not seen. There is an old golf cart in the barn. He mentioned digging that out, seeing if it ran. It'd give him wheels back and forth to the hangars."

She relaxed as they walked, shifting the hatchet to a loose grip, only using it to lop the occasional branch. The last hundred yards were easier, and the path opened out into the full heat of midday.

Mitch met them on the back veranda, sitting on the railing, arms folded. Colt immediately started scanning the area, Hawk doing the same. Nothing seemed out of place, but the rigid set to Mitch's shoulders meant something was up.

"Someone's been here," Mitch called as soon as they drew closer. "I heard something, and I'm positive a man vanished into the trees at the front of the house. About fifteen minutes ago. I checked the barn. Nothing's missing, but it feels off."

Colt split off to the left, Hawk heading right. Mitch followed, pointing where he'd last seen the guy. She ducked into the trees where he said, but the ground was too dry to see any footprints. After a quick search, she rejoined them by the house. She shook her head, telling them she'd found nothing.

"Barn and shed are clear," Hawk reported. "As Mitch said, everything is there, but I get the sense someone's been rifling through things."

Colt spun away, throwing the hatchet with all her strength. It tumbled over and over before burying itself in a nearby maple tree.

"I'm so sick of this. Not only are these jerks trespassing on our property, they're violating the memory of two people who never hurt a fly. I don't know where this idea that they stole and hid a bunch of jewels came from, but it needs to stop."

"Hey, hey. No one ever said they stole it," Hawk tried to placate her.

She stared at him. She hadn't meant to let that spill out, the fear that had been lurking in the back of her mind. "Well, it's not like they could afford it. And if it wasn't stolen, they wouldn't have hidden it, would they?" She stormed off to the hangar, needing time alone to deal with the truth she hadn't wanted to admit.

Colt flipped open the journal and settled into the old armchair she'd dug out of the pile in the hangar, planning on beating the dust off at some point in the future. Mysteriously, it had been cleaned, patched, and placed in a cozy spot in her bunk room.

No, not mysteriously. Hawk had done it. Just like he'd scrubbed the bunk room, made the bed, and stocked the mini kitchen with a kettle, microwave, and toaster. She'd found tea and coffee, snacks, and cans of soup in the cupboard, and the fridge held bottled water and yogurt. Where he'd found time for all that, she didn't know, as he had taken charge of the renovations at the house as well while she and Mitch spent their days in the hangars, either working on the planes or sorting through the piles looking for spare parts.

As much as possible, she tried to put the thoughts of the jewelry out of her mind. Dwelling on it didn't help, and the more time she spent digging through the hoarded flotsam, the more convinced she was that everyone was wrong. Nothing there was worth more than a couple hundred bucks, and that was due to the value of plane parts. Old furniture that needed refinishing. Dishes, cutlery, the paraphernalia of a life once lived, packed up in boxes and stored for posterity.

The greatest treasure they'd found was a box of her grandmother's personal items. Hawk had uncovered it, pulling out a framed picture, the glass cracked. A gangly teenager, brown hair in a long braid over her shoulder, serious but for the exultation in her eyes, stood with her arm draped over the shoulder of a tiny white-haired lady. Despite her age, she stood erect, the pride and love for the girl evident on her face. Beneath it were a few well-loved books, a couple more journals, the handwriting shaky, and a handful of postcards. Colt winced at just how few of them there were. Her favorite find thus far was the black and white wedding picture of her grandparents. Roger Stevens, resplendent in his dress whites, looking lovingly at the beautiful woman on his arm. He had died the year her mother was born, fighting in Vietnam.

Hawk had hung the picture of Colt and her grandmother in her bedroom, but she'd brought it here, where she could see it as she read her grandmother's journals. Katya documented most of her life, pouring out her heart on the page. The more she read, the more Colt was able to understand the Russian without having to look up words, although there were still occasional entries that didn't make sense.

Like the one open before her. 27 October, 1993. Sipping her tea, Colt reread the first line for the third time. It was no use — she couldn't concentrate enough to decipher the hidden meaning.

Brody was coming back tomorrow. His enthusiasm for helping with the renovations was contagious, but she couldn't help but wonder why. If he was so interested in "bringing the old place back to its former glory," as he'd told Hawk, why hadn't he kept the property for himself? And why was he still hanging around? Didn't he have a job back in the city?

When she'd mentioned her concerns to Hawk, he'd calmly reminded her that some people do genuinely want to help. Trusting his judgment, she tried to focus on how nice Brody was being, but something kept niggling in the back of her mind. Maybe residual feelings from their teenage years were influencing her thoughts. As kids, they'd run the woods together, along with her brother, Ben. When she moved back in high school, they saw each other less frequently, mostly in groups. She'd gotten the sense that he resented her — or maybe she had resented him. Either way, the situation had ended badly at the last cadet meet they'd both attended.

Unable to sit still, she poured her tea out and grabbed a flashlight. She slipped out into the soothing darkness and began running. The nearly full moon illuminated the runway enough that she didn't need the light, and she settled into a steady pace. Even so, the memories pushed through.

Brody had been bragging about that competition for the whole month prior. All the air cadets from the state would be there, and he was convinced he was going to win. He had the ability to do it too — he was a confident and practiced pilot. But his arrogance grated on Colt, and she had quietly determined to beat him. She wished she could claim that she had only been doing her best, but she had purposely set out to show him up.

The competition was strong, with several impressive scores. Brody flew in the middle of the pack, setting a mark that kept him in first place for the rest of the afternoon. As one of the youngest pilots, Colt was slated to fly at the end of the day. When she climbed into the cockpit, all thoughts of the competition fled, and she focused on flying a perfect routine. It was nearly flawless. She didn't need the announcement of her score or the cheering when she landed to know it. It had felt amazing, and she knew she couldn't have done any better.

Brody was furious. He accosted her by the hangar when they got home. What exactly he wanted, she never found out. The first violent shove sent her stumbling over the well box. But she was only down for a moment.

Six years in foster care had taught her a lot. Including how to fight.

The last time she'd seen him, he was curled in a ball against the hangar. She didn't look back as she walked away.

A winterberry shrub was taking over the spot now, and she could no longer tell where the well box had been. Brody seemed to have gotten past being bested by a girl twice in one day, but that only added to her suspicions. He'd gotten over a million dollars from the sale of the property. Why hang around with someone who humiliated you like that?

She stopped, staring at the shrubs. Unless he, too, thought there were items of great value here. And the only reason for him to think that was if he had found the necklace.

Carpaggio was waiting for him in the east sitting room. Had been waiting for quite some time in fact. But Malik stayed where he was, reclined in his favorite chair, cloth over his eyes. At first, he told himself he was just giving Carpaggio time to ensure everything was perfect. But as the afternoon wore on, his headache worsened, and he grew less and less interested in what the art expert had to say. The Italian had called him, offering to put together information on Peter Carl Fabergé and his work. Malik had agreed at the time, eager to learn all he could. Now he couldn't think why it had seemed a good idea.

A slight cough heralded the arrival of his butler. Malik motioned for him to speak.

"Sir, your nephews will be here in an hour. Do you wish for me to send Mr. Carpaggio away and invite him to return another time?"

As tempting as that was, Malik shook his head. He immediately regretted the motion, the pain flaring with the movement. "No, I'll go meet with him now. Bring me water and a paracetamol, please."

"Beside you, sir," the butler replied before exiting as quietly as he'd come.

Malik removed the cloth and sat up. The butler was eerily good at his job. Not for the first time, Malik wondered if he was paying the man enough for his attentiveness while also considering whether he should look into finding a new butler. One who was less of a mind reader. Malik dumped three of the small white tablets into his hand and washed them down with the water. He swung by the washroom to freshen up before heading to the east wing.

"Mr. Carpaggio," he said as he entered. "Thank you for your patience. I do apologize for keeping you waiting, but you know how things are." He pressed the man's hand warmly as he spoke, taking in the room.

Carpaggio shook his hand. "Ah, Mike! How good of you to join me. Yes, I do understand; business has a way of taking over, no?" He stepped back, opening his hands expansively. "As you can see here, we have an extensive collection of examples from the works of Peter Carl Fabergé. With more than thirty years' experience, I have become quite the expert in this niche field, and if I do say so myself, this is perhaps the best..."

Malik tuned him out, focusing on the objects before him. He was impressed with how the man had taken the minimally decorated room and used it as a blank canvas for setting up the display. Easels of various sizes held glossy high-res images of the Imperial Eggs. Smaller easels sat atop tables, showing more photos. In total, there were more than fifty pieces represented.

"I didn't know he was so prolific," Malik commented, stopping before an easel that held a collage of different pieces. To his surprise, none of them were Eggs. A silver place setting dominated the top corner, followed by a blue enameled cigarette case. The bottom half showed a hairpin and a gold-encrusted cup.

"Fabergé was fascinated by Japanese art, so revitalized the medium of enameling. As you can see here, he used it to make everyday items more luxurious," Carpaggio explained.

Malik moved on to the next image. Instead of a photograph, this was an artist's rendering of one of the Eggs. He glanced at the other images and realized there were several more. So many of the Eggs had been lost over the decades that only the barest descriptions remained, leaving it up to artists' imaginations to recreate what might have been. He stamped down his frustration, his head still throbbing. Carpaggio had promised insights into Fabergé, information that few had been made privy to.

"Are these photographs all you have?"

Carpaggio grinned, rubbing his hands together. "Come, come. I will show you!"

He led the way to the far end of the room. A round table held three stands, each displaying an *object deluxe*. The first was a small picture frame of pale blue enamel with gold laurels encircling the black-and-white picture of a beautiful woman. The second was a pencil, the final two inches dipped in gold and embellished with blue gemstones. The third was a translucent fish, perched on top of a gold and ruby perfume bottle, in pale green stone with golden fins, similar in shape and hue to a grape. The fish had disturbingly full lips made of gold and deep red eyes that seemed to watch Malik nervously.

"These happen to be part of my own collection," Carpaggio boasted.

Malik was impressed. Despite not being part of the Imperial collection, they would still have cost a pretty penny. But it was still not the rare insight he had been promised. Carpaggio was the kind to show these to anyone who came to visit. As if sensing his impatience, Carpaggio bustled over to another table. This one was covered in a black tablecloth, and a white board blocked his view.

"This is the pièce de résistance to my little exhibition here today. It is on loan from the owners, who have asked me to restore it for them. When I heard the rumor that they might be looking to sell, I begged permission to bring it here today. Never before has it been shown outside of their private collection."

Malik tilted his head back, considering. The man was an insufferable bore, but if he had brought him an Egg...

His heart raced at the thought of the chance of owning a Fabergé Egg. Not tomorrow, not someday when his incompetent underlings managed to find it. But today. Here. He flexed his clammy hands, his mouth suddenly dry.

Carpaggio lifted the board out of the way with a flourish. Malik sucked in his breath, immediately recognizing the Cradle with Garlands from his research. Reminiscent of a music box, the blue enameled egg lay atop an ornate stand of delicate gold craftsmanship. Garlands of jewels swooped between gold pillars holding up the Egg, which was topped with a cluster of gold and jewels like an Easter basket.

"Also known as the Love Trophies, this Egg was gifted in 1907 to Tsarina Maria Feodorovna from her son the tsar. As you can see, it is designed in the Louis XVI style." Carpaggio listed off the features.

Malik gazed at it greedily. It was even more incredible than he had imagined, the detailing so fine and precise. It would cost him millions, but he didn't care. A pair of white gloves lay on the table, and he put them on. Carpaggio showed him where to open it, and he released the clasp.

The surprises inside the Eggs were as wonderful as the Eggs themselves, often the epitome of intricate workmanship, as the pieces were tiny yet detailed. He couldn't remember what surprise was supposed to be inside the Cradle with Garlands, but he knew it would be impressive.

The Egg was empty.

Malik looked at Carpaggio, waiting for him to produce the surprise. Instead the man was beaming at him as if nothing was wrong.

"Incredible, isn't it?"

"Where's the surprise?"

"Oh, yes, it is rumored to be a miniature of —"

"Where. Not what," Malik bit out.

"Ah, yes. Sadly, it has been lost to us."

Malik closed the Egg and peeled off the gloves. Tossing them on the table, he strode from the room. Carpaggio hurried after, begging to know what was the matter.

"If I'm going to own a Fabergé Egg, I want it to be a complete one. The Egg is nothing without the surprise. Now get out."

9

Colt strode back into the hangar, the late afternoon sunlight streaming in behind her through the open hangar doors. The Polikarpov was finally in the main hangar, awaiting its turn for Mitch's attention.

Now that the planes were gone, it was easier to see the mess the hangar was in. Colt grabbed a garbage bag from the box on the bench and headed for the cardboard that had been underneath the plane. She was pleased to see it wasn't stained by oil, a good sign that the engine hadn't leaked. Dust filled the air as she stuffed the cardboard into the bag, and she covered her face as she coughed. She reached for the next piece and stopped.

A metal plate peeked out from underneath the cardboard. She kicked the covering out of the way. The plate was three feet square, rusted, and inset into the concrete floor. It was smooth, fitted to the floor with no way to pry it out. A small groove ran along the middle of one side, just wide enough for fingers to fit in. Cognizant of the possibility of spiders, Colt looked around for something to lift it with and settled on a hammer. Turning it backward, she used the prying part as a handle. The plate didn't budge. She shifted her position, adjusting the hammer. Still nothing. Grabbing a flashlight from the bench, she peered into the groove.

Nothing. The space was too narrow for the light to pick up anything.

Colt put her hand in and tugged.

The metal stuck like it was welded in place. There were no visible hinges, yet she was certain it opened. Adjusting her grip, her fingers brushed against something. She probed further, feeling a thin tab. It, too, refused to move, but this one she had a solution for.

Mitch had left a can of WD-40 on the bench, the long red straw still attached. She angled the straw into the slot. Applying a liberal dose of the lubricant, she sat down on the cardboard to give it time to work. Crossing her ankles before her, she leaned back on her hands.

Why was there a hatch in the floor of the hangar? Where did it lead?

Mitch had been so convinced about the tunnels. What if he was right? What if there was something buried here? Had her grandmother known? More importantly, had she used them? Or were they sealed when the government decided this airfield didn't fit into their nuclear defense network against the Russians?

The position of the plane felt too deliberate. Colt closed her eyes and pictured the layout of the hangar when they had first started clearing things out. The two other planes had been parked beside each other, near the front of the hangar. The Polikarpov had been further back, boxes stacked around it haphazardly. Katya had been hiding something.

"Taking a nap?"

Colt opened her eyes to see Hawk standing over her. She gestured to the metal plate beside her and explained her progress so far. "It's probably a storm drain in case the hangar flooded."

Hawk whistled. "You think it'll open?" He crouched down beside her and stuck his fingers in the slot. Grunting, he tried to shift the tab.

"Move. Your fingers are too fat." Colt pushed him aside and slid her thumb in, catching the edge of the tab. After a moment, she was able to force it over. A dull "thunk" indicated something had worked. She sat back on her heels. Hawk grinned at her.

"Time to find that buried treasure?"

She rolled her eyes. "Time to prove you wrong, you mean. But open it, if you're so curious."

"Don't you want to?"

"Wouldn't want to hog all the fun," she said, standing and dusting her hands off on her pants. Hawk grabbed the plate and pulled. The plate lifted a few inches. He let it go and found a pry bar to use for leverage. The grate groaned in protest as he drew it back all the way. The hinges held it open, stopping it from falling backward to the floor.

The opening was perfectly square, the sides once smooth metal that was now dull and pocked. The ladder was made of round poles and grated treads. Just at the edge of the light was a caged light bulb welded tight to the side opposite the ladder.

"That's no storm drain."

Colt said nothing. She retrieved a flashlight from the bunk room, refusing to let herself ponder the implications too much. It's just a ladder, she told herself. The flashlight beam revealed little more than the fact the ladder went down farther than they'd thought.

"Where's Mitch?" she asked.

"On a call with his supplier. Apparently they've sent the wrong gasket for the Piper Cub again."

She nodded. It'd be a while before he missed them. Plenty of time for a bit of exploration. So why did she not want to go?

Hawk looked at her, eagerness on his face. She shook off the weird feeling. If she wanted to prove her grandmother innocent, she had to explore every avenue. Even a secret tunnel in the hangar.

Using the flashlight, she looked around for a light switch but found only smooth walls. Shrugging, she pocketed the light and climbed onto the ladder, lowering herself into the shaft. Hawk joined her as soon as she was clear. Life aboard ships involved a lot of ladders, but none like this one. It went on and on, the darkness swallowing them. Hawk's body blocked a lot of the light from above, and she soon felt as though she'd been climbing down for an eon.

One hundred rungs later, her foot hit something other than air. "Hold up," she called before Hawk could accidentally kick her in the head. She fished the flashlight out of her pocket and turned it on.

They'd arrived in a concrete box, ten by ten. She stepped off the ladder, and Hawk soon joined her. Together they inspected the box. The walls, floor, and ceiling were all concrete, ridged with repaired cracks, while new ones splintered out from the corners. Another caged light bulb hung by the ladder, and one more beside the only exit. Two heavy metal doors dominated the opposite wall. Blue paint flaked off them, revealing rusted metal beneath. There was a door handle and a lock. Hawk stepped forward and tried the handle. It turned, but the lock kept the doors from opening.

"Well, I guess that's it. But hey, this is a good little storage space at least."

Colt gave a look like he'd grown a second head. "I don't know what's stupider about what you just said. The fact you want to lug stuff down that ladder just to leave it in this hole. Or the fact you think I can't open the door." She pulled a bobby pin from her hair. "Wait. Do you still have the keys with you?"

Hawk patted his pockets. He'd grabbed the massive set of keys that morning because they had planned on opening up the tower that day. They'd left it largely alone thus far, focusing on cleaning up the hangars. But they had noticed the windows steaming up on warm afternoons and wanted to air it out before it got too musty inside.

The rings held about fifty keys between them, all looped and connected to one another without reason. Hawk had removed the main house keys and made copies already. And they knew the set that had the hangars and other outbuildings. So that only left about thirty more keys to figure out. None of the keys were labeled or marked in any way. Even on the sets they knew, there were keys they hadn't found the locks to yet. Hawk twisted off a ring and handed it to Colt.

"These look like the right age, and there's no newer key on it like some of them."

She set the flashlight on the floor, where it made an eerie glow. Picking a key that looked the right shape, she tried it, flipped it over, tried again. No luck. Next key. She settled into a rhythm, expecting to have to run through all thirty keys.

The fourth key fit in the slot. She wiggled it around, but it still didn't work. Pulling it out, she held it over the light.

"Find me ones with this weird oval shape." She flipped ahead on the ring, searching for a similar key while Hawk did the same. She found one and shoved it in the lock. With some convincing, the pins fell into place. "Huh," she said as she twisted the handle and opened the door.

They were met with a blast of dense, dry air. Hawk returned the keys to his pocket and grabbed the flashlight. He handed it to her and retrieved his pry bar.

The tunnel stretched out before them, square, dark, with no movement of air. Based on the turns they'd made so far, Colt was sure they were headed underneath the runway. With no other option, they followed it. There was no change in scenery, the walls gray and unbroken. Out of habit, Colt counted the caged lights in her head. They were all hung on the left side at uneven intervals. Heavy wires hung between them, carrying electricity from an unseen source, although they still hadn't found a switch. Above them ran two parallel pipes. Every so often, one would branch off and vanish into the wall.

At last, they came to another set of metal doors. The lock was on the outside, so they were able to flip the bolt and push it open. They were met by a landing with two steps up to the left. After a few more short halls, landings, and low stairs, they finally came to a full flight of cement stairs, complete with metal railing.

"This feels very military, doesn't it?" Hawk asked after the second flight.

"Straight out of the pre-fab box," Colt agreed.

There were spaces on the walls where things had once hung. Fire exit signs, maybe. Or floor numbers. All that remained were squares where the paint hadn't faded at the same rate and empty screw holes. The stairs ended at another door, this time locked.

After another shuffle through the keys, they pulled the door inward and stepped into a small space.

"Ouch!" Hawk rubbed his head as Colt angled the light up. They were under a set of stairs.

"Now that's weird." She shone the light in front of them, looking for a way out. "All this time of big, open halls, clear doors, and now we're under the stairs?" She tapped the wall with her boot. It wobbled, a warped sound filling the void. Taking a guess, she kicked harder, aiming at the tiny crack of light that had appeared. The wall collapsed outward, and two panels hung to the sides like orange peels. Dull gray light flooded in, bright in comparison with the tomblike darkness of the tunnels.

Colt and Hawk waited a moment for their eyes to adjust, then stepped out into the room.

They were in the tower. The space was devoid of character, with one window and one door. The stairs disappeared into the floor above. Three old metal and fabric chairs were stacked in a corner, and a laminate table stood beside them. Telephone books, faded to brown, sat on the floor near the door, and piles of dust occupied the corners.

Colt looked up at Hawk, a number of thoughts vying for first place in her mind. Why hadn't Gram told her about this? Why was the tunnel there? Who sealed it off? She needed to figure this out. Except...a slow smile was spreading across Hawk's face until a full-blown grin broke out.

She narrowed her eyes. "What?"

"We've got a secret tunnel!"

Colt shook her head. Of course Hawk would see the good side of this. She looked around at the drab walls of the tower. Despite her earlier feelings of wanting to check it out, she'd lost interest. She turned back to the entrance under the stairs. There was nothing down there but a long, dark, dank hallway. So why did her pulse race at the thought of exploring it more?

Hawk caught her eye, his face still lit up. "Let's go back down."

"Why? There's nothing there." Even as she said it, she didn't believe it. And the look on Hawk's face said he didn't either.

"The wires in the ceiling had to lead somewhere. And the cement didn't look uniform. Like some of it was applied later."

"What are you saying?"

He held up his pry bar. "I'm saying we need to get back down there and do more investigating."

She pursed her lips, debating. She wished he weren't so convincing. A boring, straight tunnel held no further secrets, no place for long-lost treasures to be buried. "Fine. But I'm not working in the dark. Where's the electrical panel?"

They found it behind a bulletin board after a short search. None of the switches were on, the tower having been neglected for years. Colt flipped a few of them, and the building took on a distant hum.

"What did you turn on?" Hawk asked.

"Everything? Nothing's labeled, so I opted for all the switches that are wired."

"What about that one?" He pointed to the last one on the bottom row, far from the others.

"Well, it's wired, so I flipped it," she replied, feeling like a broken record.

Hawk reached over her and nudged the fuse. It made a loud clunk. "It only moved halfway. This is a pretty heavy-duty panel, especially for the age of it. More than what you'd expect for a tower at an old airfield."

Colt raised an eyebrow. "But enough to power a secret underground bunker?"

"Something like that." He wiggled his eyebrows in glee.

She waited until he moved out of her personal space, then stepped through the door into the tunnel entrance. On the wall just inside was a large red lever. She pulled it down, and a click echoed through the stairwell. Light flickered, then a buzzing filled the air as the caged light bulbs came to life. They followed the light back down the stairs to the tunnels.

"Why do you think this end has nice stairs and the other is a cramped ladder?"

She shrugged. "This was the main access point, and the other is an emergency hatch?"

"Feels like a bit of a trap though."

"Only if it's the only other exit."

"What? You think there's more?"

She wiggled her hand in the air. "It'd make sense. Why connect the smaller hangar but not the main one?"

"True. And we still don't know about the tunnel in the woods. It could be another access point like we thought."

They stopped once they got to the long hallway. Hawk pointed to the overhead wires. "See those? There's no reason for them to be branching off like that."

"Unless they're feeding something else," Colt finished. "Which means there's something beyond the wall that needs electricity."

"Yup." Hawk tapped the pry bar against the concrete, listening for a change in the sound.

Colt turned the flashlight back on, using the focused beam to look for ridges in the cement and changes in the paint color.

Below and slightly to the left of the disappearing wires, they found a tiny ridge in the smoothness of the wall. Hawk declared a variation in sound as well, so Colt stood back while he swung the pry bar back. He brought it round the side of his body, digging the sharpened end into the concrete.

"Shoulda brought an axe instead of this," he commented as he continued to smash the wall.

"A jackhammer would make the most sense," Colt replied. She stepped back from the cloud of dust that was building in the air around Hawk and continued down the tunnel. Using the flashlight, she identified another spot where the paint changed color under a vanishing wire.

Clang!

She spun on her heel in time to see Hawk bending over, clasping his elbow. "You okay?" she asked as she drew near.

"Mm."

His face was scrunched up, and he was holding his breath. Colt took the pry bar from him and waited. Pain was sometimes fleeting, she'd been told, so she gave him a moment to decide how bad it was.

"Yeah. Okay. Wasn't expecting that." Hawk let out his breath and straightened. He still held onto his elbow.

"What happened?" Now that he seemed okay, she turned her attention to the hole in the wall.

"Went through the cement and hit something behind it. Probably a metal door."

"Or we hit rebar, which means we're way off in our guess."

She stuck the end of the pry bar in the hole and pulled away the crumbling cement. Soon the hole was wide enough for them both to work at it. They could see a dark metal panel behind the layer of concrete.

"Door handle's missing," Hawk said, indicating the circle where one should have been.

"At least we now know for sure it's a door." Colt smashed the pry bar against the lower portion of concrete, sending cracks spidering out from the impact. Hawk reached above her and pulled away chunks from the top.

"Hinges are on the inside," Colt said as she cleared the edge. "We might be able to open it, which would make getting rid of the rest of the concrete easier."

"How? No handle."

Colt bent down to study it. "It's been cemented in as well. Smash it." She handed him back the pry bar. He dug the sharpened end in and levered his weight against it, trying to force the mechanism out of the door. After some digging and shoving, it fell with a clunk into the space beyond. Hawk pushed on the door.

"No go."

Colt frowned. How many hoops did they have to go through to find out what was down here? She motioned Hawk to step back, then kicked the door. Her heel struck the edge between the hole and the wall. A crack sounded, and the door flew inward. It hit the chunk of cement and bounced back, metal clanging and echoing through the tunnel.

"Well, that's one way to get in," Hawk said once the noise had died down.

Hawk pushed the door open, the chunk of concrete scraping against the floor. Stale air flooded out, dust swirling in the dim light. He found a switch on the wall, and the overhead lights flickered to life, revealing dark walls and unfinished floors. He stepped inside, Colt following.

The room was cramped. A long, scratched table sat in the center, surrounded by metal and plastic chairs. Without testing them, he knew the ridge of the back would dig into his spine, and the legs were too short to make sitting comfortable for more than thirty seconds. Blank papers were scattered about, along with a couple of pens. A stained water glass sat near the far end. Everything was covered in a thick layer of dust.

"This place feel abandoned to you?" he asked, his spine tingling.

Colt studied the room a minute before answering. "Like they left one day planning on coming right back and never did."

Hawk rolled his shoulders. "It's weird."

"Did you just shiver?"

"No."

"You sure? Definitely looked like you shivered." She stepped over to the wall where a map of the US hung, intersected by a series of arcs.

Hawk deigned not to answer. He hadn't shivered. Okay, maybe a tiny bit. But an eeriness hung in the air, a stillness felt at cemeteries. The chairs were at odd angles, as though the occupants had only moments ago stood up and walked out.

He followed Colt's eyeline. She was studying the handwritten notes on the edge of the map. A couple more maps covered the walls, and corners of paper indicated others had once hung there.

"What's it say?"

"Just a general update."

She moved on to the chalkboard that dominated one wall. It had been erased by someone who wasn't concerned about leaving a blank slate for the next person. Half words and numbers were still visible. "Take a look at this. It looks like a flight plan, doesn't it?"

Hawk squinted at the numbers. "Is this a ready room?"

"But why? There's one in the tower, and the lunch room in the main hangar doubled for briefings too."

"Because upstairs would have been too public."

She cocked her head. "You agree with Mitch's theory that this was a Cold War base?"

"It makes sense." Hawk looked around again. He pictured the pilots sitting there, a crew of young and eager men. They'd have gotten up from the briefing and left with the swagger belonging to the confident and victorious. Where had they gone from here?

"1989." Colt's voice snapped him out of the daydream.

"What?"

"This map. It was printed in 1989."

"So not Cold War exactly."

"No." There was an edge to her voice.

"Colt, when did your grandmother and Frank buy the airfield?" He guessed at the reason for her reaction.

She raised her chin, arms crossed. "Long before 1989." Her words fell like broken glass.

She left without a word, leaving him with the ghosts of the missing pilots.

10

The next morning, Colt walked down the rutted driveway to the chain. She unlocked it, then leaned against a tree to wait. Ever since the Russian guy had shown up, they'd taken to keeping the chain up and locked across the driveway. She'd even rigged a rough repair in the fence around the runway. It didn't stop people from getting closer on foot, but it was a deterrent. After the past few days of uncertainty, the chance of answers arriving soon had her on edge. She closed her eyes, letting the sounds and feel of the woods encompass her, offering a calm she had been missing. The swoosh of tires on the pavement interrupted her. The vehicle slowed, then turned and crunched up the drive. Colt stepped out and climbed into the black SUV.

Kendra smiled at her. "I still do not believe you convinced Mitch to move way out here."

"He's enjoying it."

Kendra shot her a look. "Really?"

"Well, he's not one hundred percent hating it." Colt pointed out the loop around the house, and Kendra took the turn at a crawl. The big SUV nearly scraped the bark off a tree before roaring up the sudden incline. They parked around the side of the house.

Kendra paused before turning the engine off. "Truthfully. Is he doing okay?" Worry for her brother clouded her eyes.

"He is. He's doing a fabulous job getting the airplanes back into shape. Although I worry about him in the mornings. Sounds like a cat being skinned alive can be heard from his room, and I fear for whatever is behind the door."

Kendra snorted, her hand flying to her face to cover it up. She couldn't stop the laugh that followed though. "He's singing."

"I know. Unfortunately."

Kendra dissolved into giggles, holding on to the steering wheel. Colt waited.

"Really? He is singing again?"

"Every. Bloody. Morning. I think his current favorite is 'Some Boat.'"

"Of course it is. He has always loved country." Kendra sighed, patting her hair back into place. "That makes me very happy."

"What? Knowing your brother is daily torturing us?"

"It has been a long time since he was able to sing."

"I know." The knowledge hung between the two women. After a moment, they climbed out, letting the silence pull them out of the conversation. Kendra gathered her briefcase and a long plastic tube from the back of the SUV. Colt lifted the file box and led the way into the house.

Hawk met them in the kitchen, wearing a floral apron, wooden spoon in hand. "Hey! I'm making cinnamon rolls. I'll be right with you."

Colt stared at him. "Who are you and what have you done with my WSO?" She pronounced it "Wizzo."

"A man is not known by his ability to operate weapons systems alone, doncha know."

"Said by a man who has forgotten how, clearly."

"Keep insulting me, and I won't share." He flicked a puff of flour at her. "Kendra, straight through here to the dining room. I've got coffee ready, and Mitch is in charge of tea."

"Meaning it has probably steeped for more than ten minutes by now," Kendra said as she followed Hawk's directions.

"Most likely," he agreed.

"I heard that!" Mitch called. "Not my fault if you two sat out there nattering and let the tea stew!"

Kendra set her briefcase against the wall and the tube on the table before leaning over to give her brother a hug. "I missed you too."

Colt dropped the box on the table and started unpacking the many files. "You found quite a lot. Where was all this buried?"

"In the military archives. An analyst over there owed me a favor." Kendra handed the plastic tube to Hawk. "There is no guarantee that these documents relate to this particular property. He was not able to provide that information. What we have is either generic and therefore applicable to all the bases set up during that era, or the files may refer to a completely different property altogether." She poured herself a cup of tea as she spoke, long, elegant fingers holding the heavy crockery as though it were the finest of bone china.

"Colt, look." Hawk had unrolled the papers that were in the plastic tube. He spread them out on the table, pushing the box out of his way. Colt joined him, leaning over the faded and stained blueprints.

She followed along as he traced out the lines. "This is Hangar 2, and that's the tower. Meaning this is the tunnel we found."

"You found a tunnel?" Kendra interrupted.

"We did. And we uncovered a room off it." He jabbed the paper. "A conference room of sorts. Here, I think."

"This shows there's a lot more rooms down there. It's not just a foul weather route or for keeping the runways clear. There's a whole maze buried underground," Colt said. She forced herself not to gather the papers and take them somewhere private to peruse. Or burn.

"And look at this." Hawk twisted the paper to bring the far corner closer to Colt. "This branch leads off in the direction of the cave-in we found."

"Meaning that it is connected." She wasn't sure how she felt about that. Leaning over the diagrams, she studied the lines. The tunnel Hawk found did appear to be in the right spot for the cave-in, but a large water spot damaged the blueprint where it would have connected to the main tunnel. There were marks added after they were printed in 1953 but no legend for what they could mean. She ignored them for now, focusing on an offset box in the upper corner. "There should be a tunnel leading to Hangar 1 as well. It should have tied in with the access point we found, but there was nothing there."

"We've got our own little underground cave system! Just like the Hardy Boys!" Hawk beamed around the room. A timer in the kitchen went off, and he ran out to rescue his cinnamon rolls from the oven.

"Caves I could have handled," Colt muttered. "But why seal off the tunnels and hide the rooms?" No one had an answer for her, and she really didn't expect one.

Mitch waved the blue folder he was reading. "Colt, did you know Frank had been in military intelligence?"

"Really? I thought he was in logistics."

"He was, for a while, but it says here he moved to intelligence as an attaché to the Pentagon in 1955, then was assigned to...something that's blacked out."

"That's it? Odd."

"Yeah. Not even a discharge note."

"Poor filing?" Hawk asked, returning triumphantly with a plate of cinnamon rolls, icing dripping down the sides. "No computer trail back then. If someone misplaced his file, they might not have bothered searching for it."

Kendra picked up a napkin, then helped herself to a cinnamon roll. She quickly placed it on the table and reached for another napkin, dabbing her fingers. "They are very warm."

"I wanted to make sure they were hot and fresh," Hawk said proudly. Then his face fell. "Oh, I'm sorry! Are they too hot?"

Kendra waved his concerns aside. "It looks delicious. I did not ask my analyst to look up Frank. Everything he found was filed with the project documents. So if Frank's jacket was in that box, it must have been purposely left with the property information."

"Meaning that whatever this place was, Frank was a key player."

"But if it was a centerpiece for Cold War defenses, what was a Russian operative doing here?" Kendra asked.

"You make her sound like a spy," Colt growled.

"What if she was?" Kendra tapped her fingernail on the folder. "What if she were working with the US to help end the Cold War?"

A shiver ran down Colt's spine. Looking at the faces around her, she knew they all felt that was a positive outcome. But it also meant her grandmother had betrayed her own country. A spy who had lied to her granddaughter about who she was and what the airfield was for.

"Let's adjourn to the living room," Hawk suggested. He gathered up the cinnamon rolls, icing now completely off the rolls and pooling on the plate. He sighed. Maybe there was a reason after all for why the recipe said to let them cool before serving. Thankfully, he still had half the tray from the oven un-iced. While the others gathered up the tea and coffee, he set the new rolls on the cooling rack and checked how much icing he had left. Maybe this time he wouldn't smother them like they did at the store. Remembering how his mom often drizzled toppings, he took a spoon from the drawer and tried the technique.

Beside him, Colt replaced the coffee filter and scooped fresh grounds into the percolator. Her jaw was set, eyes locked on the can of coffee with far more focus than the task warranted.

"Tell Kendra about the Egg, what Danforth shared," he prompted, spooning icing over the first roll. It landed in a dollop, not a thin line.

"Why would she care?" She didn't look up.

"One, because she's your friend. And two, maybe she can help figure it out."

Colt threw the scoop back into the can. "If she's our friend, maybe we should stop taking advantage of her position." She finished setting the coffee up with a few jerky movements, then grabbed a handful of mugs and stomped into the living room.

Hawk sighed, wishing Colt would be more open with people. Something was bothering her, and it would take him days to fish out what. He finished dressing the cinnamon rolls and moved them onto a clean plate. Well, they didn't look like Mom's, but at least the icing was still mostly on top. He gathered a stack of small plates and joined the others.

Colt was slouched in her usual chair, the only one that afforded a view of all three doors into the space. Mitch and Kendra were on either side of the fireplace, Kendra looking like she belonged in the White House in the old-fashioned wingback chair. Hawk set the refreshments on the coffee table and settled into the third chair, completing the square. Colt showed no signs of her earlier annoyance as Kendra relayed the latest information from the kidnapping case.

"As frustrating as it is, Mark's testimony is doing a lot of good. The DA has issued two additional warrants based on the information he has provided."

"And the girls? Have they all been contacted?" Colt asked. There was a hard edge to her voice.

"Yes, we are keeping them apprised of the status of the case. Many of them have applied for restraining orders. Amanda and Mackenzie are doing well — but surely you have heard from them?"

"Mackenzie sends us an update daily, but it's mostly personal," Hawk said. "She's not mentioned Mark." Not that Hawk could blame the kid. Putting the trauma of being kidnapped aside was likely the only way she could move forward. Hardly a surprise that the messages mostly talked about the walks the two girls took, the latest episode of *Avatar: The Last Airbender* they watched. And most importantly, what the two therapy dogs at the clinic were up to. She sent pictures every time the pups came to visit. It made Hawk want to get a dog, but he knew better than to broach the topic with the others just yet.

A horrible burbling sound echoed from the kitchen. Hawk sprang to his feet. The last time they'd ignored the sounds of the dying coffee maker, it had blown a fuse. He returned with the fresh pot of coffee in time to hear Kendra ask Colt what was new.

Colt shot him a glance, and he gave her an encouraging nod in response. She sighed.

"There's been rumors of an expensive necklace that turned up out of nowhere. It's making waves, and people seem to think it was found here. We spoke to a guy in the city, at the bank you sent us to. He said the necklace was most likely connected to a missing Fabergé Egg."

Kendra leaned forward. "This necklace, do you happen to know what it looks like?"

"Simple gold chain, oval sapphire in a minimal setting," Colt recited.

Kendra sat back, folding her hands in her lap.

Hawk paused at the sudden silence, bent over, mid-pour. He looked back and forth between the women, then at Mitch. The only reaction was a shrug from Mitch, who looked as lost as he did.

With a shake of her head, Kendra looked around the room, her shoulders dropping. "How do you three keep ending up in the middle of my investigations?"

"It's both a talent and a skill," Mitch quipped, grinning at his sister.

Colt dropped lower in her chair, slinging one leg over the arm. "What investigation is that?"

For all her nonchalance, Hawk knew she was deeply interested in the answer. Her gaze was on the pen she had, walking it through her fingers and back again. He finished pouring the coffee and handed around the mugs as Kendra explained.

"Our art theft division gets notified whenever items of unusual value or provenance appear for sale. Recently, a necklace triggered a response because of its value and lack of history. It also vanished shortly after being listed for sale at Rothschild's Auction House. Rothschild assures us that the transaction is all aboveboard, but they take confidentiality seriously there. Without a warrant, he sees no reason to release the name of the buyer."

"But?" Colt prompted.

A reaction flickered across Kendra's face. Hawk was surprised to see it. Many people underestimated Colt's perceptiveness, but he thought Kendra would have understood by now.

"I could use trainees as good as you," she laughed. "The 'but' is that while the buyer may have requested anonymity, the seller did not. An assessor in a small town in Pennsylvania claims to have found it at an estate sale. When questioned, he gave us the name Brody. No last name."

"Brody Farrell? That means he probably did find it here," Colt said. She stood, pacing around the chairs. "No wonder he's been hanging around."

Mitch whooped. "Any more like that hanging around, and we're set for life!"

"That's what everyone else thinks too, based on all the unwelcome visitors we've had lately," Colt grumbled.

"Any indication of where the Egg is?" Hawk asked.

Kendra shook her head. "None that we have uncovered. Most of the missing Fabergé Eggs have not been seen since the fall of Imperial Russia. If it came here, we have yet to discover how or when."

"Neither Farrell nor his uncle had any connection to Russia." Hawk frowned.

"What about —" The ringing of a cell phone interrupted her. Kendra moved into another room to answer the call, returning a moment later. "My apologies, but I need to cut this visit short. We may have a lead on how to draw this buyer out. Thank you for your hospitality. Hawk, the cinnamon rolls were delicious."

They followed her outside to wave goodbye. As she disappeared down the driveway, Hawk turned to Colt. "Something's bothering you."

Colt kept her gaze on the tree line, arms crossed, chin up. "Brody might not have any connection to Russia, but I do."

11

The Polikarpov Po-2 was an ugly little beastie, especially when compared with the fighter jets Colt usually flew. But there was something about sliding behind the stick of that little wooden crop duster that felt like coming home. She smoothed a hand over the control panel, noting that the blue elastic hair tie was still looped around the elevator lever. Katya had pulled the elastic from Colt's hair during a lesson when the little girl struggled to remember which lever did what. Even though she'd been in high school the last time she flew it, the Polikarpov felt smaller than she remembered. She should be sitting up underneath the controls, just barely able to see over the cowling.

Hawk slapped the fuselage as he approached. "Rickety old thing, isn't she?"

"You would be too, if you were nearly a hundred years old and survived a world war."

Hawk stepped back to take in the canvas and wooden structure. "You serious? This plane was used in the war? For what? Carrier pigeon backup?"

Colt snorted as she slid out of the seat and dropped to the ground. "I told you. The 588th Night Bomber Regiment used them to bomb the German lines, starting in 1942."

"So you weren't joking." He followed her to the bench and picked up a wrench.

"Why would I joke about that?" Colt changed the bit on the impact driver, and they returned to the plane to begin work on it. "The women were given men's uniforms that were far too large and boots that didn't fit. Old gear, old planes. They didn't care. They flew them and terrorized the Nazis night after night."

Hawk held the propeller while Colt braced the driver against the bolt holding it on. "She's the reason you became a pilot, isn't she?" he asked over the noise of the driver.

"Yup," she grunted.

"Why?"

"Why? What do you mean, why?"

"I know you well enough to know that young Colt was an angry, confused child. Doing the one thing the adult in your life wanted you to do should have been the last career you chose."

She gave a half laugh. "For one, she didn't want me to. She wanted me to go to law school."

Hawk struggled to keep his face straight.

"You can laugh," Colt told him. "It's a ridiculous concept."

"But didn't she teach you to fly? Why do that if she didn't want you to be a pilot?"

"Oh, she was fine with me flying small planes. Even commercial would have been okay. But she knew what it was like for women in the military. And she lost friends. A lot of them."

"She didn't want to lose you too."

Colt gave a one-armed shrug. "Didn't help that I was the only family member left either."

"She must have been a pretty good pilot to survive the war flying this little thing."

Colt shot him a look. "Oh, sure. Ace pilot and smuggler. Great role model, that."

Armed with the blueprints Kendra had provided, Colt and Hawk returned to the tunnel and began the excavation in earnest. The plans gave no indication of the purpose of each of the rooms aside from the toilet and shower rooms under the tower. They spread the plans on the table in the conference room, and Hawk stuck a sticky note labeled "Briefing" on their current location. Mitch claimed to be content working on getting the planes up and running, but Colt felt bad that he wouldn't be able to see the place.

Maybe they could figure out a way to get him down here, despite the many steps.

"What do you want to tackle first?" Hawk asked. "The bathrooms? Get them up and running so we don't have to go upstairs anytime we need a break?"

Colt shook her head. "That would take way too long. Who knows if the pipes are even functioning? Besides, we know what's in those rooms. Let's find out what is hiding further along."

"Fair enough."

Hawk hefted a multifaceted demolition tool, and Colt helped herself to one of the ten-pound sledgehammers. They had already replaced the lights in the tunnel with stronger wattage bulbs and marked potential doors with painter's tape.

Colt stepped out into the hall and swung at the midpoint of the green tape X opposite. Hawk scrambled to close the door and get out of the way.

"Why bother?" she asked between swings.

"Trying to keep a little bit of dust out of there," Hawk explained, adjusting a dust mask over his face.

"There's no door handle, and we're going to be tracking dirt and dust in and out anyway."

"Can't fault a guy for trying," he grumbled, his words muffled behind the mask.

Colt gave him a narrow look before her next swing. The hammer broke through the layer of concrete, ringing against the metal of the door underneath.

"We're going to end up with dents in all the doors at this rate." Hawk stepped forward with his demolition tool and angled it into the hole.

"Unfortunately, not much else we can do unless we want to get fancy with power tools."

"Might not be a bad idea."

Colt left him to clear away the concrete and headed for the next X on the wall. When she had three more cracked enough to see the door, she changed her focus to removing the cement. She'd cleared one door when Hawk called her back. Dropping the hammer, she jogged back down the hall to meet him. He pried the cement blocking the hole for the handle free as she approached.

The door swung inward, and the stink of chemicals overwhelmed them immediately. The narrow space was constrained further by shelves filled with heavy cameras, film canisters, and bottles of chemicals. Three feet in was another wall, a red light bulb mounted beside the door. Hawk opened the door and found the light switch inside. The red bulb turned on, and a glow emanated from the inner room. Colt covered her nose with her shirt and followed him in.

It was a dark room, filled with the paraphernalia of film development. More chemical bottles sat about, and trays lay ready. Strings with pins stretched every which way above the tables and counters. A few pictures still hung from them. Colt pulled one down.

"An aerial shot. Not of here, I don't think... That's water."

Hawk picked up a film canister and gave it a quick shake. "These are still full, waiting to be developed."

"Someone didn't finish their job."

"It's eerie, Colt. First the briefing room, and now this? What happened here?"

She looked back at the black-and-white photograph in her hand. "I don't know. It's weird. But we're not going to find any answers here. Let's keep digging." She set the photo on the counter and returned to the hall, relieved to be away from the heavy scent of chemicals that had been trapped in the room for so long.

They tackled the next two doors simultaneously. Both were nondescript offices. They decided to deal with gaining access to all the doors first before digging through what they found inside the rooms. Easier to deal with all the mess that way.

Hawk uncovered what appeared to be another hallway at first. A small antechamber with another door at the far end, about the same depth as the two offices, held clipboards of blank forms and a couple of empty dollies, their rubber wheels cracked and deflated. The double doors the width of the antechamber were locked, and Hawk dug through the key collection again till he found one that opened it.

"Not the same as the far doors?" Colt asked.

"No. On a separate ring."

"Must be more important then?" she posited.

The doors opened into a massive storeroom that stretched out in either direction. Heavy-duty shelves were stacked floor to ceiling as far as they could see. The lights didn't work, so they pulled out their flashlights. Colt went left, uncovering piles of office supplies — reams of paper, cases of pens, ink, and far too many boxes of staples.

"Expired in 1993." Hawk rattled a bottle of pills. Colt joined him in front of a rack full of medical supplies.

"That is a lot of acetaminophen," Colt said, reaching for another case. She whistled. "This stuff is hydrocodone."

"And we've got basic surgical supplies here as well." He rifled through the boxes. "Lots of bandages, bindings, et cetera. Like a field hospital."

"That would make sense if this were a base for the military, but why would Gram and Frank have needed this?"

"That's a good question." Hawk gave her a look she couldn't decipher before he shoved the case back on the shelf. "Come on, let's grab a drink and get back to work."

The question continued to dog her as they smashed the concrete up and down the hallway. They swapped jobs, Hawk wielding the sledgehammer while Colt focused on prying the chunks away from the doors. What was this place? Everything they'd found made sense if the military had kept it as a Cold War bunker until the fall of the Berlin Wall in 1989. But she was certain Frank and Katya had owned it before then. And surely the military wouldn't have abandoned so much stuff down here?

Another hour of work revealed two more rooms. One was a bunk room, four sets of bunk beds with nothing more than thin, bare mattresses. Hawk poked at them delicately, cautious of raising clouds of dust.

"This place is sealed tight."

"What do you mean?" Colt spun in a circle, looking for cracks, or the lack of them.

"No rodent activity. Even in the hangar, where there had been reasonable activity over the past few years, mice have chewed stuff. But down here, rats should have ripped this stuff to shreds. Yet everything is fine."

Colt faced him, careful to keep her smile hidden. "You know what that means?"

He raised an eyebrow.

"Snakes," she deadpanned. "Only thing likely to have kept rats out this long, right?"

Hawk swallowed hard, his eyes flicking to the shadowy corners of the room, then back to her. "Don't even joke about that."

The laugh felt good. "Come on, Hawk. It's too cold down here for snakes."

The look of relief on his face made her laugh again. "Good point."

She turned and led the way back out of the room. "I mean, you never know. They could have adapted..."

"Very funny," he grumbled as he followed her out.

The summer sun was still strong when they reappeared, despite the late afternoon. Covered in dust, the pair strolled across the runway to Hangar 1, where Mitch was stretched out in a lawn chair by the Piper Cub.

"Laying down on the job?" Colt asked.

"Reveling in my accomplishments, you mean," Mitch retorted, sitting up.

"You got it going?" Colt moved toward the little plane, tiredness slipping off her like a cloak.

"Yup. Engine's all back together. Didn't even have any leftover parts when I was done."

Colt opened the door to climb in.

"Oy, none of that. You're filthy, and I just finished detailing her," Mitch protested.

She paused, one foot on the step. Mitch's glare pulled her back down. "Fine. We'll take her up first thing in the morning."

He shook his head. "Not ready to fly yet. The window gaskets still haven't arrived, and with the state of the current ones, you're likely to blow a window."

"It's not like we need oxygen to fly in this thing. It'd just be a bit noisier," she argued.

"Colt, don't be stupid," Hawk interjected. "You'd end up with broken glass everywhere, if it didn't knock you out cold."

"Could just take the window out before taking off," she grumbled. They piled into Hawk's truck to head back to the house.

"Just wait till the parts arrive," Hawk said.

She slumped in the back seat, picking bits of concrete out of her hair. It had been too long since the last time she flew. The flurry of moving had kept her from visiting her usual airfield, and there hadn't been a plane in flying condition available yet. What was the point of owning planes if she wasn't able to fly them?

She knew she was being irrational, but the sky was where she did her best thinking, and being grounded added to her frustrations. There was too much to unravel, and even her early morning runs on the main road weren't helping. She needed the sky-high view to get a better perspective.

Hawk slammed on the brakes, and she was flung forward. She grabbed at the back of Mitch's seat in time to stop herself from slamming face-first into the headrest.

"What —?" she demanded.

"Look," Hawk said grimly.

She leaned forward between the seats. Both the side door of the house and Mitch's veranda entrance were open, the screen door banging in the wind. A small armchair lay broken on the lawn. Colt recognized it was one from her room, and sure enough, one of the second-floor windows was smashed.

Hawk peeled out of the truck, heading for the side door. Colt snatched the shotgun from under the back bench, tossing it to Mitch as she slid out. She ran for the veranda door, hand reaching for her Beretta. Too late, she remembered she wasn't wearing it. Her skin had been slow to heal, and Hawk had cautioned her to wait a bit longer. Not wanting to go in unarmed, she veered toward the chair and wrenched a leg off. Nails protruding from the end of it, she charged inside.

Caution warned her against going in without checking the way was clear, but Hawk was already inside. She heard him yell "clear" as she ran through Mitch's room.

She slowed enough to note that the bedroom was a mess, but empty. "Clear," she called in response to Hawk.

They met in the kitchen. He shook his head at her. She could see the calm on his face, the look he got when he was solely focused on one thing. But there was something else there, a reflection of the rage she felt.

She pointed upstairs and at his nod headed for the main hallway and staircase. He grabbed her arm, pointing toward the back steps. Rolling her eyes, she followed his directions and crept up the narrow steps. She heard the stairs creak under him as he went up the main flight. The crooked steps and narrow passage left little room for stealth maneuvering, so she bolted up the last few steps and into the room to the left.

Empty. A few boxes were stacked next to the only piece of furniture in the room, an old dresser. She couldn't tell if they'd been disturbed. The door into her bedroom hung open a few inches, and she crept toward it, keeping the chair leg raised and ready. Grabbing the door, she yanked it open and spun into the room.

No one was there, but they had been. The bed was torn apart, books flung off shelves, desk drawers dumped on the floor, dresser open and rifled through. She clenched her jaw at the mess but didn't stop to inspect it. Walking to avoid the old house shaking, she hurried back to the steps in the narrow hall.

Down the two, then back up three to the main hallway.

She heard Hawk call the all clear from the other end and veered into the closest bedroom. It was also a mess, but to a lesser extent, as thus far they'd only used it as storage and for old furniture that had been left behind.

The door on the opposite wall opened, and she raised the leg behind her head, ready to swing. A shadow filled the gap. A flicker of light on a gun barrel.

She spun backward, out of the line of fire.

"Colt!" Hawk froze in the doorway, quickly lowering his weapon, eyes wide at the sight of her.

She let out her breath and dropped the leg to her side. "They're gone."

He nodded. "Whoever it was had a goal in mind. Everything is rummaged through. No way to tell if they found anything. Downstairs is...bad."

A stream of blue language echoed up from the main floor.

Colt cocked her eyebrow at Hawk. "That bad?"

He nodded. "Mitch is correct this time."

They trudged down the stairs, Colt's hand tightening on the chair leg as more of the damage revealed itself. They joined Mitch in the kitchen and did a tour of the main rooms together.

Walls were smashed in, flooring pulled up. Dishes were broken in the kitchen, canisters of sugar and flour poured over the floor. In the living room, furniture had been broken with no rhyme or reason. Even the sofa cushions were cut open, stuffing oozing out of the upholstery.

Mitch kept up a litany of muttered swears as they surveyed the damage. For once, not even Hawk seemed annoyed by the language. Colt agreed with the emotion. She wanted to punch something. No, someone. Preferably the person responsible.

"Do you think they found whatever they were looking for?" Colt asked as they returned to the dining room, glass crunching under their shoes.

Hawk groaned, running his hand over his face.

"What?"

"The blueprints and notes. They're all gone." He gestured to the table, devoid of papers.

"The blueprints are in the tunnels. We took them with us this morning."

"So just the other papers then. Frank's background information. Notes I'd written down during our chats."

"None of that was in the safe?" Colt bent down to pick up a massive blue china washbasin. The edge was chipped in a couple of places, but miraculously, it was still in one piece.

"No, it wouldn't all fit. The deeds and extra keys are in there though."

"Good. Wait — is the safe —?"

Hawk stepped over a chair and yanked open a door in the long cabinet against the wall. "It's here."

Colt let out a sigh of relief. At least the ransackers hadn't gotten into that. She looked at the disaster that surrounded them. After the long day of working in the tunnels, the last thing she wanted to do was deal with this mess. But she also wasn't about to leave Hawk and Mitch to take care of it, no matter what Hawk was about to suggest. "Let's see how much of this we can get cleared up tonight. None of us will sleep well if it's like this."

The boys agreed, and they quickly got to work. Mitch stayed in the dining room, where the flooring was in the best condition and least likely to trip him. Hawk brought in boxes and shovels from the garage, and they started scooping the broken glass, wallboard, and more into garbage bags. Colt picked up the books that had been flung around, stacking them on the table for Mitch to sort through. A few had been damaged beyond repair.

"Hey, I didn't know you had a book safe," Mitch said when Colt returned to the dining room after carrying a bag of garbage outside.

"A what?"

He showed her the book, the center cut out.

"That's cool, actually. But no, I think that was one of the books that had been left here." Half the bookshelves in the living room had been emptied while the other half remained, as though someone had grown tired midway through packing. "Anything in it?"

Mitch tilted the book, letting a small piece of gold thread fall out. "No, but there had been something in there. Do you think the ransackers found it?"

Colt shook her head. "Maybe, but that's not what they were looking for. If that was all they wanted, they wouldn't have kept destroying stuff."

"Good point," Hawk said as he joined them, carrying a tray of sandwiches and a pitcher of iced tea. "Enough cleaning for tonight. Let's eat, then hit the sack."

They cleared off enough space on the table to eat. After they ate, Colt grabbed her coat.

"Where are you going?" Hawk asked.

"The hangar."

"No. No way are you staying out there alone, not after two attacks on the property."

"Too bad. I'm going. They have the papers; they know about the tunnels. If they come back, I'm going to catch them."

After a few minutes of arguing, Hawk gave in. Colt wasn't about to stay safe in the house and just let someone break in a third time. And she didn't need a babysitter. She knew it was only his desire to continue cleaning up that kept him from coming with her. She grabbed some supplies and left.

The sun was filtering through the trees, bars of orange burnishing the sky as she climbed the hill. She rolled her shoulders, feeling the stiffness from the long day of physical labor. Idly, she wondered if it should hurt. Was Hawk in pain after swinging the sledge-hammer for hours, followed by the clean-up of both the tunnel and the house? If he was, he'd never say anything. She used to think it was him not wanting to make things awkward for her. But she'd since learned that it was part of his natural stoicism. Pain was a part of life, and he dealt with it as it happened. His months of physical therapy after the crash showed her just how much he could handle.

She pondered the question as she crossed the runway to the control tower. Experts claimed that while she would never feel physical discomfort, she could suffer emotional pain. It never happened. Even when she received word that her grandmother had passed away, she felt little more than a weight on her chest and a desire to be alone. Maybe because it hadn't been a shock. Katya had been in her nineties when Colt was first deployed, and their goodbye on the dock had held a finality to it. Being back here and seeing how much the airfield had declined in the intervening years was hard. Katya sent Colt out into the world, prepared for whatever life threw at her. Here, the effects of the woman's absence were all too obvious.

The shadow of the tower reached across the tarmac to meet her, and Colt slipped inside amid the gloaming. It was gray inside, but she left the light off, not wanting its intrusiveness. Taking the spool of wire she'd brought with her, she rigged one end to the door and fed it around a few strategically placed nails in the wall. Holding the spool over the stair rail, she unwound the wire as she headed for the control room. The 360-degree windows let in enough light for her to work. The microphone for the PA system was covered in dust, but the light came on when she flicked the switch. She wrapped her hand around the controller, tightening just enough to hear a second of static emanate from the speakers mounted outside. Good, it still worked. She toggled the settings until she found the one she wanted.

A few moments of wrapping the wire and adjusting the angles, and she had it set. If anyone tried to enter the tower, the PA system would sound off an air-raid siren, waking everyone within miles.

The only problem was that Colt also couldn't open the door from the inside without setting it off. She slipped under the stairs, replacing the broken paneling back over the entrance. It was a long, dark walk back to the hangar, one she spent wondering just what her grandmother had gotten them into.

Malik took a sip of his Kopi Luwak coffee, savoring the sweet notes of plum and rose. At six hundred dollars a pound, it was an indulgence, but the unique fermentation process made for a truly special blend, and he couldn't imagine drinking anything else now.

He sipped it again, then turned his computer on. The office was often so busy that he preferred to sort his emails at home before heading in. It gave him time to review what the day would hold and tackle anything urgent without distractions. As he read down the list of addresses and subject lines, he was doubly glad he had chosen to do so today.

Two stood out as ones he would not want someone asking questions about. He opened the first.

I'll be in the US next week. Do you still need me to pick up something for you?

Driscoll

Malik frowned. It was bold of Driscoll to write so blatantly, but the request was innocent enough. He tapped his mouse. He didn't have an answer yet, and that was the problem. But maybe the answer was sitting in his inbox.

The email from his contact in the United States held only a link. He navigated to the FTP site and entered his encrypted password. The promised files were there, and his computer made quick work of the downloads.

First up was a cut sheet of the property, listing the particulars of buildings, appliances, and features. More importantly, it had the sales history. The most recent sale was listed first. He gritted his teeth. The airfield sold for far less than he had been willing to pay for it.

Before that, the only other record was in 1962, when it had sold for a mere hundred and fifty thousand dollars. He found it fascinating that such a property had not changed hands in nearly sixty years. Closing the file, he opened the next one. It was large, and Malik drummed his fingers on the desk while waiting for it to open. Blurry scans of old printed pages appeared.

He frowned, wondering why his man hadn't bothered to make it legible. After checking that his office door was closed, Malik unlocked the top drawer of his desk and pulled out a pair of gray eyeglasses trimmed in orange.

With them on, and enlarging the image size, he was able to decipher the text. By the time he finished reading Frank Farrell's service record, he was ready for another cup of coffee. If there hadn't been so much of it redacted, it might have made for an interesting read. Instead, he was left frustrated at the lack of answers. And how did the new owners come to hold a copy of it?

The next two documents were more recent. One was the land registry, outlining the details that the government had on record. The final file left him with even more questions. The title for the property listed the most recent owners. Except there were no names for the new owners. The previous owners were listed as Katya Levin and Frank Farrell, but the line for the new owners was blank.

Malik leaned back in his chair to ponder that. Was it just an administrative oversight? Why had his man not found any information about the new owners? And who was this Katya Levin? Why was there no information about her?

He was about to close the folder when he saw a small, unnamed text file.

Mike,

Found these at the airfield. The house is old, but I get the feeling the airfield was built during the Cold War. It's got that feel to it. If that's the case, there's a good chance there's an underground bunker somewhere nearby. I'll keep digging.

Malik reached for his mug, disappointed to find it empty. Katya was a decidedly Russian name, he knew. So what was someone from the USSR doing buying property in the United States during the Cuban Missile Crisis? Especially property that had "military" stamped all over it?

A glance at his watch told him he didn't have time to investigate further. He sent a quick reply to his man in the US and hurried out to meet his driver, the questions continuing to plague him as he went.

Colt bolted upright, narrowly avoiding braining herself on the bunk above. Heart racing, she swung her feet to the floor and stood. She was halfway out the door before she realized that it was no longer night. Pausing, she sought for what had awoken her. No sirens broke the stillness. No one was in the hangar. Her phone, somehow in her hand, showed no new notifications.

She read the time. 5:31 a.m.

She closed the door and sank back on the bunk. Nothing had startled her awake. Her body had simply returned to her old pattern of waking up at 5:30, and she wasn't used to it. Since moving, her sleep had been all over the place. Well, if her body was ready for the old routine, she may as well go with it. A run would do her some good anyway.

An hour later, she stopped at the house for clean clothes, a shower, and breakfast. She was ready to head out the door again before either of the guys showed signs of life.

Hawk yawned at her by way of greeting from the hall door.

"I made coffee," she told him.

He blinked, then veered to find a mug. Leaning against the door frame, she waited for the go-juice to penetrate his zombie brain.

"Sleep?" he asked after a few sips.

"Good," she answered.

"No..." He twirled his finger in the air.

"Nope, all quiet on the eastern front."

He grunted, the mug obscuring his face. "What's with the...?"

"Oh, this?" She hefted the duffel that was slung over her shoulder. "Just some clothes I'm taking to the bunk room. Don't have anything clean up there."

He gave her a funny look, but she wasn't sure if the coffee had worked enough for him to grasp the concept yet.

"Well, I'm off to work on the Mule. Join me when you're ready." A buzzing cut off whatever Hawk might have been trying to form as a response. Colt dug her phone out of her pocket and frowned. Why was Danforth calling?

She answered, turning away to give Hawk the kitchen.

"You're awake early for a banker," she said. She didn't want to poke at her own reasons for being snarky. She just knew that he irritated her.

"I made the assumption that you weren't a layabout either," he replied dryly. "I've got some interesting news for you." He said it smugly, as though she would beg him to share. Not likely.

Dropping the duffel by the door, she paced the living room. "Go on." If he called her, he wanted to tell her.

"I've been doing some digging into the history of the Fabergé Egg."

"Oh, you had time between counting all your money for something so trivial?" She took a gleeful delight in egging him on.

He took a deep breath. "Fine. I asked one of my assistants to do it. There's a lot of rumor and conjecture to filter through, but it's possible this particular one was in the possession of an Imperial guard after the demise of the Romanov family, one Pavol Rudneva."

"How do you know that? Didn't a lot of valuable jewels go missing at the time?"

"Yes, well, this man may have boasted about it enough to make the local paper."

Colt snorted. From the kitchen, Hawk waved a newly full pot of coffee at her. She nodded in reply to the unspoken question.

"He claims it was a gift from the tsar. Regardless of how he gained possession of it, he no longer has it."

"He's still alive?" She looped the living room one more time before heading to the kitchen.

"Obviously not. He'd be a hundred and forty if that were the case. And the family will no longer talk about it. My man couldn't get close to them, only speaking to neighbors, et cetera."

"You sent your guy to Russia?" Nodding her thanks to Hawk, she took the coffee with her.

"No, my guy is *in* Russia."

"Interesting." She sipped the hot coffee.

"What is?"

"Nothing. Go on."

Danforth cleared his throat. "About fifty years ago, Rudneva's granddaughter ran away, right before being forced into a marriage to an older widower with a young son. The Fabergé disappeared about the same time. My assistant said the general feeling was the family was more upset over the loss of the Egg than the plight of the girl."

"Charming." She slugged back the last of her coffee.

"Indeed," he said wryly. "Interestingly, it was the son who seemed the most offended. Her family was upset, but his response was described as one of rage, as though she had stolen from him directly."

"The question still remains — why do people think it ended up here?" Colt studied the bottom of her empty mug, swirling the dregs.

"Yes, well."

It took Colt a moment to read his silence. "You think that was my grandmother."

"You said yourself she was Russian."

She laughed. "And about thirty years too old. No, Gram was already here when the girl ran away."

"You're sure about that." He sounded disappointed.

"I am."

"There are also rumors of the Egg being in the US forty years ago."

"Did your grandmother tell you that?"

"She did work in the art industry at the time." Danforth paused. "Well, I shall let you go. Got to get back to counting my millions." The sarcasm was a surprise, but she liked it. Showed he wasn't a total ice cube.

"Wouldn't want to keep you."

"One more thing. The son she abandoned? He moved away for work years ago but recently was seen back in the village, harassing the family for information about the girl. When he left, he told them he was coming to America." With that, Danforth ended the call.

Colt made a face. She didn't like the fact he got the last word in. And she didn't like his last words either.

12

Once Hawk was awake and fed, the two of them returned to the tunnel. They made quick work of the entrance to the bathrooms, revealing larger locker rooms beyond. Colt studied the blueprints in the briefing room while Hawk made a shopping list of items needed to get the bathrooms back in working order.

"I think I've got it," she said when he joined her.

"Where?"

She used a chalk pen to circle a spot on the plans. "Here. It's inside the double doors, not in the antechamber like we thought."

He leaned over to see what she meant. They'd been trying to decipher the entrance to the second tunnel, but despite what the plans showed, they'd yet to uncover the correlating point in the tunnel. Armed with the fresh viewpoint, they grabbed their tools and headed to the far end. Once they knew where to look, it was easy to spot the variance in the wall. Working in tandem, they smashed through the concrete to the set of metal doors. The lock was still in place, crusted over. Colt used her lock-picking set to clean it out, then sorted through the keys until she found the correct one. She found it interesting that it wasn't the same key that opened the first tunnel. An extra safety precaution, or was this secondary tunnel only accessible to select people? If so, why? And who were they?

The blueprints indicated that there were more rooms off this tunnel, but Colt wasn't looking forward to the work of uncovering all of them. Hawk helped her push the double doors open, the hinges protesting after years of disuse. The now-familiar scent of stale air wafted over them as she felt for the light switch. The lights overhead came on one by one, revealing the long gray hallway, identical to the one behind them. There was one key difference — even in the dim light, she could make out several doors, uncovered, handles intact.

Colt wasted no time in opening the closest. It was a good size, a bit larger than the briefing room, laid out like a school room. Tables and chairs were lined up, facing a chalkboard on the far wall, in front of which sat a large wooden desk. Posters and banners dotted the walls, showing the alphabet and simple words. A stack of picture books sat on the teacher's desk.

"What is this place? They had a school here?" Colt flicked through one of the books, noting the simple drawings labeled with one- and two-word descriptors. "This stuff is for small kids."

"But the desks aren't," Hawk pointed out. "These are full-sized tables, not the little desks they use for kindergartners."

"So what do you think was happening here?"

Hawk waved to the movie projector sitting in the back of the room. "I think they were teaching English."

"To whom?"

"That's the question, isn't it?"

Colt punched him in the shoulder as she passed him on the way back out to the hall. "Which is why I asked it." Although she wasn't sure she wanted to know the answer. She had set out to prove everyone wrong about her grandmother, that she wasn't a jewel thief. But even though they had yet to find any evidence regarding valuables, everything they had uncovered just raised more questions.

She crossed the hall to the door opposite. The room was smaller than the last, made to feel even smaller by the overflowing shelves on two walls, material and paraphernalia spilling off. The third wall held a long table with two sewing machines. The fourth wall provided space for a dress form and chair. They flipped through the items, trying to read the patterns to understand what was being made here.

"That Russian Danforth mentioned?" Hawk asked.

"Mm?" Colt held up a floral piece of fabric, wondering if someone had really made a dress out of it or if it was meant for curtains. Either way, she wouldn't have used it.

"Any chance that's the guy we've seen around the place?"

She shuffled through the mounds of stacked fabric. "Maybe? That would make more sense than there being two crazy Russians connected to this."

"True."

"But I still don't get why or how they think the airfield is connected to anything." She tossed the material back on the shelf, at a loss for why anyone would have been making clothing in the bunker.

Hawk followed her out into the hall. "Could all of this be a leftover from the '50s when the Air Force was in control of it? And your grandmother just never bothered clearing it out?"

She shrugged. "That's one answer."

The third door was locked. There was nothing to indicate anything different from the outside, but the handle wouldn't budge. Hawk handed over the keys, and Colt ran through them, testing each till she found a small key with a round, worn bow. It opened with only a bit of resistance. She pushed the door open, revealing a tiny office.

It was the first room painted a different color than the drab gray seen everywhere in the tunnel. The pale blue added a sense of serenity. Furnished sparsely, there was only a small desk with chairs on either side, and a tall filing cabinet in the corner. For a second, Colt was sure she smelled lilacs, but the moment passed. She paused by the door, trying to find that sense of comfort the scent had brought.

Hawk pushed past her, moving to the desk. It held only three things — a lamp, an old rotary phone, and a picture frame. Colt looked up to see Hawk giving her an odd smile.

"What?"

"Is that you?" He pointed to the picture.

She joined him, reaching for the frame to get a better look. Her hands clenched around the thin metal frame as she took in the faces staring back at her. Roaring filled her ears, and she struggled to swallow. Hawk was right — it was a picture of her. A very small her, chubby cheeks smeared with icing, lopsided pigtails. Beside her, his arm around her neck, head tilted back in a laugh, was a boy of three or four. Her chest constricted, and her vision narrowed.

"Colt. Colt!"

She looked up, shaking her head, Hawk's voice finally penetrating the roaring in her ears. He pried the picture from her fingers and set it back on the desk. She couldn't take her eyes off it, convinced her brother's face would vanish if she blinked.

Hawk dropped a hand on her shoulder, a weight to ground her in the moment. "Your brother?"

She cleared her throat. "Ben. My last birthday. Before..." She didn't want to explain. How could you explain what had happened in a few simple words? She trusted Hawk to understand and not ask.

"You sure it was your birthday? He's the one wearing a birthday button." Hawk pointed to the blue button on Ben's shirt.

She frowned, picking up the picture again. The puzzle pulled her out of the memory, giving her something solid to focus on. She was sure it had been her birthday though, remembering the model airplane her grandmother had given her. Remembered, too, the argument that had followed as her mother felt a wooden airplane wasn't a suitable gift for a little girl.

But maybe Hawk was right. Maybe that had been a different day, and this photo was taken on Ben's birthday and not hers. She couldn't remember when his was. There had been no more birthdays after that.

Hawk squeezed her shoulder again, then silently slipped out of the room.

Colt pulled the chair out from behind the desk and sat down. She picked up the picture and returned it to its original spot, careful to line up the gap in the dust. Leaning back in the chair, she surveyed the room, trying to see it the way her grandmother would have. In her typical Spartan fashion, Katya had left the walls bare, the only nonfunctional thing in the room being the picture. Colt glanced at it again, seeing it through a grandmother's eyes. Two small children laughing.

Before the memories could resurface, Colt shifted her focus. The picture was the only personal thing in the room of Katya's, but it also undeniably marked this office as Katya's domain. So two questions: Why was her office separate from the others in the main tunnel? And what did she do here?

Colt pulled open the top drawer to her right. The usual assortment of office supplies was carefully arranged in the built-in dividers. Three pens, a pencil, an eraser, ruler, stapler. A small notepad, half-used. Confirming her suspicions that it held nothing of interest, she moved on to the second drawer. It was deeper, with metal rails holding file folders. Colt flipped through them quickly. Bills, invoices, receipts, all carefully organized and marked "paid."

She slammed the drawer shut, wincing at the scraping noise as the weight hung on the slides. One last drawer, a thin one in the middle of the desk. She had purposely saved it for last, knowing the others were unlikely to spill any secrets. The drawer was locked, but she still had the keys from Hawk. Next to the key for the office, there was a small key that looked like it might fit. She was right. The simple mechanism opened easily. She pulled open the drawer, the wood protesting against the movement.

The drawer held two leather-bound books and a stack of papers held together by a string. Colt pulled the journal out first. It was identical to the others she'd been reading, filled with her grandmother's elegant handwriting. This one started off in English, as though Katya were trying to stick to the new language. But the words were stilted, missing the flavor of the Russian, and after only a few entries, they switched back to her native tongue. Colt checked the dates. It started in January 1991 and ended a few months later. Unlike the other journals, this one wasn't full, with a third of the book blank.

Colt set it aside to read later. She was almost finished with the first box of journals and wanted to continue her evening ritual of reading with a cup of tea in the hangar. She lifted the stack of papers out carefully, the thin sheets crinkling beneath her fingers. Without undoing the string, she peeked at the contents. Letters, dated across the decades, signed by different names. Most of them in Russian. Colt hadn't taken her grandmother as someone with a large circle of friends with whom she swapped letters, but it was just one more thing Colt hadn't known about the woman.

The second leather-bound book was long and thin, taking up most of the bottom of the drawer. Colt had to angle it to get it out. She moved the journal and letters aside to have room to open it. Inside she found pages and pages of carefully ruled lines, columns filled in tiny, precise numbers.

Colt pulled the chain to turn the lamp on. The bulb fizzled for a moment before casting a yellow glow. Leaning over the desk, she studied the ledger. The first column showed dates spanning decades. The second column held pairs of letters. None of them seemed to be repeated, aside from the occasional two or three in a row. Next came a dollar value, all whole numbers, ranging from high hundreds to thousands. The final column wasn't completely filled out, with many boxes remaining empty. It, too, held dollar values, often similar to the previous column. There were some figures that were significantly lower than the first, while others were more than double.

Outside the office, whistling sounded, accompanied by footsteps traversing the hall.

"Hawk!" she called out.

The footsteps stopped, then grew louder again. He rapped softly on the door before pushing it open. "You alright?"

"Yeah, come take a look at this." She shifted the ledger so he could read it too. "What do you make of this?"

He ran his finger down the columns. "No totals, so not worried about overall income."

"No, it's not about income. I think it's a record of individual items and their value."

"But what?" He leaned against the wall, crossing his arms.

She met his gaze. "I know what you're thinking. This could be the missing evidence of stolen artwork."

He nodded.

"But we still don't know for sure."

"We don't."

"It's not definitive."

"Not in the least."

"We need more data."

"Absolutely."

"So I think we should find that."

"I agree."

"Good. I'm glad we're on the same page." She cleared her throat. "So. Have you found anything else?"

"Two more offices, neither locked. One's clearly Frank's — stuffed full of flight logs, weather reports, things like that. The other I think belonged to the teacher. Stacks of marked papers, all ESL assignments."

"Hmm." She pursed her lips, not sure what to suggest next.

"Have you looked in the filing cabinet yet?"

She glanced over in the corner. "Oh. Nope. Go for it."

Hawk crossed the room in a few long strides, and soon he was pulling folders and flipping through them. Colt bent over the ledger again, doing quick totals in her head. If she was reading this correctly, her grandmother had made more than one hundred thousand dollars in the first ten years listed. Of course, it could have been the other way around, and her grandmother had spent that much.

"Colt."

Something in Hawk's voice had her on her feet immediately. She met him in the middle of the room. He handed her half the stack of files in his hand. "It's girls."

Colt dropped the files on the desk and began flipping through them. Each held a single-page bio and a passport photo of a young woman. They were all from countries that had been part of the USSR. Some had additional pages, final marks from English class-es, note pages with random, meaningless words. Many of the bios had handwritten notes, including dates in the top corner.

Snatching up the ledger, Colt flipped to the year noted on the top of the open file. 1967. The girl's name: Zofia Lubeinska.

There. Halfway down the page, the letters ZL, a small check mark beside them. The final column read $21,950, nearly two thousand dollars more than the third column.

"Hawk. Names and dates." She barked out the order, fear of being right tightening her chest.

He quickly turned to the front of the file he held. "1969, Vaira Semjonova."

"VS...here." She jammed her finger on the page. "$11,990. Next."

Hawk read off more names and dates. Each time, Colt found correlating entries in the ledger, many with figures in the final column. Her hands were shaking as she turned the pages, each time hoping she wouldn't find the matching entry.

"Colt, what does...'o-tree-zat' mean?"

She looked up, and he turned the page for her to read the penciled word. "Otrezat. Uh...cut off, ended. Something like that."

"It's on most of these pages."

Colt slammed her hands down on the desk. She shoved at the ledger, sending it and the files flying. The diary caught the picture, and they both fell to the floor in a crash. The photo slid from the frame. She grabbed the lamp and flung it against the far wall.

"Hey!" Hawk cried in surprise. "What's going on inside that head of yours?"

She looked at him, eyes wide, desperately wishing she was wrong. "They were smuggling *people*, Hawk. Katya *sold* those girls."

The ringing of his phone was a jarring interruption from the bubble of his Ferrari. Malik looked at the display to see who was calling. His sister. Malik pressed the button on the steering wheel to accept the call.

"Amna. Are you —?"

She didn't let him finish. "Where are you? You were supposed to be here an hour ago."

"Be where? We're having dinner with Uncle Rashid tomorrow, no?"

"That's not what I'm talking about," she hissed into the phone. He could hear her voice echoing and knew she was pacing the foyer of her house. "Mother asked you to come over today so we could discuss her treatment. You know...her wishes."

"I'm taking care of all that, you know that." Why was she annoying him with this today? He was on his way to the stables to oversee Pozan's first cover. If it all went well, the stallion would soon be earning his weight in gold. The vet had cleared the horse after the infection but warned that the antibiotics in his system might make today's procedure ineffective.

"You're not listening to me!" Amna screeched. The car's top-of-the-line sound system took her voice and threw it back at him from all angles.

"Yes, I am. Mother is concerned about her doctors. That is why I've hired a new one. He'll be coming tomorrow morning." He clenched the steering wheel tighter, the leather creaking under his hands. He flew past a car, glaring at the idiot for driving so slowly.

"Malik." Amna spoke slowly. "Mother doesn't want a new doctor. She wants to speak to you, me, and Sulaiman about not continuing the treatment."

Her words reached through his distraction. "What are you saying?" He pulled out to pass a truck and trailer, too laden to maintain the speed limit.

"You know what I'm saying. And you need to be here."

"No. She's getting better. She has to... I'm working on something for her." He swung around a corner, narrowly avoiding an oncoming SUV.

"Brother, please. She needs you."

"No. I will not tolerate this nonsense. Mother will get better, and that is final." He mashed the button on the controls to end the call. Amna was being ridiculous. He wouldn't — couldn't — consider such negative thinking. As he flew by three vehicles in a row, he checked his speedometer, his throat catching at the sight of a number nearly double the posted limit.

His chest tightened, and he fought for air. Clammy hands struggled to keep the wheel straight as he tapped the brakes, slowly bringing the car back down to speed and then to a stop. He got out, sucking air into his lungs. Killing himself in a crash would not help Mother beat the cancer that riddled her body. No, he had to stay alive and get the Egg for her.

Unable to contain the rage that was building up inside her, Colt headed for the door. She didn't care about the mess. It could all burn for all she cared. And she certainly didn't want to listen to Hawk's attempts to convince her that maybe she was wrong. She wasn't. It was all so clearly laid out in the ledger. She stormed toward the main tunnel, letting the heavy double doors slam behind her. The silhouette of a man loomed in front of her. Stupid Hawk, didn't he know when to just drop it?

But Hawk was behind her. Her head snapped up in time to identify the large Russian man as he began running toward her, shouting in Russian. At any other moment, Colt would have chosen to use his own momentum against him. Right now, she was looking for something to hit, and he was presenting a perfect target. Her fist collided with his jaw in a punch that sent him tumbling backward to the floor. He recovered quickly, shaking his head as he clambered to his feet.

She waited, letting him get upright before moving in for a spinning back kick. Her aim was off, and she only sent him staggering back a few steps. He came at her, powerful arms throwing punches as he continued to shout.

She tuned out his words, his demands for the treasure. He claimed it belonged to him, but she wasn't interested. There was no treasure. Nothing of value here. Only the long-buried secrets of a traitor. Colt absorbed his punches, pinned against the wall. They felt no different than the sense of betrayal that flooded her soul, filling her with emptiness.

Instinct kicked in after a moment, and she fought back, ripping into him until at last he lay panting on the ground.

"The treasure...is still...mine..." he sneered.

"Enough!" she roared. "There is no treasure. There's nothing here."

Grabbing him by the ear, she dragged him into Katya's office. Hawk looked up, startled.

"No treasure!" She shoved the man into the wall.

He slumped down, holding his side.

"I don't know what more you want. There's nothing here. Now. *Get. Out.*"

He lunged forward, waving his hand at her. A flash of steel, and she felt something tug at her side. Before she could react, he snatched the photo and other files off the floor and bolted out the door.

Hawk looked at her, his mouth open.

227

"Shut up."

Malik strode into the restaurant, Dalal on his arm. Uncle Rashid glowered at him from the head of the table. He was late and would pay for the slight by sitting at the foot of the table. Malik guided Dalal around a white marble column to the two empty chairs at the end. He held the chair for Dalal to sit down and leaned to kiss his elderly aunt before sinking into his own velveted chair.

The table was a series of smaller ones pushed together to make room for their large party. It was set with floral placemats, white plates topped with folded napkins, and wine glasses. Down the center were plates of peppers and olives, baskets of flatbread, and bottles of condiments, as well as water.

"You're late," said his cousin's daughter. At thirteen, she was hovering between child and adult and didn't know how to fit into either world. He ignored the jibe in her words, wondering where the girl who used to beg him to go to the stables had gone.

With the whole party assembled, the servers soon appeared with the food. He popped an olive in his mouth as dishes laden with his favorites were delivered. Malik's stomach growled at the smell of grilled kebab. He piled his plate full of arayes, tabboula, kebab, pieces of chicken tikka, and a couple of vegetable samboosas.

His aunt started telling him all about the young women she knew who would be "just perfect for him, women who wanted families." Dalal glared at him, and he stepped in to remind his aunt that he was in a committed relationship. Dalal smirked while his aunt glared at her.

"If you were so committed, then why are you together for three years and no ring, huh? You tell me that, Malik."

Now both women were glaring at him. He wasn't going to get out of this easily. Malik was relieved when his phone buzzed in his pocket. He slid it from his jacket and held it in his lap to open the email.

His source had sent a black-and-white picture of a woman in her fifties, cut from a newspaper.

Malik looked up. His aunt was now talking to her son, seated on the other side of her. Dalal was refusing to look at him. The only person who was looking at him was his cousin's daughter. He looked down at his phone again.

Found this picture of the old woman who owned the airfield. Have taken it around the art shops in the area, but no one seems to recognize her.

I've got a couple more places on my list. Will hit them up tomorrow. She lived here for 60 yrs, someone's got to know her.

Malik returned the phone to his pocket. Good news at last.

13

The sounds of someone arriving drifted up to where Colt lay stretched out on her bed. She listened as though it were happening to someone else. Car doors opened and shut, Hawk welcoming someone, a quiet voice in reply. The voices moved inside, and Colt slipped back into the void of nothing where she'd been residing for the past few hours. Hawk had dragged her to the house after the fight with the Russian, but she'd refused to let him look at her injuries.

The step near her room creaked under a heavy weight, then again, lighter. The dresser in the outer room rattled as the floor dipped with someone crossing it. Someone knocked on the door. She didn't answer. It came again.

Go away. It was too much effort to say the words aloud.

A third knock, louder.

"Go away."

"Colt, come on. Mackenzie's here," Hawk wheedled.

Mackenzie? Why Mac — oh. "I'm fine."

"Colt, you're not fine. There's blood everywhere. Let her take a look." He pulled the door open as he spoke but let Mackenzie enter the room first. The tiny blonde held up a plastic case that weighed as much as she did.

"I passed my certification exam!" she exclaimed, giving a shy smile from behind her curtain of hair.

"That's great." Colt knew she should be more enthusiastic, but she couldn't dig up the energy.

Hawk pulled a chair close to the bed, and Mackenzie set her kit down on it. Hawk handed her something he'd been holding, then slipped out of the room. Colt was aware of his movements but without curiosity. Mackenzie flicked the lights on and opened her kit, then twisted her hair up in a bun before snapping on a pair of blue gloves. She leaned over Colt to get a better look at her.

"Ohh. That's why...where are they? Here." She picked up an ice pack and placed it on Colt's eye. Then immediately removed it, flustered. "Oh no, sorry! Did that hurt? Here, I'll be more gentle. But you've got a nasty black eye."

Colt summoned the energy to give her a half smile. "It doesn't hurt. I can't, remember?"

Mackenzie nodded. "Oh, right."

"Calm down, you're doing great. Do what you need to. You won't hurt me. I promise."

Mackenzie took a deep breath, reassessing her tools. "I'm supposed to ask where it hurts the most."

"Hmm. Well, what would you do if I were unconscious and couldn't tell you?"

"ABCs! But you're awake and talking, so I know your breathing is okay. Which means your heart is beating too."

"Good. What next?"

"Well, your eye is pretty bad. And your hands are a mess. But Hawk said you were bleeding a lot, and it's not from either of those. So why don't you tell me?"

Colt sighed and finally moved her arm. She was wearing a black long-sleeved shirt, lying on top of a black throw blanket, and had a black towel pressed against her side, all of which did a good job of masking the blood. She peeled the towel away, revealing the tear in her shirt and the gaping wound below it.

"It's not that bad, I swear. He only just caught me with the edge of his knife."

Mackenzie wrinkled her nose, ripping open a pack of wipes. "It needs stitches."

"Can't you just tape it shut?"

"It won't heal properly, and that's assuming he didn't nick any internal organs or arteries."

"He didn't. Look, it's only a couple inches long, and blood isn't gushing out. It's been three hours since it happened, and I'm still conscious and talking. No signs of shock, correct?"

Mackenzie pressed her lips together as she wiped the blood away to get a better look at the wound. "This is going to —"

"Hurt?" Colt supplied. "It's fine."

With a tiny nod, Mackenzie pressed down on the edges of the cut. Blood seeped out, filling the space as quickly as she wiped it away. She grabbed a bandage and covered the cut again. "I'm not good enough for this. I can't tell how deep that is."

"Mac, listen to me. You're doing great. Just bandage it up. If it gets worse, I'll find a doctor."

"You need stitches."

"Okay. So put in stitches."

"No way! I can't do that!"

"You learned, right?"

"Ye...esss."

"Time to put it to use. Mackenzie, I'm the perfect person to practice on. You can't hurt me, and I don't care about scarring."

Tears filled the younger woman's eyes. "What if I screw up?" she whispered.

Twinges of guilt stabbed at Colt. "If you really don't want to, I won't make you. But I believe you can do this."

Mackenzie took a shuddering breath. "Okay, I can try."

"Good girl. Go tell Hawk what you need."

Mackenzie hurried downstairs, returning a few minutes later with a stack of towels and Hawk in tow. He carried a basin of steaming water.

"Colt, give me one good reason not to pour this on your head. Why are you making Mackenzie do this?"

Colt glared at him. "I'm not making her. I just think she's perfectly capable of doing it. Don't you?"

She watched him struggle with a response. She'd backed him into a corner, where he couldn't argue without upsetting Mackenzie.

"Fine. But only if she wants to."

Mackenzie tugged on his arm, pointing for him to set the basin down. "I want to. And she needs it. But if you're going to argue, you can leave. I need Colt calm, and you're upsetting her."

Hawk's mouth fell open, and he gaped at the two women in turn. "Okay, but if you need anything, I'll be right outside."

Mackenzie giggled. "Is he always that much of a mother hen?"

"Always. You wouldn't believe the things he'd get worked up over on the ship."

With a crease of concentration between her eyes, Mackenzie opened a clean sheet of gauze and laid it on the bed, then carefully set out the instruments she'd need. She washed her hands in the hot water and donned a fresh pair of gloves. Standing beside Colt, she let out a shuddering breath, shaking her hands.

"Can you talk to me? I need to think about something else while I'm doing this."

"About what?" Colt moved her arm under her head to get it out of Mackenzie's way.

"Anything. Hawk said you'd found your grandmother's journals."

Colt shifted. "Yeah, well. I've decided to stop reading them."

"Why? It sounds cool to be able to read about what life was like for your grandmother." Mackenzie threaded the needle and picked up a pair of forceps.

"It was great, until we discovered she wasn't so nice of a person." Colt didn't want to go into details. She didn't really want to talk about her grandmother at all, but it was worse looking at Mackenzie and remembering how they met. She was bitterly aware of what it did to someone to be stolen away from their life, and she didn't want to reopen that wound for either of them.

"Well, tell me about some of the good things you read."

As Mackenzie focused on suturing the cut, Colt did her best to share nicer memories from her grandmother's journals. There were a lot of stories of flying adventures and working on the planes, with the occasional anecdote about Colt and the other cadets.

Sooner than Colt expected, Mackenzie was tying off the thread. "There. All done. But you have to take it easy for the next few days, or you'll pull them out."

"Okay." Colt leaned on her elbow to take a look at Mackenzie's handiwork.

The girl pushed her back down. "I mean it! Stay in bed as much as possible. No lifting things. No raising your arms above your head."

Colt flopped back down. "Yes, doctor," she said contritely, earning a small smile from Mackenzie.

"Thank you for sharing the stories from your grandmother. You should keep reading the journals." Mackenzie said as she gathered up her equipment.

"You don't know what she did."

"I don't need to. I know she's not as bad as you think she is."

"How can you know that?"

"Someone who raised you to be such a wonderful person can't be all that bad." Laden with the kit bag and the basin of water, Mackenzie slipped out of the room, leaving Colt to ponder if that was true.

Despite Mackenzie's warnings, Colt threw herself into work around the airfield. Hawk watched her with concern, keeping his thoughts to himself. She needed time to deal with all she'd learned. His worry grew as the days passed and she kept working. The grass was long past due a trim, and the tarmac was overgrown. She helped Hawk repaint the house after the ransacking. Taking the tractor out, she spent hours in the woods, clearing the trails. When Mitch requested help with the planes, she was there. As long as it wasn't the Mule he was working on. She refused to go near Katya's plane, and she avoided the tunnels.

After a long day of replacing the wiring in the tunnels alone, Hawk returned to the house. While he didn't mind the work, he wished Colt were down there with him. They worked well together, and he was worried about the way all three of them were going off in different directions. Mitch was perfectly content repairing the planes by himself. He said that way, no one judged him for talking to the planes. But when Colt went off alone like that, he knew she was brooding.

The sight of a vehicle in the driveway pulled him from his reverie. Brody climbed out of the car, two bags of take-out food containers in his hand.

"Hawk! Great timing, my man. Here, take one of these." He thrust one of the bags at Hawk and led the way into the house.

Hawk gave a loud whistle as he entered the house, a signal to the others. Colt looked up from the box she was reading in the kitchen.

"Oh, good. I don't have to cook. What is a monoglyceride anyway?" She tossed the prepackaged pasta kit on the table.

"I don't know," Brody laughed. "But there's probably plenty of it in this stuff too. Come here, cuz, give me a hug. You look like you could use one with that black eye."

Hawk saw the look on Colt's face before Brody's outstretched arm blocked it. Whether it was the "cuz" or the demand for a hug, he wasn't sure. But she didn't punch him, for which Hawk was very grateful.

She ducked out of reach. "I'd rather hug the food, if it's all the same to you."

The conversation over supper extended to all the work being done around the property. Mitch outlined the current status of the three planes he had on deck. Hawk and Colt made a point not to mention the tunnels or the Russian man. Hawk watched Brody closely. If Kendra's research was correct, then Brody was the one who had found the necklace and sold it.

"Looks like you redid the dining room, too. Removed the doors?" Brody waved his shrimp-laden fork in the air.

Colt took a deliberate bite out of her egg roll.

"Yeah," Mitch drawled. "Decided we didn't like them any-more."

Hawk focused on his own plate of food. The doors had been smashed by the ransackers.

"Lots of changes, for sure," Brody observed. "You'll double the value of the property in no time at this rate."

"That's the plan," Hawk said, wondering where he was going with this.

Brody laughed. "If that happens, you'll have to send me part of the proceeds."

"What?" Colt looked at Hawk. No, she wasn't missing any-thing. They owed Brody nothing.

"Just kidding. But hey — if you do find something of value on the property, I should get a share of that. You know, for being the heir to everything."

Colt twirled noodles around her fork. "If you're so invested in this place and the value it holds, why'd you sell it in the first place?"

"I would have loved to have kept it, believe me. No time, no money, you know. But it makes me so happy inside to know that it's in such good hands."

Hawk wasn't sure he'd ever heard anyone lie so badly in his life. What Brody's purpose was, he couldn't fathom. But they might have let it go if he'd left it at that.

"Although, I think there is a law about that. If you make any money off the planes, or find anything else of value here, I'm entitled to part."

Hawk saw the look on Colt's face, and he knew what it meant. He had the time. He could have stopped her. But he couldn't bring himself to do anything about it.

She dropped her fork with a clatter. "Get out." Her voice was calm, a sign of her inner rage.

"What? I'm just teasing you."

"No, you weren't. Get out." Standing, she purposely knocked her chair over. Brody clambered to his feet. "If you cared an ounce for this place, you'd have kept it."

"Fine! If that's how you're going to treat a guest, you can pay me back for the meal." He ripped the receipt from his pocket and slammed it down on the table before storming out. "Email it to me."

Hawk beat him to the front door by way of a different route from the dining room. He pulled a couple bills from his wallet and slapped them against Brody's chest. Colt hustled him out the door.

"You'll regret this," he called as he slid behind the wheel of his car.

"I doubt it. But you will," she replied.

Hawk was so proud of her for not slugging the little weasel.

Colt let out a deep breath as she watched the taillights to Brody's rental car disappear down the driveway. It felt good to feel something again, even if it was anger. Ever since finding out her grandmother's secret, she had been living in a fog.

She ignored the knowing look Hawk gave her as they rejoined Mitch inside. He was holding a wrinkled pink piece of paper. Smirking, he handed it to Colt.

"I think our friend left something important behind with his receipt."

Colt spread the thin page out on the table. It was a triplicated page from a carbon copy form. Stamped in the top corner was the name and address of a pawnshop. The item details were faded and nearly impossible to read. The signature was the only legible piece of information.

"Katya Levin."

"What's Brody doing with a pawn ticket from your grandmother?"

"Something not good, I'm guessing."

Colt held the paper up to the light. "I can't see what the item was. Whoever wrote this had terrible handwriting."

"Maybe a hair dryer would help?" Hawk suggested. "My mom does that with faded receipts."

"Not sure it would help — there's a water stain in the center."

"What's the name of the shop? They'd have a copy too, wouldn't they?" Mitch grabbed his tablet and started typing. "Looks like it's still there. Been in the family for a hundred and fifty years is the claim."

Colt pulled out her phone.

"Says they're closed already," Mitch pointed out.

"Not calling them. Calling Glitch."

Hawk gave her a surprised look. She shrugged back. In the year that Glitch had been helping her search for her missing brother, they'd moved past encrypted messages. She counted the hacker a friend now.

He answered on the second ring.

"I've got a question, and I'm betting you know the answer to it."

"I'll take that bet," he replied immediately.

She read off the name of the pawnshop. "What can you tell me about it?"

"Give me five minutes, and I'll get back to you."

Nearly an hour passed before he called back. Colt took pictures of the receipt with her phone and fiddled with the settings to see if she could make the text more legible. The one thing she determined was that the value box was empty. No prices were noted at all.

"Alright," Glitch said when she answered. "You find me the best puzzles. That pawnshop has a long history of selling to the auction house you asked about a few days ago. An interestingly high number of eastern European artworks have passed between them. Even some that were believed to have been lost to the Nazis."

"Any indication of where they came from?"

"None of those pieces have sellers on record, beyond the pawn-shop. Which, of course, means lots have been sold without proper provenance. Nothing's ever been flagged as stolen."

"I think I want to talk to the pawnshop owner."

"If he's still alive."

"What do you mean?"

"Well, it's been nearly thirty years since he last brought anything of value to the auction house. The few pieces they have seen in recent years were delivered via courier. And none of them of controversial origin."

"So you think the one with contacts might have passed away and a new generation taken over the shop?"

"Looks that way to me," Glitch replied.

"Alright, thanks," Colt said, ready to hang up.

"There's one more thing," Glitch stopped her. "The FBI's fingerprints are all over this data as well. I dug a bit more, and there's definitely some chatter."

"Chatter?"

"Yeah. Dunno details, but I'd say they're working on something related to all this."

Colt ended the call, dismissing his comments about the FBI. Kendra would loop them in if there was anything happening. But she wasn't convinced by Glitch's argument. What if it wasn't the pawnbroker who stopped selling the pieces, but his supplier who stopped bringing them to him? And how did her grandmother and the women she had trafficked fit into this?

14

The menagerie was an oasis of tropical flora and exotic fauna. Coconut palms created a canopy under which flourished orchids, jasmine, and anthurium. A variety of hibiscus threw splashes of color around the space, and bougainvillea climbed the latticework. The leaves were dewy from the early morning watering they had received, making the whole area feel fresh and revitalizing.

Malik offered another piece of pomegranate to his cockatoo. The bird took it daintily in her beak and swallowed, immediately looking for more. Laughing, Malik gave her the last of the fruit, then stroked the cockatoo's back.

"Greedy little bird," he said affectionately. The bird preened, raising her crest. The yellow feathers looked like a spiky mohawk. She cocked her head, looking for more.

"That's the last of it," Malik told her, showing the empty dish. The cockatoo poked at it, then flew to a nearby branch. She proceeded to tell Malik off, berating him for not bringing more fruit.

"Well, if you didn't eat it so fast, there'd still be some left," he explained. The ringing of a phone had him looking around for the parrot. The brightly colored bird refused to be hand-fed, but that didn't stop him from being jealous of the attention the cockatoo got.

Unfortunately, the sound was coming from his pocket, so Malik set aside the little bowl and wiped his hands on the damp cloth he had brought with him.

"Ah, good, you are awake," the man on the other end said when Malik answered. "Wasn't sure if it was too early for you."

"Early for me is very early for you," Malik responded.

"Or very late," the man countered. "Which it is. I've had a busy day."

Malik waited for him to elaborate.

"... Right. Okay, I took the photo around to a few more places, especially shops that have been in business for a long time. Old family places, you know. Found a pawnshop owned by a ratty little Jew."

Malik sighed. He didn't care who owned the shop. He just wanted the man to get to the point. "And..."

"And, well. He wasn't very cooperative. At first he was super friendly, when he thought I was about to drop a load of cash, but when I showed him the picture, he denied recognizing her.

Then this super old dude came out, wanted to know what was happening. The first guy showed the old dude the photo. The old dude went nuts. Ranting about treasure hunters knocking on his door for forty years, and for forty years, he's had to chase them away. Kicked us out of the shop, real rude like."

Malik rubbed his face. "So what you're saying is that you have nothing."

"Well, not nothin'. The old guy wasn't having it, but I think the first guy might know what's up. So we're going to keep an eye on the place, maybe go back."

"Leave it."

"What? This is a real lead."

"No, the lead is the airfield. Him recognizing the previous owner only confirms it. You said the hangars were full of boxes. Go back and find what we need." He ended the call and looked up at the cockatoo.

The bird stretched out her neck and gave a piercing call.

"My thoughts exactly," Malik said, heading inside. He had things to take care of.

Hawk pulled the truck to the curb and leaned forward over the steering wheel. The pawnshop was three buildings down, across the street. The sign that stretched the length of the storefront was smashed, reading "Caplan's -awn Shop." The windows were dirty and barred, and dried leaves sat piled in the corner of the sidewalk and building despite the summer warmth.

"Drive around again," Colt said beside him.

He sighed and leaned back. "We've driven by twice already. People are going to call the cops. Colt, I know how hard this is for you, but isn't it better to know than not?"

She glared at him. "I was only trying to gain as much intel as possible. Don't want to go in blindly."

Hawk turned the engine off. "Come on. No more stalling."

Reaching into the back seat, he grabbed his messenger bag. Colt would have thrown a fit if she knew what was inside. He hadn't told her for the same reason he was pushing her to talk to Caplan. If she continued in this downward spiral, he was scared he was going to lose his friend. This person she'd been the past few days was so different from anything he'd seen from her before. It wasn't something he was willing to watch grow worse.

He joined her as they crossed the street and approached the shop, the hot summer air amplified by the black pavement. Even up close, the window displays were hard to make out through the grungy glass. A bell tingled over the door as they entered.

Despite the early hour, the inside of the shop was already sweltering. An air conditioner mounted on the wall was rattling away, but it made little difference to the temperature. Hawk's eyes took a moment to adjust to the gloom after the bright sun outside.

Shelves lined the walls, and the middle held a long display case, all filled with items. He noted the tiny paper tags tied to each with a black thread. A glass counter stretched the length of the back wall, save for a section that opened in front of a door that led to a back room.

Behind the counter stood an old man, hunched over, a brown cardigan over his thin shoulders. Wisps of white hair were combed in straight lines over his head.

"Welcome to Caplan's," he said in a surprisingly strong voice.

"Are you the owner?" Colt asked.

"I am Jethro Caplan," he confirmed. "What can I help you with?"

Colt walked up and placed the pawn ticket on the counter, smoothing out the wrinkles. The man reached for it with liver-spotted hands.

"I'd like to redeem this ticket," Colt said.

"Of course, my dear," Jethro said. He patted his head, then his pocket. "This is an old ticket though, so no guarantee we still have the item."

"Well, maybe you can tell me what it was for, at least."

Hawk joined them, leaning his hip against the counter, his bag making a dull thunk as it hit the glass.

Jethro found what he was looking for by the cash register and slipped a pair of frameless spectacles on his nose. "I'll do my best. Now, where were we? Oh, yes." Lifting the paper to the end of his nose, he muttered as he read the ticket. He stiffened, then set the paper down with care. "No. I can tell you nothing about this."

Colt went rigid, and Hawk silently willed her to stand down. Brute force wasn't going to convince the man to share what he knew.

"Can't you check your records? It's from your shop — surely you know something about it."

"No. It is too old."

Hawk cleared his throat, earning him a glare from her. He nodded his head at the man encouragingly. *Come on, Colt. Tell him.* She said nothing.

"Please, sir," Hawk asked, using his best "respect your elders" voice. "It's important."

Jethro sighed, then picked up the ticket again. His shoulders were rigid, and he narrowed his eyes at them through his thick lenses. "Wait here," he said curtly. Clutching the ticket, he shuffled to the back room, closing the door securely behind him. Hawk could hear him muttering, but the words were muffled by the clattering of the air conditioner.

He was gone for a long time. Hawk studied the collection of assorted coins under the glass counter while Colt paced like a caged panther. At last, the door creaked open, and Jethro limped through, carrying a paper bag by the handles. He set it on the counter and pushed it toward Hawk. "Here we are. It was brought in around 1995. Seemed sentimental, so I kept it. Thought the person would come back for it." He didn't make eye contact as he spoke.

Hawk peered down into the bag. Inside was a wooden jewelry box with a painted glass insert, covered in dust. "That's it?" he asked.

"Yes." Jethro folded his hands on the counter and raised his chin.

Colt joined them and took a look in the bag. She shook her head. "No —"

"I want you out of my shop," Jethro declared before she could say anything more. "Now."

Colt took the bag from Hawk as soon as they got in the truck. There was no way the jewelry box belonged to Katya, but she might as well check it out. Lifting it out, she was surprised at how heavy it was. She tossed the bag in the back seat and set the box on the dash. Her fingers left smears in the dust on the dark wood. A stained glass insert in the shape of a heart displayed simple pink and purple flowers. Six inches long and four deep, the box had two small drawers on top and one larger on bottom. Colt pulled the tiny handle on the top left drawer, but it wouldn't budge. Same with the right.

"It's jammed," she said. Maybe that's why the guy had given it to them. He knew they couldn't open it.

Hawk started the engine to get the air conditioning running, then reached over and lifted the top of the box, revealing the contents. "My sisters had similar ones," he explained.

Colt gave him a skeptical look but didn't comment. She turned back to the box and started sifting through the contents. A smell drifted up as she stirred the cheap jewelry. It wasn't lilacs. It was different, cloying. The pieces gave her the same feeling. They were chintzy. Oversized rings, once bright and shiny, now dull and black, their glass stones fogged over with neglect. An owl broach fell out, its ruby eyes glaring eerily. Colt picked it up and laid it on a stack of old coins in one corner.

She pulled open the bottom drawer, and more of the sickly sweet smell filled the truck. A tiny glass vial lay on top, the letters YSL stamped into the cap. Colt held it up to the light. The vial was empty except for a coating of brown on the inside.

"The perfume must have spilled," Hawk said. She handed him the bottle, and he tucked it into the cupholder on his door that held a variety of small, useful things.

Colt stirred the tangle of pearls, beads, and plastic earrings. "Katya wouldn't have worn anything like this, and none of it has any value. The pawn ticket might have had her name on it, but this isn't what we were looking for." She closed the box and shoved it onto the back seat.

She slouched in her seat as Hawk put the truck in gear and pulled away from the curb. Another dead end. Had the old man lied to them, or had Katya really pawned a box of costume jewelry?

Hawk slowed, turning onto the highway in the opposite direction of the airfield. She shot him a questioning look.

"We promised Mackenzie we'd visit this week. Now seems like as good a time as any," he explained.

Colt gave a quick nod. She wasn't eager to return to the airfield just yet. The amount of work was overwhelming, not least because of the emotional toll the unsettling discoveries were starting to take. Catching up with Mackenzie would be a nice reprieve. She found herself looking forward to the visit as they drove past fields of flourishing crops.

Colt did her best to shove the mystery aside as they pulled into the parking lot of the care home where Mackenzie and Amanda were staying. After being held captive together, Colt felt responsible for the younger women. They deserved her full attention.

Willow Grove Retreat was nothing like the government-funded facility where Hawk and Mitch had recovered from their own battles. A 250-year-old brick mansion adorned the top of the sloping lawns. Expansive grounds held two ponds ringed by willows, shady trails, and rambling gardens. Amanda's dad was a wealthy businessman and politician and had paid for both girls to stay here.

Mackenzie and Amanda were sitting in the shady gazebo, their bare feet stretched out into a sunbeam, blond head and red together as they pored over a shared book. Both wore light sundresses, but Amanda had a blue cardigan over her thin shoulders.

As soon as Hawk's shadow blocked out the sun on their legs, Mackenzie jumped up to give him a hug. Colt stood back, hands in the back pocket of her jeans. Mackenzie gave her a quick smile, then settled back on the bench beside Amanda, who gave them a small wave. Recently, Amanda had started being more outgoing, but the news of Mark's release had made the shell reappear. Colt leaned against one of the pillars, keeping an eye on the area around them. Other small groups of people were scattered around the grounds, but the closest was a pair of boys playing by the pond with a dog.

Hawk took a seat in the shade near Amanda. He set the jewelry box on the bench and nudged it toward the girl but kept his focus on Mackenzie. When he had suggested they give the box to Mackenzie, Colt had quickly agreed. Mackenzie loved making earrings and necklaces, and the pieces in the box would provide her with gems she could incorporate into new designs.

"What book are you reading?" Hawk asked. Mackenzie picked it up to show him the cover. It was a collection of illustrated fairy tales.

"We found it in the library," Mackenzie said, flipping to one of the pages to show him a color plate. "Amanda is practicing her drawing by copying the pictures."

Colt noted for the first time the small sketchbook that Amanda had tucked half under her skirt. Shifting positions against the pole, Colt changed her focus from outside of the gazebo to inside. Her fears about Mackenzie withdrawing again were unfounded. The girl was animated and open, chatting with Hawk easily. Even Amanda was better than she had expected. Although the woman had yet to say anything, she wasn't cowering from her visitors, and she had no reaction to the gentle giant sitting near her.

Colt wanted to ask how they felt about Mark being released, but she wasn't sure if that was a taboo topic. If it were up to her, she'd take the two girls to a firing range, tape a picture of Mark's face over the target, and let them blast the image to smithereens. But any facility burdened with the name Willow Grove Retreat probably wouldn't sanction that sort of therapy.

"What's your favorite fairy tale, Colt?" Mackenzie asked suddenly.

"Mine?" Colt replied stupidly. She wasn't sure she'd ever read one.

Mackenzie giggled, holding up the book. "Yes. Amanda wants to draw you a picture."

Colt hadn't seen any sort of communication between the two, so she assumed it had taken place before their arrival. Stalling for time while she thought of an answer, Colt yawned. "Uh...the Ugly Duckling?"

"Oh, good! We've not done that one yet!" Mackenzie flipped through the pages, then looked back to Colt. "You're tired. Why don't you lay down in the hammock, and Hawk can read to us?"

Colt turned toward the netting that was strung across the other side of the gazebo, hiding a smile at Mackenzie's sudden mothering. Tactically, the hammock was a terrible decision. Getting out would put her at a severe disadvantage in a fight. She shook off the thought. The property was secluded, and nothing evil lurked in the trees. The midday sun was warm, the breeze pleasant, and Hawk was there to keep watch. Maybe a nap would be a good idea. She climbed into the hammock, stretching out at an angle to keep it from swallowing her completely.

Hawk held the book so that Amanda could see the pictures as he read. The young woman pulled the notebook from under her skirt and carefully turned through the pages until she found a blank one. Considering the pencils in the slim pouch, Amanda selected one and started drawing loose lines on the page. Beside her, Mackenzie tucked her legs up under her cross-legged and pulled the jewelry box onto her lap. She pulled a broach out, watching stones catch the light as she turned it. Mackenzie showed it to Amanda, then laid it on the bench.

Tucking one arm behind her head, Colt let her eyes drift half-closed and listened as Hawk started reading to the girls.

"It was so beautiful in the country," Hawk read the opening of the story. "It was the summertime. The wheat fields were golden, the oats were green, and the hay stood in great stacks in the green meadows..."

His rich baritone blended with the buzzing of the bees in the flowers ringing the gazebo. The muggy heat made her drowsy, and Colt dozed off.

She was awoken a short time later by the whistled notes of a familiar song. She waved her hand, too comfortable to make her mouth move.

Something plonked onto her chest. A penny. "Wake up," Hawk said. Giggles followed.

With an exaggerated groan, Colt swung her legs over the side of the hammock and sat up. She must have been asleep longer than she thought. Hawk had finished reading, and the book was now propped up by Amanda, her sketchbook lying beside it on the bench. Mackenzie had finished sorting the items from the jewelry box and was playing with a gold necklace that had several flowers made out of gemstones.

Colt raised an eyebrow at Hawk, wondering what was up. He grinned in reply, then flicked another coin at her. She snatched it out of the air before it could hit her in the face. The coin was similar to a quarter in size and color. "50 FORINT" was stamped on it above the mintmark. She flipped it over. The second side showed a bird of prey perched on a tree stump. The letters "MAGYAR

KÖZTÁRSASÁG" ringed the outer edge, along with the year 2001 on the bottom.

"Hungarian?" she asked, looking up at Hawk.

He shrugged but couldn't hide the smile tugging the side of his mouth. "What year did Caplan say the jewelry box was pawned?"

"1995."

His grin matched hers. "Precisely."

Colt snapped her fist closed. "He lied."

Colt fumed. She drove this time, giving Hawk a chance to rest his leg. After a week of heavy work around the airfield, she was sure she'd noticed him limping on the old injury — at least, that's what she said to convince him to toss her the keys. In reality, she was too impatient. Even though her efforts to push the speed limit would only shave a few minutes off their time, this way she at least felt as though she were doing something. She couldn't believe she'd let the old man lie to her like that. She should have trusted her instincts.

Hawk stretched out beside her, walking the coin through his fingers. "It was Amanda's idea to give me the coin," he said, breaking the silence.

"Really?" Colt pulled her thoughts away from the talking-to she was giving Caplan in her mind.

"Mm-hmm. She thought the bird was a hawk."

"That's good, right?" Colt asked. She should have paid more attention to Amanda.

"Very good. She didn't talk to me but did whisper occasionally to Mac."

Colt shifted her grip on the steering wheel. "So she's doing okay?"

"She is. Willow Grove is a safe place, but I don't think she needs it like she did last year."

Colt drew in a long, slow breath. Even if the facility was secure, she shouldn't have fallen asleep. She'd promised to look out for the younger women.

"Stop that," Hawk ordered.

She let it out in a hurry. "Stop what?"

"You needed the nap. You've been strung out ever since we moved to the airfield. It's okay to relax sometimes."

Colt gave her head a quick shake. She wasn't disagreeing with him; she was trying to dislodge the invasive thoughts before they could get a foothold.

Concentrating on the road for the next few minutes, Colt cleared her mind as she passed car after car. Acknowledging each thought, then tossing them one by one in the rearview mirror.

Caplan wouldn't be easily convinced to tell the truth. Not now that he'd already thrown them out once. The answer was easy, but

Colt went around in circles, refusing to admit that it was the best option. She pulled to a stop across the street, staring at the barred windows and broken sign as her mind churned.

"You got the coin?" she asked Hawk.

He handed it over before climbing out. She waited for him by the hood while he dug his messenger bag out of the back. The heat from the engine made ripples in the air. She narrowed her eyes at the worn leather flap, wondering what was inside. Twice he'd brought it along to the shop, but he'd left it in the truck at Willow Grove.

The coin gripped tight in her fist, Colt led the way inside the shop, her boots sticky on the sun-softened blacktop. This time she marched straight to the back counter before the bell even finished ringing. Jethro Caplan appeared in the doorway, a frown instantly forming on his face.

"I told you to get out."

Colt leaned against the counter, flipping the coin in the air and catching it. "I know. We came back." She caught the coin and slapped it on the counter. "You lied to us."

Jethro peered at the coin but didn't pick it up. "What do you want?"

"The real item for that pawn ticket."

The old man drew himself to his full height with the air of one who'd faced a thousand bullies and not backed down. "Why? It's not yours."

Colt sucked in a breath and looked at Hawk. He jerked his chin toward Caplan. Of course he'd think that was the best route. She turned back to Caplan. "It belonged to my grandmother."

Jethro paused. "You're Katya's granddaughter?"

15

Colt accepted the teacup and saucer from Jethro, his shaky hands spilling some of the hot liquid onto the delicate china. She took a sip, noting the bitter taste but not the burning sensation on her tongue. Hawk glared at her, shaking his head. Lowering the cup, she kicked herself for forgetting to watch his reaction. He could tell if the tea was too hot to drink; she couldn't. Although based on the sweat forming on his forehead, she wasn't sure if it was the tea he found too hot or the room in general.

The apartment was a restful break from the clutter of the pawnshop downstairs. Even though the furniture and decor were dated, everything was tastefully arranged. Two glass-doored cabinets stuffed with books flanked a fireplace on one wall. Above the mantel hung a beautiful oil painting of a peaceful lake scene. Hawk was sitting opposite her on a sofa that matched the chair she was sitting in. Two other chairs completed the seating around a circular statement table. A third wall held more paintings, mounted above an elegant secretary-style desk. In the corner sat a monumental grandfather clock carved with intricate details.

Jethro returned, carrying a plate of Fig Newtons that he set on the table. He took his time settling into his armchair. "What would you like to know?"

Everything, Colt thought. I want to know everything about this woman who lied and stole and was so horrible.

"Why don't you start off by telling us about the store?" Hawk suggested.

Jethro nodded, a smile of pride filling his face.

"I was just a boy when my father was killed in the war. My mother took over the running of the shop until I was old enough to help out. After the war...many people brought their family heirlooms here. They wanted to buy new and exciting things. And other people...my people...came here looking for the heirlooms they had to leave behind in Germany." He paused to sip his tea.

"Katya was neither. She would come in with a piece that needed a home. She would never say where she got the pieces from but insisted I be discreet when finding buyers. A few times, she turned down offers I had for her for lower prices. Never wanted to draw attention to the piece or herself."

Colt put the tea down on the table beside her, setting her emotions aside with it. A clear head would make this go faster. She could deal with the fallout later. "Did she ever say where the pieces came from?"

He shook his head. "No, never. She would come in with it carefully wrapped up and say in that low voice of hers, 'Jethro, I have a surprise for you.' And we would bring it up here and unwrap it. And she was always right. It was always a surprise." His voice grew soft as he remembered.

"Why you? Why here?" Colt asked.

"My family is Jewish," he explained simply.

She cocked her head. "Why did that matter?"

"The Jews who fled Germany were not allowed to bring items of value or any amount of money with them. My mother welcomed them into our home and helped them find their feet again. I think Katya knew that and wanted to help in some way. And I think she was also lonely for her people."

Colt frowned. "What are you saying?"

Jethro gave her a benevolent smile. "Katya's family — your family — was Jewish, my dear."

Colt tucked that away to consider later. She was too busy trying to reconcile this man's pleasant memories of her grandmother with the knowledge of the woman's actions.

"Didn't it bother you that she never told you where she got the items?"

He shrugged. "Is it not better for them to be in the hands of people who would appreciate them than in the hands of the Nazis?" He spat the last word.

"But you don't know that's where they were from." She kept her voice flat, locking away the anger that wanted to pour out.

"How many pieces did you handle over the years?" Hawk asked, not giving Jethro a chance to reply to the accusation.

He wiggled his hand in the air. "Maybe a hundred or so?"

"That's all?" The way Hawk posed the question had Colt looking at him carefully. What was he getting at?

Jethro cleared his throat. "That's all she brought to me. But I believe she had other brokers, people she went to instead of me. She was careful. So careful."

"Can you show us which ones she brought to you?" Hawk reached into the bag he'd brought with him, pulling out Katya's ledger.

Colt's fist tightened on the chair beside her. Hawk had no right to bring that ledger. To even have taken it out of the office. It was too late to argue though, so she clenched her jaw and watched as Hawk passed the ledger to Jethro.

"It looks as though she had estimates for the items' values and then final sales prices. We don't know what she was selling though. Or buying?" Hawk pointed out details and what they thought each meant, without mentioning the files or the girls.

Jethro pulled the ledger closer, hunching over it. His fingers traveled over the page, tapping on an entry every so often. "Yes,

yes," he muttered, more to himself than his audience. "Mm, perhaps that one. We will have to see."

He continued like that for a few minutes before passing the ledger back to Hawk and pushing himself unsteadily to his feet. He waved off Hawk's offer of assistance and shuffled over to the grandfather clock in the corner. Reaching up behind a carved swirl, he pulled out a little gold key. After opening the glass in front of the clock face, he wound the time back until the two hands pointed at the twelve. He then took the key and fumbled at the side of the massive clock. With a click, a panel opened. Jethro stood, clutching something to his chest. Limping over to the table, he set the long, thin volume down.

"I have a ledger of my own," he declared proudly.

Colt joined him, taking their ledger from Hawk. If this man had information on just what Katya had been doing, she wanted to see it firsthand. Right now, she was still having trouble reconciling all the evidence before her.

Jethro flipped to the first page in his ledger, reading down the row until he found what he was looking for. "Aha. 1962. What do you have for that year?"

Colt found the corresponding year in Katya's. The first two entries. "One for eight hundred dollars and one for three thousand dollars."

Jethro gave a delighted laugh. "Yes, yes. Here. It was a vase. I remember it. One-thousand-dollar sale and eight hundred dollars to Katya."

"Twenty percent is a hefty cut," Hawk commented, helping himself to a Fig Newton.

Jethro shrugged. "Maybe, maybe not. Katya never disputed it. And I would say I earned it, providing her a way to sell the items without the buyers knowing her identity."

"What's next?" Colt nudged him back to the ledgers.

"1965."

"Seven thousand," Colt read off.

"Yes, yes! That was a Monet."

"Cheap for a Monet, no?" Hawk interjected.

"Ah, but we could not prove for sure that it was a Monet." Jethro tapped his nose and winked. "Of course, we knew it was, but that was how these things worked."

Colt reached over and pulled the pen Hawk carried in the front pocket of his shirt. She made a tiny mark next to the two entries Jethro had identified so far. They continued working through the ledgers, cross-referencing the dates and prices. There were a few maybes, and Jethro couldn't always remember what the piece was, but in all, Colt figured they had crossed off fifteen percent of Katya's records. She wanted to ask him about the other entries in his own ledger but guessed that Katya wouldn't have been his first or only client. There would have been a reason she came to him, and that would have been the recommendation of someone she trusted.

"These ones without second prices — she didn't sell those?" Colt showed him what she meant.

Jethro peered down his nose at them. "We couldn't always find buyers. Not without drawing greater attention, you understand. I was willing to take them off her hands and sell them at a later date, but she said it was too risky. The only piece she let me buy was that one." He nodded to the painting over the fireplace.

"Who's it by?" Hawk asked.

"I have no idea." Jethro chuckled. "It could be worthless. But I find the serenity in the colors restful, and I value it more than some of my pieces with far higher price tags."

"Apparently Katya preferred the pricier stuff," Colt muttered.

"My dear girl," he said, cupping Colt's cheek in his hand. She willed herself not to flinch from the touch of this kind old man. "You look so much like her. I may not know how Katya came to own these, but just because they were in her possession does not make her a thief. Many had already been stolen from their rightful owners by the Nazis. As for the others..." He shrugged. "It's far too late now to wonder about that."

"If that's the case, why was she so secretive about them?"

He sighed. "She was secretive about so much in her life. She did not want the attention. I never told anyone where I found any of the more...select pieces I sold. And most of my buyers were also reluctant to ask."

Colt nodded. Fear had lingered in the refugee community years after the end of World War II.

Hawk cleared his throat. "We should go. We've taken up enough of your day, Mr. Caplan."

"Thank you for letting this old man wander the paths of memory lane," Jethro replied. As they headed out the door, he stopped Colt with a hand on her arm. "Did you happen to find anything? Any of the pieces she didn't sell, I mean?"

Colt studied him before answering. "No. Why?"

He shrugged with a small smile. "There was a piece...something special. She mentioned it a few times, wanting to know if I could handle something much more...unique than the other pieces. I assured her I could. Offered to put feelers out to line up a buyer outside my usual clientele. She kept saying, 'Maybe next time.' But she was too nervous to bring it over for my evaluation. And in the end, she just stopped coming."

"No, we haven't found anything like that," Colt said.

"Ah, well. It would have been nice to see such a piece once in my lifetime."

Malik poured the last of the Balvenie into the glass. He took a sip, letting the liquid slide down his throat.

That *fool* of a doctor.

He knocked back the rest of the whisky. The new doctor he had hired insisted on talking to his mother's former care provider. And of course the fool had shared his pessimistic viewpoint. Now the new doctor was offering the same prognosis. Malik refused to believe it. His mother was not dying.

With a furious motion, he threw the glass across the room. It smashed against the mahogany panel, shattering. Malik paced the office, avoiding the damp patch of carpet by the wall. There had to be something he could do. Accepting the doctor's words wasn't an option.

Turning on his computer, he navigated to a browser on his desktop. It wasn't his usual one. In fact, he'd only used it a few times in the past. He entered a series of passwords until he reached the page he wanted. After a few minutes, he decided on what to say.

"Rare artifact recovery in Pennsylvania. Required immediately. Self-driven individuals only need apply."

In the payment box, he entered "$2,000,000."

After carefully signing out of all the pages, he texted his man. "I'm coming to the States. Enough of this fooling around. I can't wait any longer."

Before leaving town, Hawk swung through the drive-through of a fast-food joint. He ordered two ultimate burgers for himself and Colt's favorite spicy chicken burger and a couple drinks. She said nothing as they pulled out onto the highway. Only at his urging did she open the bag of food and share out the burgers.

"Cheer up, Colt," he finally said. "At least we know now that she wasn't a thief."

She dropped her half-eaten burger back onto the paper. "No, but she was definitely a smuggler. And it still doesn't explain the women. Where do they fit in?"

He sighed, not sure how to respond to the barrage. "You can't lose hope. Surely there's a good explanation for it."

"Stop being so optimistic. Not everything has a silver lining. Sometimes life just sucks."

"Colt —"

"No. Enough. I'm done talking about this. When we get home, I'm going to seal off the tunnels again. It's time we get back on track with fixing up the airfield and planes. That's what we should be worried about."

Hawk opened his mouth to respond, then shut it again. He locked his jaw and took a deep breath. His friend was hurting, and pushing the issue wasn't going to heal her aching heart. He couldn't imagine finding out the one family member you idolized wasn't who you thought they were. His own family was the quintessential American picture. Mom, Dad, five younger sisters. Home-cooked meals and church on Sunday.

They drove in silence for a while. Hawk considered turning the radio on just to break up the heaviness in the air. He couldn't think of a station that would fit the mood, so he left it off. He finished his lunch, dismissing conversation starters as soon as they came to mind. There was a fine line between letting Colt sort through her thoughts on her own and letting her stew too long. He wasn't sure where they were after meeting with Jethro.

A buzzing filled the air. Hawk glanced at his phone on the console. The screen remained blank. The buzzing continued.

"Are you going to get that?" he asked.

Colt gave him a dirty look before pulling her phone out. Her finger hovered over the red button a moment before accepting the call.

"What?" She switched to speaker and dropped the phone on the armrest.

"Hey," Glitch's rumbly voice filled the cab. "Found something interesting." The whirring of a high-speed fan filled the background.

"About Ben?" Colt replied. Finally some good news. She could put the airfield nonsense behind her and focus on her missing brother.

"Uh, no. Sorry. About the necklace business." The rapid clicking of a keyboard told her he continued to type as he spoke.

"Ah. Right." Colt tamped down her disappointment. Hawk's look of curiosity was the only thing keeping her from ending the call.

"I did some digging. The guy who bought the necklace is known as 'The Collector,' and —"

"The Collector?" Colt snorted. "Like some sort of James Bond supervillain?"

Glitch laughed. "Sadly, no. He's super private, and no one's been able to figure out his identity, so they use the code name."

"But?" She sensed Glitch had more.

"But…" Glitch couldn't hide the triumph in his voice. "I figured it out. Or at least partially figured it out. He's a Kuwaiti business-man. Ruthless in pursuing deals he wants. Outbidding the others and driving up prices because he's determined not to lose."

Colt sipped her drink, wondering where this was going.

"He doesn't seem the type to give up. If he wants the Fabergé Egg — and it would appear that he does — he's going to stop at nothing to get it." His words were punctuated by mouse clicks.

"But I don't *have* an Egg." She banged the console beside her with her fist. "There's nothing here."

"I don't think that matters anymore. He thinks you have it, and he's not going to stop."

That sounded a bit dark. "Wait — what?" Hawk interjected.

Glitch paused his rapid typing. "He's posted a very generous ransom to anyone who brings it to him. He's not shared your address yet, but that won't take long for them to find."

"What are you saying?" Hawk asked because Colt wasn't about to.

"If there's any chance of there being anything worth finding on that property, I'd find it soon. And maybe put the local police on speed dial."

Colt shook herself as Hawk pulled into their driveway. Glitch's words might be dire, but she didn't believe them. Time to stop moping about, stop chasing ghost stories. She jumped out to lower the chain and put it back in place once Hawk drove through. She climbed back in.

"Let's head to the hangars, see what Mitch has on the go. We need to see where we are with the planes."

"You don't think we should do anything about what Glitch said?" Hawk asked.

"No. We know there's nothing here. Anyone comes, we can show them the empty tunnels. With any luck, they'll get lost down there and won't bother us." Now that was a pleasing thought. "We've got work to do."

"You still want to reopen the flight school?" he asked.

"Makes the most sense, if we can get the insurance. At the very least, I know I've got one student."

"Oh yeah, who?"

"You, idiot. It's about time you stopped napping in the back while I do all the work."

"Yeah, and what will you be doing while I'm doing your job?"

She grinned. "Flying something else."

He laughed, and she settled into her seat, pleased the tension of the past few days had been set aside. She knew she'd have to deal with Glitch's intel at some point, but there was little she could do about other people's beliefs.

They parked between the two hangars. The main one was open, but no sign of Mitch beyond the Piper Cub on the tarmac. They headed for the second hangar and found him sitting on the floor, rifling through boxes of manuals. He'd taken to not putting his prosthetics on every day and not using the wheelchair as much. He used the golf cart to get from the house to the hangars. Colt was glad to see him becoming more comfortable with his new reality and just being himself.

He looked up, waving a piece of paper at them. "You're back finally. I found something. Take a look at this."

Colt took the page from him, the weight surprising her before she realized it was a much larger page, folded over. She spread it out on the hangar floor.

"It's another copy of the blueprints Kendra brought us," she said.

"Yes, but better," Mitch gloated. "See if you can figure out why."

She scanned the lines, matching them up to where she knew the rooms were located far beneath them.

"It's dated the same year," Hawk said. "But all marked up. It's hard to tell."

"There's another tunnel." Colt couldn't help being curious.

"Not just that," Mitch said. "It's hidden. Look. It starts behind one of the rooms you guys have already found. And there's no door."

"That could just be that no one bothered to mark it on the plans," Hawk argued.

"Did you see a door when you were down there?" Mitch demanded, and Hawk had to admit that he hadn't.

"What room is it?" Colt asked. She couldn't remember if she'd been that far down the second tunnel.

"The library!" Hawk blurted out.

"What?" She hadn't seen a library or anything that would have been close.

He nodded vigorously. "Yeah, it's just past the —"

Bang!

Colt was flung backward, tumbling into Hawk. Smoke filled the air, making her cough. Her ears were ringing, and she couldn't find her balance to get up. Huge bugs moved through the haze. She saw one lean down and bite Hawk.

"No, no," she moaned, pulling herself across the floor.

A glassy-eyed bug-man grabbed her. She felt his claw on her neck. Then everything went black.

16

Consciousness returned slowly. Colt blinked the crustiness out of her eyes and sat up. Mitch was slumped against the workbench, his hands strapped to the metal legs. Beside her, Hawk groaned as he fought against his bindings. She looked down. Her hands were pulled behind her, and her feet were tied together. Her mouth felt dry. Probably due to the gag wrapped around her head. Rubbing her face against her shoulder, she managed to pull the gag down. Hawk glared at her.

"What? I didn't tie you up." She rocked back, bringing her hands under herself. Rolling forward, she stood up, hands in front. She shuffled over to the bench and found a pair of pliers. With a few quick snips, the plastic ties around her wrists and ankles fell to the floor. She released Hawk next, and they moved to help Mitch together.

"Maybe we should leave the gag on for a bit?" Hawk suggested.

"Why?" She snipped the tie on his right hand. It dropped to the ground. "Oops."

Hawk held Mitch's other wrist as she cut the tie. "Because when he wakes up, he's not going to be happy."

"True." Together they laid him down. "But we can't have him choking."

Colt removed the gag as Mitch's eyes popped open. His mouth followed soon after, confirming Hawk's fears as he made his opinion of the men who did this very well known.

"Colt," Hawk interrupted, pointing.

She followed his gaze, noticing the hatch to the tunnels was propped open. "Mitch, shut up. Hawk, there's a shotgun under the bench."

"What? Why?" he demanded even as he hurried to get it.

Colt ignored him as she ran to the bunk room, returning moments later with her Beretta. "Give the shotgun to Mitch. Let's go."

"What do I get then?" Hawk asked.

"You're big enough, you don't need anything." She stuffed the Beretta down her waistband and grabbed a pair of gloves off the bench. "Mitch, shoot anyone who comes up that hatch." She glanced at Hawk. "See you down there."

"Colt, what are you..." Hawk called.

She left him muttering as she climbed down the first few rungs of the ladder. Taking a deep breath, she wrapped her hands around the side rails and stepped off, bracing one foot and then the other against the metal so she could slide down quickly. Adjusting the pressure on her hands, she was able to control her rate of descent. Once, her hand hit a mounting bracket, nearly throwing her off, but she caught herself and kept going. Above, she could hear Hawk clambering down.

As she neared the bottom, she slowed and descended normally, straining her ears for sounds of anyone in the tunnel. Silence. She dropped into the antechamber and pulled out her Beretta. Holding it ready, she crept to the door to the tunnel. She turned the handle slowly, wincing at the squeak. No shouts or running footsteps from the other side, so she pulled it open.

The lights were on, illuminating the empty passage. The doors to the second tunnel were also closed tight. Hearing Hawk getting near, she decided to go for it and yanked the door open.

Another empty hallway. She ran down it, footsteps echoing off the concrete walls.

"Fifth on the left," Hawk called behind her, just loudly enough for her to hear.

She counted doors, then slid to a stop. The door was open a few inches, and she held her gun ready. Hawk caught up and pressed himself against the wall on the other side. Colt pushed the door open, dropping low as Hawk swung around above her.

The room was trashed, books pulled off every shelf and thrown in piles. Colt was really getting annoyed at people coming in and making a mess of things.

Along the back wall, one of the bookcases was angled out into the room, revealing a dark space beyond it. Hawk flicked the light on, and both rooms lit up. Colt picked her way through the books, trying not to step on any. Peering in to ensure it was empty, her breath caught.

The inner room was long and narrow, more hall than room, and filled with shelving like the storeroom they had found in the main tunnel. There was no one there, but evidence of their work was clear. Colt tucked her gun away and stepped into the room, gazing around in wonder.

Paintings were stacked in rows, some wrapped in burlap, others with their gilt frames visible. Vases, sculptures, and other pieces of art were scattered around the shelves. Everything was coated in a thick layer of dust.

"Why didn't they take it?" she asked.

Hawk looked around. "They did. Some things, anyway. You can see the smudges in the dust."

Colt nodded. They were looking for something. All the spaces void of dust were small squares or rectangles. She walked up and down the rows. The shelves were far from full, but there was still enough to tell a story.

"Well, that's it, isn't it?" She shoved her hands in her pockets, looking over the room one more time.

"What is?"

"Definitive proof that Katya, my grandmother, was a thief, a smuggler, and a kidnapper."

She spun on her heel and marched back out to the hall, ignoring Hawk as he called her name. He followed her all the way through the tunnels, eventually falling silent.

Colt was quiet as they climbed the stairs to the tower and crossed the tarmac. With every step, the weight inside of her grew. It wasn't something she could articulate or push aside. She needed to confront Katya, to demand the truth. But that wasn't possible.

Mitch nodded from his position by the bench, shotgun at his side. She scanned the hangar to make sure he was okay, then veered off. The Piper Cub was sitting on the tarmac. The skies were calling to her, and she could no longer resist.

"Colt, wait! It's not ready yet," Mitch shouted.

She paused, trying to remember what he'd said wasn't working on it. No matter. She needed the release only flying could offer. She slammed the door and started the engine.

The headlights of the taxi struggled to cut through the downpour. The driver turned into the parking lot, splashing water over the windows. The taxi stopped by the front doors, and the driver shifted into park.

"You sure you want me to drop you here?" he asked dubiously, peering up at the storage facility.

Malik grunted his reply, not willing to let on he shared the feeling of unease.

The driver punched the buttons on the meter, and Malik tapped his card against the reader.

"I can wait for you. Might be hard to get another cab out here."

"That won't be necessary, thank you." Malik opened the car door and stepped out, ducking his head against the rain. His foot landed in a puddle, soaking his ankle. Slamming the car door, he hurried to the building's doors. The keypad was old, the screen impossible to read in the dark. Malik entered the code he'd been given. Rain poured down his collar as he waited for the doors to release.

Once inside, he brushed the water off himself as best he could. The lobby was empty but brightly lit, a damp musk permeating despite the "Climate Controlled" signs everywhere. He took the elevator to the third floor. Two halls opened on opposite sides, and he chose the one to the left, following it as it made a sharp right angle. He was immediately enclosed in a long, narrow hall with blue roller doors on either side. The smell of mothballs followed him. His footsteps echoed in the silence, and he wondered if he had gotten the time wrong.

Ahead, he noticed one of the roller doors was opened. As he drew near, a man stepped out into the hall to greet him. Pushing fifty, with a fit body going soft, he wore a plaid shirt open over a T-shirt and a ball cap pulled low on his head. His trimmed beard was in contrast to the hair that hung over his collar.

"Mike," he said, holding out his hand. "Glad you could make it."

Malik shook hands, flinching at being reminded once again of the familiarity with which Americans treated everyone.

"I went in with a team of three. Surprised them all. And as I mentioned on the phone, they had a map of the tunnel system. Which came in very handy, as you'll see." He grinned. "Come in and see what we've found." The American gestured toward the open roller door.

Malik followed him into the ten-by-ten storage locker. Folding tables were set up, displaying a variety of expensive items. Malik eyed them greedily, his gaze tripping from one to the next, searching for anything the right size, shape, or color. When nothing stood out, he looked more carefully. Using a handkerchief, he opened a couple of jewelry boxes, peered into vases, and checked velvet cases.

The Egg wasn't there.

He swallowed and folded the handkerchief carefully, giving himself time to control his anger.

"Impressive, huh?" The American smirked. "And there's more if we want to go back for it."

"No, it's not. In fact, it's quite disappointing."

The American uncrossed his arms and took a step closer to Malik. "What did you just say?"

"I sent you in to find an Egg." He waved a hand at the tables. "Nothing here is even remotely close to egg-shaped, something even a schoolboy could identify."

"This stuff is worth a lot of money." A vein bulged on the side of the man's head.

"This is pennies in comparison to what I asked you to find for me." Malik took a deep breath, trying to keep his rage at bay. He turned and strode down the hall. He'd had enough of the stench of this place.

"What do you want me to do with this stuff then?"

"Keep it. If you find me the Egg, it's yours. If you fail again, I'll tell the authorities where to find you."

Colt went through the takeoff procedures by rote, her hands and eyes moving across the instrument panel of their own accord. She made adjustments without thinking. The familiar motions helped ground her, but it was as though she were watching it through someone else's eyes. The little plane hopped over the rugged tarmac, bouncing as it picked up speed. She pulled back on the stick, lifting off the ground and over the trees.

Circling away from the major cities to the southeast, she leveled out at ten thousand feet, heading north. She listened to the engine for a few minutes, keeping a close eye on the instruments. There was a slight rumble, but it smoothed out as the engine warmed up. She hadn't given it time to do so on the ground like she should have. She didn't want to admit that waiting would have given Hawk time to argue her out of it. Or come with her.

She was glad he wasn't there. As much as she appreciated his perspective, she needed time alone to think. Below her, the mountains rolled away in never-ending cascades of green, vermilion, emerald, and black. Updrafts pushed the little plane, and she had to concentrate to keep it level, yet the quietness of being aloft settled into her.

For the first time since moving to the airfield, she let herself face her emotions and was surprised to find that the overwhelming one was disappointment. Even before they knew anything about treasures or tunnels or smuggling, something had been lacking. She took her time examining that. After a while, she decided it was okay. When she was small, the airfield had been a safe haven, away from the confusion and hurt of the outside world. As a teenager, it was her proving ground, where she found herself and who she wanted to be. And through it all, her grandmother had been there, comforting her, guiding her in that soft Russian accent.

When the enemy thinks they've got you, cut the engine, and scream to your death.

It was an odd thing for the dainty woman to say, but it was all about subtlety and sleight of hand. It was also about knowing when to make a clean break.

Colt sighed as she changed her trajectory. To the west, a bank of clouds built and thickened. The airfield felt different because Katya wasn't there. And never would be again. It was time Colt stopped looking for her and stepped into her new life.

But that only solved one of her problems. The woman Colt had known growing up was the last person anyone would suspect of being a thief, a smuggler. A trafficker. Maybe that was the point. Winds buffeted the Cub, and Colt banked to find a smoother pocket of air.

There was no denying that Katya had items of great value. And according to Caplan and his ledger, she had sold many of them for a great deal of money. So where was the money? Sure, the airfield and the tunnels would have taken a lot to maintain. But not the millions she'd tallied up from the amounts in Katya's ledger.

Colt thought back to her childhood. While she didn't remember feeling poor, there hadn't always been money for extras. The tiny apartment she'd shared with her grandmother during high school hadn't been lavish. And Frank certainly hadn't spent that kind of money around the airfield. It was always in a state of near disrepair.

A flash of light filled the cockpit. Colt looked out the side window to find the bank of clouds had grown into a storm. She sighed. The tiny plane wasn't an ideal place to be amidst lightning.

As she pulled the plane around to head home, Colt made a decision. No more hiding from the truth in front of her. She would clear out the tunnels and do her best to return the artwork to its rightful owners. And then she would track down the women and help them get home too.

The storm chased her all the way home, winds buffeting the little plane, making the loose window rattle. She landed a bit too far to the left but quickly pulled it back and applied the brakes. The rain started as she taxied to the main hangar.

Mitch was waiting for her inside, shotgun leaning against the workbench beside him. "Getting a bit dark," he said cautiously.

Colt gave him a direct look, and they shared a nod. "Storm came up faster than expected. She did good though, and the window held."

"Thank the bayou for that. Would have been a noisy ride otherwise." He checked the shotgun, then tucked it away behind the bench.

Together they put the Piper Cub to bed. Mitch headed for his golf cart, parked just inside out of the rain. "You coming?"

She shook her head. "I've got some reading to do."

"Sounds good. I'm going to go catch the tail end of the ballgame. The Braves are playing the Yankees tonight." He levered a two-by-four against the pedal to get it going.

Colt waved as he drove off, then lowered the hangar door. Darting through the rain, she ran to the second hangar. She ducked into the bunk room for a bottle of water and a snack and tossed them into a small bag that she slung over her shoulder. Then she opened the hatch in the floor and climbed down the long ladder for the second time that day, albeit at a much slower pace than last time. Munching on an apple, she headed for Katya's office. Now that she knew the items in the ledger were pieces of art and not the women in the files, she wanted to find a list of the artwork Katya had handled over the years.

The door was unlocked, and she expected it to be in the same state of disorder she'd left it in. Instead, it was tidy, with floors swept and surfaces dusted. Even the overhead light seemed brighter. Hawk. She smiled. Of course he'd come back and cleaned things for her. It wasn't that she was a dirty person; she just didn't see the dust the way he did. And her cleaning habits were more aligned with "do everything once a week" while his were "clean it all now!" He was a good friend, and she should remind him that she knew that. She'd get him ice cream the next time she was out. That weird fluorescent blue and pink kind he loved.

She settled behind the desk, the chair squeaking loudly. Reaching into the top drawer for the journal, she was surprised to see the ledger had been returned. Hawk must have brought it down while she was gone. Flipping open to the first item Caplan had told them about, she decided to start there. The broker had said it was a vase, sold for one thousand dollars. The initials next to it were RD. Colt went over to the filing cabinet, digging through to find a girl with a name that matched. Reveka Dyedishev. Colt lifted it out, bringing it back to the desk to study. Maybe there was something in the notes to explain why Reveka had a valuable vase.

A soft knock on the door made her look up. Hawk pushed the door open, wearing a soft smile.

"Hey."

"Hey yourself."

"You busy?"

She motioned to the files in front of her. "Trying to piece together the connection between the girls and the art."

"I think I have something that can help with that. Come with me."

She followed, wondering at the odd look of excitement in his eyes. He led her down the hall to the library. She stopped in the doorway, impressed by the transformation. All the books had been returned to the shelves. Many were stacked sideways or facing the wrong way, but the floor was clear. Two wingback chairs with a small table that she hadn't noticed before sat at one end.

Hawk beckoned her to the far corner. The shelves here were all filled with leather-bound books. "There are a lot of books in here, many old and worth a lot. But I think these are the most valuable."

She looked at him, wanting confirmation of what she suspected. He nodded, motioning for her to take one. Carefully, she lifted one of the books down off the shelf. Undid the small metal clasp. The leather creaked as it fell open to a page with a lilac branch pressed and dried. The scent filled the air, mingled with oil and leather. Colt jerked her head back, swallowing hard.

Hawk squeezed her shoulder. "I can't read them, but I think I got them sorted by date."

She nodded, unable to speak. Did she want to read these? Dive any further into the mind of the woman who had betrayed her? She slammed the book shut and put it back on the shelf.

"Colt, I know you don't want to, but I think you owe it to your grandmother to find out the full story. And these journals are the only way you're going to know for sure." He took the first journal off the top shelf and pressed it into her hands. "There's a thermos of coffee on the table. Go read."

She raised her fist and tapped him a couple times on the arm before following his directions and settling into the chair.

"Don't forget to get up and move," Hawk admonished as he left.

The room was pitch dark when the ringing of the phone awakened him. Malik sat up, blinking at the bright device. As always, the jet lag was messing with his internal clock, and he was certain he had only just fallen asleep.

His sister's name on the screen registered, and he found the correct spot to tap.

"Hello?" he mumbled.

Silence.

"Amna?"

A muffled sob sounded. He sat up, concern wiping away the last of the sleep. "Amna, what is it?"

Another sob, followed by ragged breathing. "It's Mother," Amna finally managed. "She's...she's gone, Malik."

A weight grew inside him until he felt as though he was under a boulder. "No, she can't..."

"How soon can you get here? There's so much to do, and I don't know, and..." She broke off, unable to stop the tears.

"Mother's... I can't come yet. I'm away on business."

Amna stopped crying, her voice turning icy. "I hope this 'business' is worth it. She called for you, you know."

Her words slapped him across the face. Why did no one understand? He was here for Mother! Why couldn't she have held on a little longer? "It's unavoidable."

"The funeral is in three days. You had better not avoid that." She hung up the phone, leaving him staring at it in the dark.

He staggered to the bathroom and splashed water on his face. The reality that his mother was gone had yet to sink in. All he could think of was the Egg. It didn't make sense. He was supposed to find it. It would make her better. She couldn't have died before he brought her the Egg.

Returning to the bedroom, he looked at the phone where it lay on the floor, the dimmed screen the only light.

Surely the call had been a dream. That was it. A dream. He hadn't failed yet.

But it was a warning. He needed to find the Egg before it was too late. He was running out of time.

17

The early morning sun was burning off the rain from the night before as Colt walked down the hill. Hands in her pockets, head high, she breathed in the peaceful quiet of the woods. She slipped in the side door to find Hawk scrambling eggs in the kitchen.

He looked up, scanning her face. She stood still for the scrutiny.

"You look..."

"Exhausted?" she offered, knowing her eyes were probably red from being up all night reading. At least the black eye was starting to fade.

"Better. I was going to say better."

She laughed and helped herself to the coffee. Hawk cracked a couple more eggs into the pan.

"So tell me what you found?"

She sipped the coffee, pondering where to start. Before she could decide, Hawk's phone rang. He answered it on speaker-phone, setting it on the table.

"Kendra, good morning."

"Hawk, I dug into those names you provided."

Colt raised an eyebrow at Hawk. He just shrugged, cha-grined.

Kendra continued. "I found some interesting information on three of them so far. Each of them has a registered death certificate from when they were younger than five years old. But there are social security numbers issued to them, tax re-turns, and marriage certificates. And in one instance, a sec-ond death certificate. She died in a car accident at the age of fifty-seven, if you were wondering."

Hawk looked at Colt with concern. She knew what he was thinking. But he was wrong.

"You can stop looking, Kendra," Colt said. "Katya wasn't kidnapping girls. She was rescuing them." She grinned at Hawk's goofy look of triumph. "When my grandfather, Roger Stevens, married her and brought her over, she realized how hard it was for women to escape the awful conditions in the USSR. As the situation got worse, women were marginalized more and more. When they met Frank and discovered the bunker under the airfield, they decided to do something about it. The first were some of the women she flew with in the 588th."

"Well," Kendra said. "If you will excuse me, I need to go delete my recent searches from the system and get back to this sting I'm working on." She hung up.

Colt met Hawk's eyes over her mug of coffee. He was smiling.

"So Katya wasn't evil."

"She wasn't evil."

He brandished the smoking frying pan at her. "Told you so."

She took a couple slow sips. "Hawk, we have to keep the files safe."

"Because of the women?"

She nodded. "Some secrets are worth protecting."

Colt led the way into the tunnels with a very different mood than the past few times. Instead of the dread she had carried of finding something worse, she was looking forward to exploring and uncovering her grandmother's operations. It was also Mitch's first time in the tunnels. It was an awkward solution, one they would have to update soon, but he hung on Hawk's back down the many flights of stairs. Colt carried his wheelchair, the distances in the tunnels making the transportation necessary.

They did a full tour of the two branches, showing Mitch everything and ensuring their blueprint was accurately labeled. They ended in the library.

"So we know the women were here for a noble purpose," Hawk said. "What about the artwork?"

Colt grinned devilishly. "That's how they funded the whole thing. The girls brought pieces with them. Some did belong to them, but often it was a simultaneous transport. The women were responsible for making sure a painting made it through. And if both girl and art made it to the States, that was her ransom, essentially. Katya would then sell it, and the money from the sale went to help the girl get on her feet in her new life."

"What about the pieces that didn't sell? Or the women who couldn't bring anything with them?"

Colt shrugged. "That's why I think there is a second list. The ledger we found denotes what was given to the women, but it isn't a definitive listing of all the pieces. There's more pieces in the hidden room than are marked as unsold in the ledger."

Mitch whistled. "Granny had a multilayered smuggling operation going on to screw the Commies. I love it."

Colt rolled her eyes but had to agree with the sentiment. Now that she knew the truth, she was pretty proud of what her grandmother had built.

"We've still got one problem though," Hawk said. "The missing Fabergé Egg."

Colt opened the door to the inner room. "Right. None of the pieces are ever named in Katya's journals. She mentions them only with the vaguest of details."

The boys followed her inside. "There is one that she keeps coming back to. She was worried about it, about the girl who brought it over."

Hawk looked over at what remained on the shelves. "They took anything that the Egg could have fit in," he said.

Colt nodded. "Except...I don't think Katya kept it with the rest. Even with the extra security and the hidden door, I think she wanted to keep it separate."

"That's dumb," Mitch said, picking up a small gold statuette. "Why not keep it in the vault?"

"Because she didn't tell Frank about it."

They let that sink in. A secret between people who kept secrets.

"Well, if she didn't keep it in here, then the ransackers didn't get it," Mitch said. "Fifty bucks says I find it first."

Colt laughed. "Deal."

They split off, each heading to the location they figured the most likely to be a hiding spot. She went back to Katya's office. It was the most obvious, but maybe Katya had wanted to keep it close. Mitch went to the storeroom, and Hawk took a more methodical approach, starting with the farthest room in the tunnel.

Eight hours later and Colt had lost her enthusiasm. She looked down the rows of shelves in the store room. Mitch had a point, that it would take years for someone to stumble on it here, but she couldn't see it as a viable option. Maybe the ransackers had found it after all. There was nowhere that was left in the bunker that would be a reasonable hiding place for something as valuable and delicate as the Egg.

"I'm going topside to grab a drink. You guys want anything?" she asked.

They both declined. "We're going to take a look at the stairwell, see if we can find a way to squeeze an elevator in there."

"Good plan." She headed up the stairs, looking forward to the fresh air to clear her head. She was sure Katya had hidden the Egg here somewhere. She just had to think harder.

If you want something done right, do it yourself. The mantra ran repeatedly through his mind as Malik navigated to the secret browser on this computer. When he reached the forum, he was pleased to see that his offer had received plenty of replies. Maybe he had a chance at getting the Egg after all.

He scrolled through the responses, curious about the people who were interested in helping with his little problem. He quickly realized his mistake. By offering such a large reward, he set himself up for a lot of offers, many of which were not what he needed. He dismissed the most obvious ones, but there were still far too many for him to decide who to hire. He wasn't even sure how many he should hire.

Much as he hated to admit it, he was unqualified to evaluate the skills on offer. He copied out the responses and sent them to the American.

Sort through these and set up a team. I'm not waiting any longer. As you're clearly incapable of identifying an Egg, I'll be coming with you. Don't waste my time.

He hit send on the email. Before closing his computer, he sent a second email to his courier.

The piece will soon be in my possession. I trust you're still able to get it out of the country?

Malik smiled as he put the laptop away. Sometimes delegation was the way to go. Let the American redeem himself. In the meantime, Malik had a lunch meeting at the embassy.

Raiding the fridge in the bunk room, Colt decided to give Danforth a call. Maybe he had some updated information on the Egg. She slid her earbuds into her ears and dialed.

"You have the most unfortunate habit of calling at the worst possible time," he said as he answered the call.

"Oh, yeah? Did I interrupt them washing your soul?"

"Being a banker doesn't mean I'm a terrible person."

"No, but being a jerk does." She opened the chocolate milk and sniffed. Seemed okay.

"So why do you keep calling me?"

"Being nice. Don't want you to miss me." She took a swig.

"Can you get to the point? I'm having dinner with my grandmother."

Colt immediately felt bad. Then again, a woman who had replicas worth millions was probably as stuck up as her grandson. "Run me through everything you know about the Egg again."

He sighed. "Its last known location was a small town in Russia in the 1970s. And even that was rumors. No photographs to confirm that it was an Imperial Egg. The first hint of it still being in existence was the sale of a necklace that is presumed to be part of the piece a few months ago."

Colt heard coughing in the background. "And now we've got this Collector guy thinking it's here."

"About that..." Danforth moved the phone away from his mouth. "Grandma, are you okay?"

"About what?"

Danforth hesitated. "That FBI friend of yours called. She wanted photos of my grandmother's replica to set up a sting operation. We're doing a press conference to announce that it's been found. I need to go. My grandmother isn't well."

Colt could hear the continued coughing in the background. "One more thing, Danforth."

"What?"

"Skip the photos. Take the replica. May as well go all out if you're going to be on camera."

Closing the fridge, she grabbed an apple off the table and turned to leave. Her phone rang in her hand.

"Kendra, what's up?"

"Where are you?"

"At the hangar. Why?"

"You all need to leave. Now."

"Elaborate." Colt set the apple back on the table and reached under one of the bunks.

"One of my analysts uncovered a post on a forum. It seems the man who is looking for the Egg —"

"The Collector." She grabbed the black case and jogged to the front of the hangar.

"How do you know that? You know what, it is probably better if you do not tell me." There was a pause, and Colt heard a car door slam, followed by the starting of a powerful engine. "We set up a sting operation to lure him out. Unfortunately, it appears he has preempted us. He has hired a group of mercenaries and is planning an attack on the location where he believes it is hidden. Colt, these guys are serious trouble. Get Hawk and Mitch, and get out of there."

"It might be too late for that." Colt hung up and shoved the phone into her pocket. Peering out the personnel door, she scanned the tree line. She couldn't see it yet, but the distinctive

steady thumping was hard to miss. A Black Hawk assault helicopter.

18

Running across the tarmac was out of the question. She had to give them credit for the audacity though. A full assault before the sun had even set. Colt slammed the door and headed for the workbench. Opening the case, she tucked the contents into her pockets and grabbed a screwdriver, then ran to the hatch. She climbed down a few rungs and pulled the hatch closed over her, then shoved the screwdriver into the bracket to pin it shut. Using the same technique as the day before, she slid down the ladder.

At the intersection of the two tunnels, she paused. "Hawk! Mitch!"

No answer. She sprinted down the main tunnel, calling out as she went.

"Here!" finally came the response from the storeroom. She spun on her toes and darted in, finding them in a far corner.

"What's wrong?" Hawk asked as she drew close, out of breath.

"Incoming. At least eight of them. In a Black Hawk. Possibly two."

Mitch whistled. "They ain't foolin' around."

"Nope."

"Can we get out?" Hawk asked.

"If we go now, I think we can make it. And they'd probably let us go as long as they don't think we have the Egg."

"What are you going to do?"

"Stay here," she said simply. "I'm not about to let them walk in and burn this place to the ground."

"Good, then I'm staying too," Hawk said.

"Me too," Mitch added. "Besides, I think we can do a little fighting back of our own." He motioned to the door beside him that Colt hadn't paid any attention to yet.

She peered around him. "I like you. I like you a lot."

The deep closet was stacked with racks of weapons. At least twenty rifles and half as many handguns. A row of grenades sat on a shelf beside boxes of ammunition.

"What's the chance any of this will still work?" she asked.

Mitch shrugged and picked up the first rifle. "They've been stored properly. We could clean a couple."

"Well, grab what you need. It won't be long before they are down here."

They each grabbed a rifle and two handguns along with cases of ammunition. Mitch added a cleaning kit to the pile on his lap and stuffed a couple grenades in his shirt pockets.

"Where to?" Hawk asked.

"Katya's office. There's something I need to check."

They ran, Mitch leading the way in his chair. At the intersection, Mitch and Colt went on ahead while Hawk paused to lock both the doors. It wouldn't hold long, but every second would give them a chance to arm themselves. Along the way, Colt dropped small black disks on the ground.

"What is that?" Hawk asked.

"Think pop caps on steroids. A friend gave them to me to hold on to for him."

"Why?"

She shrugged. "Don't step on them."

They piled into Katya's office. Hawk and Colt barricaded the door with the filing cabinet. Mitch set up at the desk and began breaking down the weapons.

"So what's the plan?" Hawk asked.

"Honestly, beyond 'not die,' I'm not a hundred percent sure. But the more time we can give Kendra to alert the troops, the better."

"Stall. Fine. We can do that." He joined Mitch in breaking down the rifles, then paused. "Are we actually going to be shooting at people?"

Colt looked at him. "If they shoot first, I'm guessing they're pretty clear on the rules of engagement at that point."

"Fair."

"Shoot to disable, not kill if you're so inclined. But keep in mind they'll probably be wearing body armor." She pulled open the top drawer of the filing cabinet.

"What are you looking for?"

"A file on a girl named Masha."

A shudder rippled through the office, followed by a muted boom. Colt grabbed the cabinet to keep her footing.

"Was that one of yours?" Hawk asked.

She shook her head. "I really hope not."

Shouts sounded in the distance, drawing closer. Hawk frowned.

"They're in the tunnels already! What's he saying?"

Colt strained to hear. "Sem'ya. It means family. I think he's saying it belongs to the family."

"The Russian guy? How did he get down here?"

"I'm getting the impression that he's working with the Collector. Unfortunately."

The shouting drew nearer, the same phrase repeated over and over. Banging joined in as doors were opened and slammed shut.

Colt looked around, the realization of what they were doing sinking in. "Guys, I —"

"Colt, don't be foolish," Hawk said.

"Oh, please. Don't tell me you're about to get mushy on us, are you?" Mitch groaned dramatically.

"It's just...things have been weird."

Hawk finished putting the cleaned rifle back together. "No matter what you think, she really did love you."

"You could say she kept it from you to protect you," Mitch chipped in.

Colt gave a rueful grin. "She was always trying to protect me. Sem'ya prevyshe vsyevo."

"What's that mean?" Mitch asked.

Colt thought about the phrase for a minute. "Family is above all," she whispered. She looked up at the guys, a smile spreading across her face. "I know where it is."

"The Egg?" Hawk asked incredulously.

"Sem'ya prevyshe vsyevo. Katya would say it before we'd go up, especially in the Mule."

"So it's in her plane?"

"No. It's in the parachute."

Colt paced the tiny office. "She had this big old parachute she'd insist I take with me. It was heavy and awkward. I hated it. The Night Witches didn't have parachutes — they were too heavy with the bombs. But she told me that if anything happened to her, the parachute would protect me. I thought she was referring to another stroke, but I think she meant the Egg."

"Go." Hawk set the handgun down and came around to the door.

"What about you guys?"

"We'll be fine. We'll stall them. You get to the Mule and find the Egg." He and Colt moved the filing cabinet away from the door.

"Here, you're going to need this." Hawk handed her a key. "Lock the doors behind you."

"I'm not trapping you down here."

"It's a duplicate. There's at least four of them."

"Well, that's secure," Colt said, tucking the key in the front pocket of her jeans. She glanced at the rifles on the desk. Even with Mitch having just cleaned them, she didn't trust them not to jam at the worst possible moment. She had her regular weapon, and her backup on her ankle. Mitch shoved one of the Colt M1911s across the desk along with a couple of spare magazines.

"Take it. They're brand new, so should have no problem firing, and better to have the extra ammo..."

He was right. She swapped her Beretta for the M1911 and slid the magazines into her pockets. With a deep breath and a last nod to Hawk, she eased the door open and peered out. Clear. She sprinted down the hall, keeping her steps as light as possible. The Russian had been around, and she was sure the mercenaries wouldn't be far behind. She watched each of the doors as she passed, ready to dart out of the way if they should burst open.

He rose out of the shadows with a roar, and she plowed into him, sending them both staggering backward.

"Give it to me!" the Russian shouted.

"I don't even have it," she retorted, circling around. She was faster. If she could get past him and to the door, he wouldn't be able to keep up.

Unfortunately, he seemed intent on not letting her pass.

"Move," she told him, watching his eyes.

"She stole it from my family! Either give it to me or tell me where she is!" He swung at her, and she replied with a kick to his stomach. He was wearing body armor, strengthening her belief that he was working with the Collector.

Gunfire burst from behind her. Colt dropped to the floor, the man landing beside her with a heavy thump. The door to the schoolroom was open, and she crawled toward it. Beside her, the Russian man groaned. With a sigh, she reached for his collar and dragged him into the room with her. She kicked the door closed and flopped to the ground, panting.

"Who are you?" She rolled to her knees, checking him for weapons.

He moaned again in pain. "George Kulik. My stepmother stole from my family. Tell me where she is." His voice caught and burbled as he spoke, blood spilling from his lips.

Colt shook her head, trying to find where he was hit. "She was never married to your father. And whatever you think she stole, it belonged to her, not you."

"My family...sem'ya..." He slipped into Russian, murmuring phrases Colt couldn't catch.

She found the flow of blood, the warm liquid pooling over her hands as she pressed them to the side of his neck. "Sem'ya prevyshe vsyevo," she replied. "Family is above all. Family, not greed."

"Moya...sem'ya," the man whispered one last time before falling still.

Colt sat back, wiping her hands on his pants. There was nothing more she could do for him. No time to sit around though. She took a deep breath, switching gears.

Key in one hand, her M1911 in the other, she approached the door. The double doors were about five running strides to her right. Unlock it, get through, relock it. Of course, she had no way of knowing what was on the other side.

And there were already people in this tunnel. Which meant they'd either opened the doors, or they'd found the tunnel from Hangar 1. Great. She'd deal with that later.

She opened the door with one hand, staying to the side. In the passage, a mercenary crept past. Glancing down at his feet, she smiled and closed the door again.

Two seconds later and his boot landed on one of her pop caps, filling the passage with gunpowder and a loud bang. As soon as it went off, Colt burst through the door, leaping on top of the guy. He was screaming, standing on one foot. She knocked him to the ground, her arm slipping around his neck. She applied steady pressure until he stopped fighting and went still. Dragging him into the schoolroom, she stripped him of his weapon and radio.

She clipped the radio to her belt and put the earpiece in. Chatter about positions immediately filled her ears, and she quickly determined no one was near the ladder.

She made it to the door this time without any more delays and slipped into the main tunnel, locking the door behind her. Shouts came as she unlocked the second set of doors, followed by bullets slamming into the door beside her. She returned fire. Yanking the door open, she fell inside and kicked the door shut and locked it. Leaving the mercenary's gun on the floor, she sprang up the ladder, climbing as fast as she could, her movements steady and controlled.

The screwdriver was still in the hatch, pinning it closed. She pried it out, losing her grip on it as it jerked free. It fell, clanging against the ladder on its way down. She winced at the noise. The hatch was even heavier to open from below, but she pressed it open enough to determine no one was about to shoot her. Darkness had closed in during the hour she'd been in the tunnel. Though the sky was still gray, there were enough shadows to give her protection.

She climbed out of the hatch, letting it fall on her rather than risking the open door being spotted. When she was almost out, she flipped over and held the hatch with her hands as she wriggled her foot free, then lowered it carefully. Sticking to the shadows, she crossed the hangar to the corner by the open main door.

In her ear, the succinct commands continued, so she knew Hawk and Mitch were still undiscovered, as were her own movements topside. She looked around, flagging the men who were standing guard. In the tower, they'd set up a spotlight and were sweeping the grounds.

Two Black Hawk helicopters sat in the middle of the tarmac, and there, in front of Hangar 1, was Katya's airplane.

19

Hawk shut the door behind Colt and leaned against it. Everything was telling him to go with her. That's what they did. She led the charge, and he was on her tail, following her every move, anticipating threats. Except this time, they weren't in an F/A-18.

"Why don't you go with her?" Mitch asked.

Hawk shrugged.

"Dude, you didn't have to stay with me."

"I know." Hawk winced as he heard the roar of the Russian. Colt would shout if she needed help, but for now, his job was to stay here.

He waited a minute longer, straining to hear if Colt called, then crossed to help Mitch with the weapons.

"I certainly hope the plan isn't to stay here like snakes in a barrel," Mitch said, loading one of the rifles.

Gunfire broke out in the hall, making them both freeze. A moment later, a small pop sounded, followed by a man screaming in pain.

"Nope." Hawk picked up a rifle and a couple of spare magazines from the desk. "Are you good?" He was prepared to go out there to help Colt, regardless of the risk. But the last time Mitch had seen combat had resulted in his helicopter being shot down.

Mitch grabbed two rifles. "You push. I shoot."

Hawk gave a laugh. "Alright." He swapped the rifle for one of the M1911s, tucking it into his pocket. Grasping the handles on Mitch's wheelchair, he brought them closer to the door. He could hear nothing.

He took a deep breath and opened the door. The hall was clear, so he backed Mitch out of the room and headed away from the doors and the main hallway.

"Hey! Wrong way."

"There's no way we can get to the stairs. If they're coming in this way, they must have found the other entrance."

The far end of the passage was dark, obscured by a cloud of dust. Hawk strained his eyes to see what was lurking there. He was certain he saw movement, then there was a shout, a warning for them to stop.

Hawk swung the chair around and backed through the nearest door. The library. Mitch swore when he realized.

"The exact spot they're aiming for."

"I know." Hawk pulled the heavy table over and blocked the door. "And they saw us come in."

"That's not going to hold them long," Mitch maneuvered his chair around to give himself the best angle for shooting someone coming through the entryway.

Someone banged on the door. "Let us in, and no one needs to get hurt!" a voice shouted.

"That's exactly why we're *not* letting you in," Mitch retorted.

"We're not interested in hurting you. We only want the Egg!"

"Yeah, right."

"Hand over the Egg, and we'll leave!"

Hawk looked at the former Marine — sweat beading on his forehead, snarl on his face, rifle in each hand, grenades sticking out of his shirt pockets. "I've got an idea."

Hawk rushed into the treasure room. If they wanted an Egg, he'd give them one. On a back shelf, he found what he needed. Using his pocketknife, he pried the top off a small wooden crate and removed the vase from inside.

He ran back to the library and set the box on the table. Mitch handed him one of the grenades, a grin forming as he understood Hawk's plan. With careful fingers, he loosened the pin, jamming the ring into a crack in the lid. The grenade nestled into the straw, and he bunched the bedding up to keep the explosive in position.

The pounding came again. "Open up!"

"In a minute!" Hawk shouted back. He glanced at Mitch. He didn't want to think too deeply about what he was preparing to do. Hopefully the mercenaries had enough body armor on. "You good with this?"

Mitch laughed. "Scramble 'em."

Hawk pulled the table away from the door, putting it on its side. "Sending it out," he called. He opened the door slowly, staying to one side, then slid the box out as far as he could. It was yanked from his grasp. Hawk slammed the door shut and ducked behind the table.

"It's a grenade!" The shout was repeated, paired with running footsteps.

A heavy thump echoed through the tunnels. The ground shuddered under his feet, and dust rained from the ceiling. A second thump came from the hall, followed by a crashing.

"That didn't sound good," Mitch said when things stayed silent.

Hawk stood up and dusted himself off. There were no sounds from the hall, no guns being fired at the door. He hoped all the men had made it to safety, but if they hadn't been using deadly force before, they certainly were going to now.

Prying the door open, he peered out. Dust swirled in the air, but he could just make out a pile of broken cement and rocks in the tunnel.

"Well, looks like we're definitely taking the new route. We caused a cave-in, so the main tunnel is blocked off."

Mitch pushed himself over to the door, then picked up the rifles again. "Doesn't mean they're not still out there. Let's go."

Hawk grabbed the handles and headed out of the library. Debris littered the floor, forcing him to go slowly to avoid pitching Mitch out of his chair. One of the mercenaries lay under a pile of stone. Hawk paused long enough to find the man's pulse and shift the rubble from his chest. Once they were clear, he jogged. If the tunnel entrance was near the main hangar, it shouldn't be too far. But he'd not finished his explorations down this end, so it could be anywhere.

A pair of double doors on the side wall stood open. He had dismissed it as a storage room as it had been empty when he checked it. Now, there was a pile of cement revealing the larger chamber. Against the far wall was a ladder, much like the first entrance they had found.

"That's not going to work," Hawk said.

"I can climb that," Mitch replied.

"Don't be ridiculous. It's at least a hundred feet."

Mitch looked ready to argue, then changed his mind. "You go first, then you can pull me up." He leaned over and grabbed a heavy nylon rope that was hanging down the shaft. "Tie their rope to my chair. They'll have some sort of pulley system at the top if they dropped in like this."

"I'm not leaving you here."

"We can't stay here. We're sitting ducks if they come back. You go up; I'll cover you."

"And what if there's more at the top?"

"Colt's up there. I'm sure she could come up with some sort of distraction."

Colt counted the men on the airfield again. Three were pacing, watching the perimeter. There was at least one in the tower. And two were by the farther Black Hawk, one standing on the step looking down at the gestures of the other man. From his silhouette, he was the only one not wearing tactical gear. In fact, he seemed to be wearing a three-piece suit, his tie flapping in the wind. Hawk's truck was parked by the tower, in clear sight of the men patrolling.

But no one was watching the airplanes. The spotlight flashed in her direction, and she ducked back inside the hangar. Once the light had passed, she dropped to her knees and crawled out of the hangar.

Shifting to a full-belly crawl, she inched her way across the rough ground toward the Mule. Only fifty yards separated them, but the distance stretched out with every second it took her to get there. The spotlight continued to weave back and forth, threatening to light her up at any second. A guard came near, and she pressed herself into the ground, hardly breathing until he moved on.

At last, she reached the Mule. No one was near, so she pulled herself upright against the wheel and climbed into the plane. The parachute wasn't in the cramped pilot's seat. If she stood up, her silhouette would be visible to anyone who glanced over.

As quietly as she could, she climbed back out onto the wing and over to the gunner's position. There, in the bottom of the footwell. Her fingers wrapped around the rough canvas, and she pulled the parachute onto her lap. She dug into the small pockets on the pack, hoping the Egg wasn't buried inside the silk. If it was, she wouldn't be able to find it without releasing the chute.

A piece of material was stuffed in the bottom of the second pocket. It was folded over, stiff and creased. Velvet. She thought about the box Danforth had kept the replica Egg in.

Katya wouldn't have left the velvet there without reason. Colt wanted to believe it was a clue. But was it enough to go on for what she had in mind next?

Screw it. She didn't need the parachute to act as a lifesaving device. She just needed it to not burst out in a pile of white silk. Taking her knife from her pocket, she slit the brittle fabric, stabbing deep into the silk. It spilled out, enough for her to wedge her hand inside.

In her ear, the mercenaries sounded off as they cleared the rooms far below her. And still no sign of Kendra and the rescue squad. If Colt was going to do something to save Mitch and Hawk, she needed to do it soon. She dug deeper, feeling through the millions of layers of silk for something that felt different.

There. Velvet, wrapped around something hard and textured. She yanked her arm out and stuffed the silk back in as best she could. The Egg could stay wrapped up for now. She needed to call Danforth.

Checking her phone, she muttered a less savory word her grandmother had taught her. Of course the cell signal was down. The Collector had hired a top crew; the first thing they would have done would be to cut the phone lines and jam the cell signal.

She studied the airfield. Getting to Hawk's truck was out of the question. She could head for the trees and run to the house. If her phone still didn't work there, she could hop on her motorbike. Except she didn't have her keys with her. And she doubted the mercenaries had left the driveway clear for her to make an easy getaway.

Escaping with the Egg would be the easy part. She could disappear into the woods, and they'd need dogs to be able to find her, if they even saw her leave. But that would do nothing to help Mitch and Hawk.

She tapped her fingers together. The only recourse was obvious, but was it foolhardy? Yes. Absolutely. Would Hawk kill her if he knew what she was thinking? Most definitely.

But Hawk wasn't here, and she was out of options.

Slipping the parachute over her shoulders, she climbed out of the Mule and slid down the wing to the ground. She needed to get inside to the Piper Cub. Another glance around for the position of the guards had her pausing. With the two Black Hawks in the middle of the runway, she'd never get the Cub off the ground.

But the Mule could make it.

She racked her brain to remember what Mitch had said about the plane. He had only spent one day on it, claiming the engine was in perfect condition. It was back together and fueled up, awaiting her to do a test flight. Now was as good a time as any.

Decision made, Colt wasted no time in getting ready for takeoff. As soon as she started the engine, the mercenaries would be on her. She tossed the parachute back in the gunner's seat and flipped a switch in the pilot's seat. Ducking low, she ran her hands over the plane as she moved around it. Everything seemed locked in place. And if it wasn't, well, this was a plane renowned for working with no engine. She kicked the chocks out from in front of the wheels and moved to the front.

Noting the positions of the guards, she took a deep breath. As soon as she swung the propeller, they'd be alerted to her presence. Her pocketful of little pop caps would do nothing here. But the spare magazines Mitch gave her just might.

Running back to the cockpit, she used her knife to cut the blue hair tie off the lever. It had lost its elasticity but would work well enough for what she needed. Taking one of the magazines, she laid the flat detonator against the side and tied them together with the hair tie, careful not to tighten it too much.

She moved away from the Mule and threw the magazine as far as she could. Hawk had taught her how to pitch a fastball for the squadron baseball games. She didn't stand around to watch it, running to the propeller. She was only half convinced her diversion would work. With any luck, the clatter of its landing would draw their attention.

The blasting cap went off as she grabbed the long wooden blade and jumped. Landing, she put all of her strength into rotating the propeller. In the distance, the rounds in the magazine went off one after another. The engine caught with a deafening roar. Ducking out of the way, Colt flung herself into the cockpit and immediately opened the fuel wide. She angled the Mule down the apron, gathering speed as she passed the Black Hawks.

In her ear, shouts and confusion sounded over the radio. The little plane gathered speed, bucking down the uneven tarmac. Over the noise of the wind and engine, she heard gunfire break out. She drew back on the stick, lifting the nose off the ground. The wall of trees loomed before her.

Bullets slapped against the plane, sending wooden splinters flying through her field of vision. Colt squinted through them, willing the plane higher. The radio earpiece was yanked from her ear by the wind.

The trees were close enough that she could make out individual trunks.

"Come on, Kerosinka," she muttered, using the name Katya had called the plane. She was pretty sure it wasn't a complimentary term, but the plane seemed to respond to it, lifting higher.

One particularly tall tree loomed to her left. If she kept on straight, it would clip her wing. Turning before gaining enough altitude and speed could likewise be fatal.

But a turn right after takeoff was something Colt had practiced for years. When being catapulted off the bow of a ship, fighter jets needed to bank immediately. If they didn't and something happened, the ship would plow right over them.

She checked her airspeed, trying to remember the numbers for the Mule. Using her recent flight in the Cub as a baseline, she decided she was going fast enough to make the turn.

She nudged the stick right, and the plane responded immediately. Watching the top of the tree, she ducked as the left wing grazed the top of the tree. She braced for the resulting loss of control.

The Mule rocked to the right, giving Colt a great view of even more trees. She drew the stick back as far as it would go, bracing against the rocking of the plane. After a moment, it leveled out, and she breathed again.

She gained altitude before turning east. No GPS or nav systems meant she wasn't entirely sure where she was headed, but the light pollution from New York City would soon provide a beacon. She settled down into the seat, and her foot knocked something under the pedal. Checking that everything remained balanced, she poked the thing with her foot again, dislodging it and drawing it closer to her.

She bent down and picked it up. Ear protectors. The big heavy kind that protected your hearing from extended loud noises. The leather was old and cracked, but it was better than nothing, so she slipped them over her head.

Feeling around on the seat beside her, she found the earpiece to the radio and tucked it up under the ear protectors. There was only static. She fiddled with the dial in case she'd knocked it, but no sounds of angry mercenaries appeared. Too far away, she guessed. But that meant that maybe she was far enough from the jammer for her cell phone to work. She lifted out of the seat until she could retrieve it from her back pocket.

Full bars. Good. The radio and her phone used the same connection for earphones, so she switched it over and dialed Danforth.

"Are you nuts?" he demanded.

"Quite possibly," she replied.

"My grandmother is in the hospital, yet she insisted that I come here, with her replica, and run this farce."

"I didn't really catch all that. Tell me you've got the press conference set up."

"Yes. Where are you? It's really noisy."

About that. He was right. It was really noisy. Noisier than it should have been. She looked down at the instruments, using the phone's screen to light up the dials. Everything seemed fine. But the deep thrumming continued.

She twisted in her seat as a Black Hawk swooped into view.

Colt opened the throttle, then laughed. The maximum speed for the Mule was far below the helicopter's cruising speed. Unfortunately, because it was a helicopter, she couldn't outmaneuver it like the Night Witches did to the Messerschmitt pilots. They could try to force her out of the sky, but she was banking on them not wanting to risk the Egg. For now, they would have to follow her and attack when she landed.

"Where are you?" she asked Danforth.

"Integrated Broadcasting, on Broadway. I've got an art expert here who's willing to attest to the replica being the real thing, but only if I promised that the real one was on the verge of being discovered." He took a deep breath. "It is, isn't it? Tell me I didn't just lie to the head of the art department at Columbia."

"I've got it."

"What?" His voice pitched to a screech.

"Calm down. You might break a nail." She wished the Black Hawk pilot would back off a bit. The vortex of air created by the massive rotor blades on top of the helicopter was causing the Mule a lot of turbulence.

"But how?" he sputtered.

"We'll get to that. First, does the building you're in have a helicopter pad on the roof?"

She heard him move the phone to ask someone. "Yes, it does."

"Good. Get up there. Make sure it's clear. Let me know if there's anything nearby in the airspace." She let up on the throttle, reducing her speed even more.

"You're in a helicopter?"

"Not exactly. Look, I'll be there in an hour. Be ready, because I'm not going to be able to land." The Black Hawk finally took the hint and moved up to give her room. It could easily outpace her, but without knowing her destination, they were stuck following her.

"You can't fly a plane through New York City!"

"Technically, I can…because what I'm flying isn't exactly going to show up on any radar." She opened the throttle and banked right. "Look, send me your location on one of those sharing apps. And call Kendra. There's an attack helicopter heading straight for downtown Manhattan."

Colt ended the call and secured her phone in her pocket. She couldn't outfly the Black Hawk. The tiny five-cylinder engine in the Polikarpov had gumption but not power. No matter what she tried, the massive helicopter could match her every move.

However, she was a fighter pilot. A trained and experienced adrenaline junkie. More importantly, she had a stomach of iron. She couldn't stop the wicked grin from forming.

The pilot might be able to maintain equilibrium. But she doubted a fancy businessman who threw millions at attaining the unattainable was accustomed to sudden plunges and abrupt changes. And with any luck, the other mercenaries would be a bit green around the gills when they landed.

Keeping one hand on the stick, she climbed up onto her seat and stretched as far as she could to reach the gunner's seat. She grabbed the parachute and pulled it back to the front seat with her. She slipped it around her shoulders. The bulkiness pushed her closer to the controls, but she wasn't about to risk it falling out during the next few minutes.

The Black Hawk was back in position directly behind her. She shoved the stick all the way forward, the nose of the Mule dropping to the ground. Wind screamed past her as she watched the altimeter spinning closer and closer to zero. In the dark, she couldn't see what was below her, so when she got under one thousand feet, she started pulling back to level off. At five hundred feet, she rolled left. The little plane responded immediately.

Something bumped and tumbled around her. She grabbed for it, her fingers grazing against the radio as it fell out of the plane. Good thing she wasn't using that.

She climbed steadily, knowing the helicopter would easily regain altitude. When she heard it alongside once more, she looked over and gave the pilot a wave. Right before she put the stick all the way over to the right, spinning into an aileron roll. The Black Hawk followed her descent once more. She continued through a series of maneuvers designed to keep the other pilot guessing, always favoring the right. While he didn't need to invert to follow, she hoped it was enough that his passengers were struggling to keep their lunches.

The glow on the horizon from New York City was growing. If she was going to lose them, now was the time. She leveled out once more at eight thousand feet and waited. A flare gun would have been really handy as a diversion, but she had only the M1911, and she wasn't about to get into a gunfight with an assault helicopter while flying little more than canvas and wood.

When she heard the Black Hawk drawing close on her tail once more, she slowly opened the throttle, pushing the Mule to its top speed, willing the Black Hawk to speed up too. Before the helicopter got too close, she shoved the stick to the left and down.

She circled around behind it, taking advantage of the darkness. Heading for the deck, she planned on using the terrain to help keep her hidden for a few minutes. The plane settled into an easy cruising speed of seventy knots, giving her a minute to catch her breath. She checked the gauges, ensuring she still had enough fuel. New York wouldn't be a problem. Making it back to the airfield might be tight.

As the light pollution from the city spilled out to meet her, she pulled her phone out of her pocket. Danforth sent a link to his location in a map app, so she opened that and requested directions from her current location. The app got a bit confused as she wasn't following a road, but it soon showed a route up NJ-3 West.

A house flashed by below her, then another. Time to gain some altitude so residents wouldn't complain about a sewing machine buzzing their homes. Following the highway seemed as good an idea as any, so she banked south and soon found the lines of red and white lights below her.

The all-too-familiar thumping in her chest returned, and she glanced over to see the Black Hawk lower into position beside her. So much for a peaceful trip into the city.

The side door slid open, and a man holding an assault rifle appeared. Colt gritted her teeth. Shooting her down now would mean not just her death but the death of anyone she happened to crash into, whether that be in a house or a vehicle on the road. They weren't that foolish. Were they?

There was little she could do at that moment. The wash from their rotors was causing the Mule to buck and veer away. She fought to keep it steady, wanting to go higher but worried she might end up flipped on top of the Black Hawk.

From the other side, another thumping joined the first. She couldn't risk looking over her shoulder, but she groaned.

She wasn't going to make it the last ten miles to New York.

20

Malik braced himself against anything that looked safe, terrified of touching any of the switches. The Black Hawk helicopter had been decommissioned from military use, but there were still a lot of buttons needed to keep it aloft.

He glanced over at the pilot, who seemed relaxed. Too relaxed. In fact, Malik suspected the man was enjoying himself. The tiny plane in front of them jigged right again, and the helicopter followed with a lurch.

Malik's stomach responded with a backflip, and he struggled to maintain his equilibrium. He refused to let on how much the roller-coaster maneuvers were affecting him, but he was sure that the pilot was doing it on purpose.

The helicopter dropped a hundred feet in the air, and bile filled his mouth. He regretted choosing to join the chase rather than waiting at the airfield. His man had offered to go instead, but

Malik wasn't about to be left behind. He was certain the woman had the Egg, and he wasn't interested in standing around waiting.

A certain level of distrust had eked into their relationship as well. Even though the American was paid well, Malik wouldn't put it past the man to hold the Egg hostage until Malik paid him more. And he didn't have time for that.

The pilot cribbed the Black Hawk to the right, following the ghost of a plane in front of them. Retching came from the back seat, causing Malik's stomach to heave again. His hand shot out to catch his balance and knocked a switch. The pilot glared at him as he corrected whatever had happened.

Malik had to admit that the pilot was impressive. He had trouble making out the shadow of the little plane they were following as it darted around the sky, but the pilot kept close behind it, never losing sight.

The plane pulled away, increasing speed.

"It's getting away!" Malik cried, waving for the pilot to catch up.

"It can't get away," the pilot retorted. "It's too slow."

"Well, it's getting away now, isn't it? Speed up!"

The pilot obliged, closing the gap between them. Suddenly the plane disappeared from view. The pilot swung to the left, following, but there was no sign of the plane.

"Lost it," he said.

"Find it!" Malik screamed into the headset. No way was he losing the Egg when they were this close. "Don't let her get away!"

A tense few minutes passed as they searched the dark skies for the plane. It was so old it had no lights of any kind to indicate its location. Finally, one of the men in the back seat spotted it.

"We're getting close to the city," the pilot told him as they drew near. "We'll have to fall back."

"You'll go wherever she goes," Malik retorted.

"No way. I'm not losing my license for this. New York City has restricted airspace."

"Fine. We'll force her to land then."

"How do you suggest we do that?"

"Shoot her down."

"Are you insane?" the pilot demanded. "This isn't Iraq."

Malik turned around to face the men in the back, ignoring the pilot. "You heard me! Shoot her down! Do it!"

After a moment's hesitation, one of the men reached for the side door and pulled it open. Immediately, the helicopter was filled with swirling, roaring air. The helicopter drew alongside the plane.

"Fire!" screamed Malik.

The man lifted his assault rifle and took aim.

"Hold your fire! Hold your fire!" shouted the pilot.

Malik looked at him, wondering if he'd lost his mind. The pilot was pointing at the plane. Malik followed his finger. A second helicopter settled into place, sandwiching the plane between them. On the side were three large white letters.

FBI.

Tuning out the two helicopters, Colt called Danforth. There was nothing she could do about them. If they wanted to shoot her out of the sky, she'd only be able to hold on and hope she could make it to the Hudson River.

"How close are you?" he demanded when he answered. "I've been trying to call you."

"Sorry, been a little distracted. Less than five minutes out now." The lights from the roads ended in front of her, a black expanse indicating the river. She veered for a spot between the two bridges, thankful for their lights.

"Okay, good. What are you flying?"

"A Polikarpov Po-2."

"A what?"

"A crop duster." She climbed higher, knowing she was going to need the altitude to pull off what she had in mind. She peeled the parachute off her back and braced it on her lap.

"You can't land a crop duster on a helipad!"

Don't tell me what I can't do, she thought, even though he was right. She pushed the thought of trying out of her mind. No way could she take off afterward, even if she did manage to stop on a postage stamp. "I'm not. I'm going to do a flyby and toss the Egg to you."

"*What?*" The poor man sounded ready to join his grandmother in the hospital.

"Hope you're good at football."

"You want me to *catch it*?"

"Yup."

"Do you know how much that is worth?"

"Relax. It's in a parachute. Wrapped up all cozy and secure. All you have to do is catch it." She took a deep breath, checking her altitude. "Are you sure about the location? And you've got the lights on?"

"All lit up like a Christmas tree," he promised, still sounding dazed.

"Right. See you soon." She leaned forward and flipped the switch on the engine. Time to be a Night Witch. For a moment, her ears rang from the sudden silence, then the rushing of the wind took over.

Katya's voice echoed in her ears. *When the enemy thinks they've got you, cut the engine, and scream to your death.*

She scanned the buildings below, looking for the right spot. There were too many lights and too many buildings with helicopter landing pads. "Danforth. Give me a two-one flash."

A pause that felt like an eternity, then she saw it. An orange square flashing in one- and two-second increments.

"Call the ball," he said in her ear.

She laughed. Maybe he had served on a real ship after all. "Roger ball."

"I see you!" he cried. "You're a little left."

She nudged over, following his directions. She lined up her nose with the left-hand line of lights. The square grew, tall buildings flashing close beneath her.

"You're still left!"

"Stand by for catch," she replied, eyes locked on the far corner of the lights. She lifted the parachute and balanced it on the edge of the fuselage.

Three...two...one...

"Release!" She flung the heavy chute as far as she could. A figure ran forward to catch it, but she was past and couldn't turn to see what had happened.

Buildings loomed in front of her. She punched the button to restart the engine. Nothing happened.

21

Buildings flashed by as she dropped under the thirty-story mark. Colt pressed the button again, holding it down.

"Come on, Kerosinka, don't burn out now," she begged.

The engine sputtered to life, coughing once before the propeller caught. She sighed with relief as the Mule finally responded to her commands, the nose no longer pointing straight at the cars below her.

A box truck blared its horn at her. She looked up into its headlights. Pulling back with all her strength, the Mule began climbing. She braced herself, hoping to hit the East River before anything else went wrong.

Buildings and cars and parks flew by underneath her. She readied to bank left once she hit the river, turning to follow its length rather than crossing into Brooklyn.

A bright light flashed in her eyes. She raised her arm to see around it. The thumping of a helicopter filled the air, and she groaned.

But this one was different. Not the deep, chest-pounding vibration of the Black Hawk. Beyond the blinding light, she could just make out the smaller bulbous silhouette of a commercial model helicopter.

"This is the police!" The words filled the air, followed by the squawking of a loudspeaker. "Land this plane now, or we will shoot you down."

"Sure. I'll land. Where exactly would you like me to do that?" she muttered. The plane was still dangerously low. The river spread out beneath her, so she made a wide turn, the helicopter cribbing sideways to keep up.

"Turn to frequency seven-seven-oh and acknowledge!"

She laughed. The Mule wasn't equipped with a radio, and she'd lost the one she'd taken from the mercenary.

"Turn to frequency seven-seven-oh and acknowledge!" The command was repeated more fiercely this time.

She raised one arm over her head and waved. There was no universal signal for "no radio," so she hoped they got the point.

After a minute of silence, the voice returned, giving her a new vector heading. She waggled her wings in response and followed their directions to RC Flying Airfield.

Vehicles roared toward her before she even rolled to a stop. She powered down the engine and leaned back in the seat. Silence deafened her as she took off the hearing protectors. She unclipped her ankle holster and pulled the M1911 from her waistband. Adding her pocket knife, she made a little pile in the footwell.

Taking a deep breath, she raised her arms over her head and started climbing out. Immediately, spotlights shone in her face, voices shouting at her to get down on the ground.

What do you think I'm doing? she wondered. Ensuring her hands were visible at all times, she slid down the wing and walked a few steps away from it. She lowered herself to her knees, then to her stomach. Someone ran up and shoved her face into the tarmac, yanking her arms behind her back to cuff them.

"Are you armed?" he screamed at her.

"Not currently," she replied.

"Sir!" came a cry from one of them swarming the plane. "We've got a weapons stash here!"

The man cuffing her pressed his knee into her back. "Is that everything? What else do you have on you?"

She ran through the things she'd been carrying. "A cell phone, keys, ID. Earphones. Oh, and a spare magazine and pop caps."

He dug through her pockets without flipping her over. She ignored the groping by taking pleasure in the fact he was suffering more pain from scraping his knuckles on the tarmac than she was experiencing.

Another cop joined him, and her belongings were dumped into a plastic evidence bag. The two grabbed an arm each and hauled her to her feet. They pushed her into a van and sped off to a nearby building, where she was marched inside. Two men moved in front of her, clearing a path, two held her tight, and the rest of the parade brought up the rear, weapons trained on her.

She scanned the room. There were a lot of officers milling about, all of them pausing to look at her, shock on most of their faces. The only one trying to hide a smile was a young female cop. Colt gave her a knowing nod. None of the others had expected a woman.

But she had places to be, and promoting women's rights would have to wait. She planted her feet, forcing the cops holding her to stop.

"I want to speak to Special Agent Kendra Mitchell of the FBI," she proclaimed loudly.

"You'll talk to who we tell you to talk to," the cop on her left said, yanking on her arm.

She ignored him. "I flew here from Pennsylvania, followed by a Black Hawk and an assault crew."

"Yeah, we know about them. They were stopped in New Jersey by the feds."

"Do you know where the second one is?"

He glared at her.

"I thought not. F. B. I." She waited while they all looked at each other in confusion. "I can call her for you if you like?"

"Shut up."

A shout came from an office in the corner. "Chief says to put her in holding."

Her escort pulled on her arm but was stopped by the female cop. Colt read her name tag. Garcia.

"She's bleeding."

"It's just a few scratches. She's fine."

"No, not there." Garcia pointed to Colt's midsection.

She looked down to see what the fuss was about. Her shirt was ripped and wet with blood. "Yup. I'm bleeding."

"Doesn't seem to be bothering her. She can wait for the FBI if she's so chummy with them." The parade of cops led her down a hall to a row of holding cells. The door beeped open, and she was shoved inside.

Colt looked around at the other occupants. They'd passed two empty cells, so she wondered why they put her in with two guys. To make everyone uncomfortable, most likely. There was only one bench, on which a very large man was snoring. The back corner was occupied by a man with a mullet and a bad sunburn showing the shape of his sunglasses.

She pulled her shirt up to show him her wound. "I got stabbed," she told him proudly.

He blanched and went back to minding his own business.

Garcia approached and handed Colt a sanitary pad. "Sorry, it's the only thing I'm allowed to give you."

"Thanks, this will do fine for now." She unwrapped it and pressed it against the wound. Mackenzie's stitches had ripped out, but she couldn't tell if any further damage had been done.

"You okay?"

"Oh, yeah. Adrenaline, you know. It'll catch up to me soon." She kicked herself for not remembering to act like she was in pain.

"I'll see what I can do about getting you to a hospital if the FBI agent doesn't get here soon."

"Thanks, appreciate it." Colt leaned against the bars.

"Anything else I can do for you?"

"Turn the TV a little bit more this way?"

Garcia looked where Colt was pointing. She walked away, returning to her desk by way of the water cooler. She stopped and stretched. Her hand brushed the ceiling-mounted TV. It shifted a couple of inches, giving Colt enough of an angle to read the captions on the screen.

The news was still rolling with the story of an averted kamikaze attack on New York City by a vintage biplane.

"It wasn't a kamikaze attempt," Colt muttered.

"How do you know?"

Colt jerked around to see Mullet Man leaning on the bars behind her, eyes on the TV.

"Because I'm still alive, aren't I?"

"Yeah, but maybe you was stopped before you could."

His logic was baffling, but she didn't have time to argue. "Shut up. I'm reading," she told him.

Commercials flashed on the screen, and Colt took the time to adjust the bandage. Blood was still seeping out. Maybe a little faster than when she'd first been cut. Reasonable, considering what she'd been doing for the past hour.

The commercials ended, and the screen panned back to the two news anchors, who chatted briefly about an incredible piece of missing art that had been found, "right here in New York City, John."

The screen shifted to show two additional people at the desk, Danforth and a guy with a man bun and a tweed jacket. The art professor.

A black velvet box sat between them. Colt ignored the captioned chatter and focused on Danforth. Did he have the real Fabergé Egg, or were they about to reveal the replica? It took her only a moment to decide they had the real one. Danforth was grinning like a canary that had outwitted the cat.

At last, the art professor donned a pair of white cotton gloves and lifted the lid from the box. The two news anchors nearly fell off their seats at the opulence before them.

Colt grinned. The Collector had lost.

A flurry of activity in the bullpen caught her eye. Kendra walked in, her height complementing her poise and command. Officers leaped out of her way while pointing in the direction of the chief's office. Garcia stopped her before she could enter, whispering something in her ear. Kendra continued on into the office, and mere seconds later, she reappeared with the chief in tow.

The cop who had frog-marched her inside rushed to obey as the chief shouted orders. "Hands," he said to Colt as he drew near.

"No cuffs," Kendra said from behind him.

He started, then opened the door for Colt to exit. "No hard feelings then?" He held out his hand for her to shake.

"None at all. You were just doing your job," she replied. She dropped the dirty bandage in his hand and followed Kendra out to her car.

No time to think. The projectile was inches from her head when Colt snatched it out of the air. An empty soda can.

She stepped through the doorway to see everyone in the room wincing.

"Mitch. Seriously, you need to work on your aim," she dropped the can in the garbage beside the door.

"What do you think I was doing?" he protested.

"Never mind that," Hawk argued. "You need to learn to keep your arm in the sling. Mackenzie, check her, please?"

Colt dropped into her favorite chair. "I'm fine, stop fussing. Toss me one of those drinks, Mitch?"

He obliged, an underhanded throw that had her reaching with her left arm. Hawk groaned.

"If you rip your stitches again, I will tie your arms to your side."

Mackenzie stood up from the sofa she was sharing with Amanda and shuffled over, gesturing for Colt to lift her shirt. Colt glared at Hawk as she opened her soda, then leaned to the side to let Mackenzie check her bandage. Colt took a sip and looked around the room, and at the friends gathered there. The only one missing was Kendra, who had made excuses about additional paperwork for why she couldn't be there.

A car drove up the driveway and stopped outside. Hawk motioned for her to stay seated as he went to the door. Colt was too content to pay much attention to what was happening until he returned, two people in tow.

Danforth walked in, a tiny white-haired woman on his arm.

Colt set her drink down and stood up. "Masha," she said.

The woman smiled. "It has been a long time since anyone has called me that."

Three Months Later

The walls were gray. The floors were gray. The ceilings were gray. Even the table and chair where he sat were gray.

Malik decided that if he never saw gray again, it would be too soon. Unfortunately, it seemed as though gray was the color of his life now. Despite the myriad of promises from his friends at the embassy, he'd been left in this monotone wasteland for far too long already. He'd not even been granted permission to attend his mother's funeral.

He tapped his foot impatiently, sitting upright in his chair. It hadn't taken long for prison life to erode his free will, but he refused to give in completely. He wouldn't slouch, and he certainly wasn't going to touch the filthy table.

Besides, the lawyer worked for him. He might be able to walk out of here after their meeting, but Malik was still the one calling the shots, and it was best the lawyer remembered that.

However, it was difficult to maintain control of a meeting when the other party had yet to make an appearance. Malik shifted in the uncomfortable seat. If it weren't for the mail his lawyer was bringing, he would request to return to his cell. But in order to avoid unpleasant conversations, all his mail was sent via the law office. Yet another thing for the lawyer to hold over Malik's head.

The door opened, and a stranger walked in. Tall, about thirty years old, he was dressed in a suit that cost well north of a thousand dollars. In fact, Malik was sure that the tie alone cost that much. The man moved with an air of supreme confidence in himself, in his place in society, and in the status of his bank account. Setting the tooled leather briefcase he carried on the table, he sat down and smoothed the tie, the gold ring he wore on his right pinky flashing as he did so.

"Mr. Al Kandari, I am Chauncey Danforth IV, of Danforth & Briggs." He slid a black and gold embossed business card across the table as he spoke.

"Danforth & Briggs, as in the company that facilitated the purchase of the airfield in Pennsylvania." Malik ignored the card. He wouldn't need it.

The younger man smiled. "You've done your homework."

"I always do my homework. But what I don't know is why you are here and my lawyer is not."

"Forgive me, but I convinced him that it would be better if he were not present at this meeting, and I do hope you'll agree."

"Thus far, I'm not so inclined."

Danforth smiled again. He leaned back in his chair and crossed his legs. Malik seethed. The man not only flaunted his attire in the face of Malik's own forced orange wardrobe, but he was toying with him as well.

"Now, don't be like that, Mr. Al Kandari. I believe we can help each other."

"And how is that?"

Danforth opened the briefcase and removed two full-sized glossy images. He centered them in front of Malik.

"This, you may recognize, is the surprise necklace from the Hen with the Sapphire Necklace Fabergé Egg. I am in possession of the Egg, and I would like to make the set complete."

"And why would I want to help you with that?"

"Because of what I offer in return." He tapped the second picture, a photograph of a letter on a desk. In the corner of the image, Malik could see the walnut nameplate that his lawyer was so proud of. "This letter is from me to the governor. He's a good friend of my father's, you know."

Malik risked a glance at Danforth's face. The man wasn't joking. But if his own lawyer had the letter already...

"Here's how this will work. The letter is with your lawyer, yes. But it's post-dated for the end of the month. If by that time I do not have the necklace, or at least confirmation that it is on its way to me, a different letter will be sent to the governor. The contents of that letter will depend on whether you and your lawyer try to screw me."

"You're very trusting," Malik said.

"Am I?"

Malik looked him in the eye for the first time and there saw the first thing that truly frightened him since entering the prison. "I could out you, report you for extortion."

"You won't."

Malik hated the arrogance in those two words, hated that he was right. "Why do you want the necklace that you're willing to risk your reputation like this?"

"It belongs to my grandmother. It is time it was returned to her."

Author's Note

Thank you so much for reading *Angels Zero*. It means so much to me, and I really hope you enjoyed it!

If you'd like to find out how Colt and Hawk crashed, you can discover the full story in the free novella, *Out of Options*, by signing up to my newsletter here:

I send emails with book news, exclusive free content, and promotions, and I'll always let you know first when a new book is on its way.

If you'd like to contact me, my email is Arleigh@ArleighJaco bs.com, and you can find me on Facebook @ArleighJacobs, or on Instagram @ArleighJacobs.

You can find all the Team Colt books and more about me at .

Delving into the past of a character can take a story in directions the writer never thought possible. When I wrote the short story "Hellcat One-One" for a charity anthology last year, I realized I wanted to learn more about the Russian Night Witches, and that it was a legacy I felt Colt shared. But the more I discovered about her grandmother, the more I realized that this woman wasn't as simple as I first thought. (Honestly, what was I thinking? Any woman who flew in combat during World War II wasn't going to be plain vanilla.)

Having Colt explore this part of her past was really interesting to me — maybe because I'm somewhat sadistic to my characters. To take the one person Colt trusted and have her doubt that relationship was perhaps cruel on my part. But I think confronting those secrets can bring closure and help you understand what has been lost and what has been gained.

This book took me far longer to write than I had anticipated, but throughout it all I had an amazing group of people cheering me on. Without their support, I would not have had the strength to complete it.

Rebecca Goodwin — My editor, friend, chocolate co-conspirator. Thank you for pushing me to keep making this story better.

Nicole Schroeder — Typo-squasher and comma wrangler. Thank you for not screaming in frustration every time I mix up em dashes and ellipses.

Susan Odev — Thank you for rightly calling me out for making things too easy for Colt.

Angela Marshall — Thank you for giving me permission to put my writing first.

Fatima Fayez — Thank you for helping me bring Malik to life and ensuring I got all things Kuwait correct.

Liz, Tara, Nicole, Denise, Mark, Jac — Thank you for the support and the early feedback.

The Coronitas Writing Group — Thank you for being the best writing sisters anyone could ask for.

The BXP Team — Thank you for being the best group of cheerleaders ever. Special thanks to Julian Barr for his help and to the Word Race crew for the monthly challenges.

My amazing husband — Thank you for your unwavering support. And for buying me a puppy. You and Toblerone are my life, and I wouldn't be me without you.

And I also want to thank you for reading *Angels Zero*. I hope you've enjoyed it. If you have, it would mean a great deal to me if you were to leave a review on the bookstore of your choice. Reviews help make my story visible to more readers, and they fill me with joy every time I read them.

Arleigh Jacobs